MW01131260

A Black Rose

A Detective Mike Mastro Mystery

A Black Rose

By Judi Ciance
judiciance@gmail.com
judiciance.com

Published: June, 2017

ISBN-13:978-1547071746
ISBN-10:1547071745

Other Books by this author:
The Casey Quinby Mystery Series:

Empty Rocker (November 2012)
Paint Her Dead (October 2013)
Caught With A Quahog (October 2014)
A Tale of Two Lobsters (October 2015)
18 Buzzy Lane (October 2016)

Dedication

To My Husband
Paul Ciance
His encouragement to continue,
his patience to listen and
his help in keeping me in line
are why Detective Mike Mastro
came onto the scene.

Acknowledgements

This author wants to thank Beverly Blackwell, Judy Pinkham, and Brenda Rizer. Because of their support, expertise, and guidance, I was able to bring the reader the first book in the Detective Mike Mastro series.

I also thank my critique group for keeping me on track and helping me develop more as a writer. David, Ray, and Mark ... you guys are the best.

A Black Rose

A Detective Mike Mastro Mystery

by

Judi Ciance

CHAPTER 1

Wednesday night

Jeni Johnson's naked body lay peacefully still on the shiny white satin sheets—her face buried deep in the pillow—her strawberry blonde curls framed the outline.

Frank Sinatra's *My Way* played softly in the background.

He got up from the crimson and gray striped wing back he'd been sitting in for the last hour. A half empty glass of 2008 *Spottswoode* Cabernet Sauvignon sat on a side table. "It's time for a toast." He lifted his glass, swirled the dark red liquid, lightly coating the sides, and saluted the array of football trophies that adorned the marble fireplace mantel. He took a taste, then gently lifted the black rose that rested beside the bottle of wine. He knelt down and laced the stem between her fingers, then stood to admire his work.

"Sleep, my child. Sleep." He sealed his words with another mouthful, then set the glass back down in the same spot he'd taken it from.

He ran his fingers tenderly down her spine. Her skin was soft, still warm. He leaned over to rest his face next to hers. "Beautiful Jeni," he whispered. "You're an angel now. You know why I made you an angel. The world doesn't, not yet."

CHAPTER 2

Thursday

"Mike, you talked to the Captain yet?" asked Detective Sal Petruca.

"No, I just got here."

"Grab your coffee. I'll fill you in on the way to the squad room. Another day in paradise. A jogger called the station about forty-five minutes ago. She was frantic. Dispatch sent out a black and white."

"Okay, a frantic jogger. What happened? Did this person encounter somebody's overfed Bobtail and think it was a rabid Bobcat?" I asked.

Sal frowned. "You've got too many years on the job. Listen up."

I smirked.

We were steps away from the squad room when Sal put his arm up in front of me. "Another murder victim, just like the one we found in Hull a couple months ago."

I stopped. "Where was this one?"

"Behind the seawall on the Boulevard."

Two uniforms came up behind us and spoke in unison. "Morning, Detectives. It's going to be a busy day."

I nodded. I had thirty-two years on the job—twenty-two in the North End precinct, and going on eleven years in my current position in Revere, been offered the position of lead detective several times, but turned it down. I still had two hands, all my fingers, my limbs and most of my mind working and I wanted to keep it that way. I was married once, but it didn't last long. She loved the uniform, but didn't like the job. Since the two went hand-in-hand, I had to choose which hand I wanted to hold. Five years later, she filed for divorce. I signed the papers and haven't been in a lasting relationship since—that was twenty three years ago.

"Mike, you with me?"

"Yeah, reflecting—just reflecting. Here comes the Captain. Let's grab a seat."

The squad room went silent. Captain Bosworth took his position behind the podium at the front of the room. He put his papers down, clasped his hands behind his back and perused all the faces as we waited for him to start the morning briefing.

"Good morning. Unfortunately, I have to confirm what you probably already know. About an hour ago, a jogger called to report the body of a woman in the sand beside the bath house, across from the Do-Drop-In Lounge." He cleared his throat, then resumed. "One of the officers I sent out to authenticate the story was the same officer who assisted the Hull PD two months ago with a body found on Nantasket Beach. When he viewed the victim, he called me directly to let me know there were similarities."

I knew what he was about to say and didn't want to hear it.

"Detectives Mastro and Petruca have been working the Hull murder." He looked in our direction. "To date, we don't have anything concrete. After this briefing is over, they'll head the Revere Beach case. The rest of you cover your assigned routes, but be on call should a problem arise. Dismissed."

We stayed behind to talk to the Captain. I spoke first. "Anything we should know before we head out?"

"The responding officers figure the victim to be somewhere in her twenties. They got contact information and took a statement from the caller. I sent out four cars to secure the area. They're waiting for you. The Medical Examiner will also meet you there."

CHAPTER 3

A crowd gathered close to where the victim lay motionless on the sand. Yellow crime scene tape defined the restricted space privy only to assigned law enforcement personnel. News vultures scrambled for pictures and statements to fill prime spots on the evening broadcast.

Someone called my name. "Detective Mike Mastro."

I turned toward the voice. "Vinny Balls, what brings you out from under your rock?"

"I heard somebody found a body this morning. News travels fast, especially if it's bad."

"What if I told you it was a rubber blowup doll? Oh, wait a minute, I'm sorry I forgot that's your kind of girl. Maybe I should be questioning you. When was the last time you sucked a balloon?" I crossed my arms over my chest. "Now get out of my face. I've got work to do."

"Nice to see you too." Vinny, in his true fashion, flashed me the bird.

I laughed, knowing it would aggravate him even more.

Sal knelt down beside the victim. "Mike, check this out. No bruises or cuts. No blood on or around her. No apparent cause of death. But, since she's fully clothed, we can't verify the facts until the ME does a post-mortem exam."

I put my hand on Sal's shoulder and squatted next to him. "Do you remember the Doll murders in Quincy a year ago?"

"I'm trying not to."

"Think about it. The cause of death in the Doll murders was cocaine overdose. Both of them were raped. Neither of them had any signs of a struggle or abuse. They were young, pretty and fully dressed, all except for their underpants, just like our Hull girl. I'll bet my paycheck our victim here isn't wearing panties either. The Quincy murders were dubbed Doll murders because the two victims looked like Barbie dolls."

"Our Hull girl also fit that category. As soon as the ME gets here and we turn this one over, I'm sure we'll find ourselves a fourth Barbie." Sal got up to take a few more pictures.

"He'll also be able to confirm if she's missing her underpants." I moved to the other side of the victim. "The Quincy murders were never solved. The girls were never identified. Our Hull girl is also a Jane Doe. I'm sure our Revere girl will share the name."

Sal stared out over the harbor. "A serial killer."

We turned to greet Irving Bailey, the Medical Examiner, and his team.

The ME looked down at the girl on the sand. "Looks like a repeat of Quincy and Hull."

"I think so, Doc." I moved back to let him do his thing.

Sal canvassed the area, taking pictures.

I stayed with Irving and took notes.

"She's been dead approximately nine hours." The ME signaled his team to gently turn the body over. "There are no apparent abrasions or bruises to the face, neck, arms or legs. I'll check the rest of her body at the lab."

"Her clothes aren't ripped or hardly wrinkled." I bent down beside Irving. "Hull girl was missing her underpants. Can you check to see if this victim is missing hers?"

Irving took his flashlight and looked up her skirt. "She doesn't have any on. Same as the other girls."

"Our little lady was lifted very carefully over the seawall. She wasn't dropped, she was placed. I know it's not season, but I can't imagine nobody saw what happened."

"There's nothing more I can do here. I'm going to have her moved to my lab for an autopsy."

"We'll stay until you load her up. Most of the crowd has dispersed, but all it takes is one asshole to compromise evidence."

"Stop by the lab on your way to the station. That'll give me time to compare this case with my notes from Hull."

Sal finished taking pictures of the victim, the immediate area and the surrounding area so we could re-create the scene back at the office.

"I'll ask some of the rubber-necks if they saw anything."

Looking over the crowd of people behind the yellow tape, I'd be surprised if half of them could write their own name.

"I'll take the ones in front of the Clam Shack." Sal draped the camera strap over his shoulder and took a pad and pen from his jacket pocket. "Meet you at the car in a few."

I glanced to my left. Vinny Balducci leaned against the side wall of the bath house watching our every move. "Hey, Balls, what scandal sheet you working for now?"

"Anyone who'll pay me for a good story."

"You must be unemployed then. You've never written a good story in your life." I moved closer. "What time did you get here this morning?"

"I don't remember."

"I suggest you search that short term memory of yours and answer my question, unless of course, you'd like to take a ride to the station."

"Once a pig—always a pig." His expression hardened.

I stood my ground. "Well, what time?"

"Around seven-thirty. I heard a broad scream and ran over to see if she needed assistance. She already had her cell in her hand making a call. I assumed it was to your office."

"Is that when you saw the body?"

"Yep."

"Did you touch the victim?"

"You think I'm stupid?"

"You really want an answer?"

"No, I didn't touch her."

"Did you see anybody else around her?"

"Not around her, but that Hummer parked across the street was here. They had tent signs blocking the sidewalk, so people had to walk on the grassy area to pass. Then, they paraded on the street carrying the same message. I was about to cross over to get a story when I heard the aforementioned scream. They heard it too and quickly threw all their paraphernalia in the back of the Hummer."

"Okay." I walked away without saying another word. I didn't have to turn around to know he was pissed.

There was a group of five standing beside a canary-yellow Hummer parked across from the entry to the beach. They stopped talking as I approached. "Morning." I flashed my badge.

A young man with hair halfway down his back and a beard that touched his chest stepped forward.

"Your car?" I asked.

"Yeah."

Business must be good.

"I've got a few questions."

"So ask."

Cocky bastard. I flipped the page in my notebook and noted his plate number.

"What's that for?"

"Because I feel like writing. Now, if you're ready I'll ask those questions." I positioned myself so I could see Jesus and his four disciples. "Mr. Spokesman, you got a name?"

"Richard."

"Okay, Richard, what time did you and your friends get here?"

"I got here about a half hour ago. I don't know what time they got here."

"This is your car, right?"

"I already told you it was."

"Indeed you did." I unbuttoned my jacket. "This car was parked here when we arrived and we've been here an hour. I'll ask you again." I backed up slightly. "What time did you get here?"

"It was just before seven o'clock."

"I'd like to see your license."

"What for? I didn't do anything wrong."

"I didn't say you did." I held out my hand. "Your license, please."

Richard played pocket pool for a couple seconds, then produced a well-worn document.

"This is a Vermont license. Do you have a Massachusetts one?" I asked.

"No."

It was expired, but I didn't want 'our' fearless leader to run, so I didn't acknowledge the fact I'd noticed it. "Did you drive here?"

"Yes."

"And your reason for being here?"

He moved closer to me.

"I'd suggest you stay right where you are unless you'd rather spend the rest of your day at the station. I repeat, why are you here?"

"We meet here a couple times a week to discuss issues."

I sensed an uneasiness building amongst his friends. Out of the corner of my eye, I saw Sal cross the street. I gave him a wrist signal to join me.

He circled the Hummer and stopped a few feet away from where I was standing.

"So you and your friends were here at seven o'clock and didn't notice a body lying on the beach behind the seawall?"

"We didn't go over to the beach."

"And you didn't hear a girl scream when she discovered the body?"

"No."

"Where did you hold your 'discussion' meeting?"

"Right herc."

"Let me get this straight. You've been here since seven a.m. babbling some bullshit to anyone who'll listen?"

"We talk about the pros and cons surrounding current concerns."

"Okay if I take a look in your car?"

"Got a warrant?"

Sal moved around behind Richard's four buddies.

"We can do this without incident, unless you want to be detained for several hours until we get your requested piece of paper."

"This is bullshit."

"Bullshit, cow shit, horse shit or human shit—I don't really care—open the back of your car."

Richard shuffled, but didn't say a word.

I handed Sal my notebook opened to the page where I'd written the plate number. "Detective Petruca, please call the station and have them run this." I kept my eyes focused on Richard. "Also, radio one of the black and whites across the street. Have them come over here."

Richard's attitude changed. Without saying a word, he opened the back of the Hummer and stepped aside.

Sal unbuttoned his jacket and moved behind Richard while I looked inside.

There were two tent signs and a number of home-made picket signs. 'KILL THE SINNERS' was printed in black with red droplets painted to look like blood dripping from the letters.

The black and white pulled up behind the Hummer. Two officers walked to where Sal and I stood. I backed away from Richard and his disciples and turned to face the officers. "I want these five cuffed and taken to the station. I'm charging them with parading without a permit, blocking a public walkway and disrupting the flow of traffic. Call over one of the other black and whites to assist. We'll take their fearless leader."

The two officers nodded.

I looked at Richard's friends. "You four come over here and lean against the car. Richard, I want you to step over by Detective Petruca."

"What's going on?"

"Here's what's going to happen, Richard. You and your little band of holy rollers are being arrested for parading without a permit, blocking a public walkway and disrupting the flow of traffic."

One of the four leaning against the car tried to break away, but was immediately grabbed and cuffed by the officer standing at the end of the Hummer.

I shrugged and threw my hands up. "How stupid was that? Anyone else want to leave without permission?"

The second black and white pulled up.

"You guys take these two to the station. Make sure they're in separate rooms." I turned to the first two officers. "You do the same with the other two."

Sal looked at Richard. "Where's the keys?"

"In my pocket."

"Get them."

"You get them."

I walked over behind Richard and grabbed him by the back of his neck. "Give me the fuckin' keys."

He reluctantly fished them from his pocket. I locked up the Hummer to secure any evidence it harbored.

"He's all yours, Detective Petruca."

Sal guided Richard to the unmarked and stuffed him into the back seat.

"Mike, the Hummer is registered to a Martin Rucci."

"The same Martin Rucci who owns Pinky's Powder Lounge on Lee Burbank Highway?"

Sal turned to look at Richard. "Yep. One and the same."

I radioed the station to let them know we were on our way in with the ringleader of our 'Revere Beach anti-sinners' group. "Is room four empty?"

"It is. We'll be waiting at the back door."

As I rounded the last corner, and pulled into the police lot, I glanced in the mirror. Richard was staring out the side window. "You've had twenty minutes to do some hard thinking. I hope you used the time wisely."

Two uniforms walked up to the car as we pulled in front of the door behind the station.

"Bring our guest to room four. Stay with him till we get there."

Richard didn't flinch. Flanked by the two officers, he was led inside.

I leaned against the car. "What do you make of this asshole?"

"I was about to ask you the same question." Sal shrugged. "Have you ever met Martin Rucci?"

"I have. He's the scum of the earth. About twelve years ago, we questioned him in a child pornography case. He was guilty as hell, but he beat it. I wanted to pound the brains out of his pea-sized head. Probably would have if the boss hadn't stepped in." I grimaced at the thought of Rucci being involved with our dead girls. "Then just before you transferred over from Beacon Hill, his name came up in a drug bust the department worked. He walked away clean."

"Question before us now is, why does Richard have Rucci's Hummer?"

CHAPTER 4

"Be right back, I'm going to hit the head, then grab a coffee before we start on Jesus," I said.

"Coffee sounds good. It might even be fresh enough to drink. Meet you in front of four."

I left the breakroom.

Sal poured himself a cup, then headed to room four. He took a drink as he watched Richard through the one-way glass. Richard sat straight up with his hands, still cuffed at the wrists, folded in front of him, as if in prayer.

I walked up behind Sal. "Things would be much easier if we corralled all these critters and shipped them to an uninhabitable island, miles out in the ocean, where the only thing they'd have to drink is salt water."

Sal raised his eyebrows. "Remind me not to get on your bad side."

"It's showtime. Let's go entertain our guest."

Sal grinned. "Right behind you, partner."

Richard didn't look up when we walked through the door. Sal sat across from him. I sauntered around the table, stood behind Richard long enough to make him uncomfortable, then walked back and took the chair beside Sal.

Richard raised his head and looked at our coffees. "Can I have one of those?"

I lifted my cup. "You mean one of these?"

"Yes."

"Do you think it might help you talk better?"

"It might."

"Let's see how you do without it, then I'll think about it."

Sal rested his elbows on the table. "Does Martin Rucci know you have his vehicle?"

Richard squirmed in his chair. "Yes."

Sal moved forward, his upper body stretched almost halfway across the table. "Does he know about your merry band of followers and the messages you were trying to communicate with passersby on Revere Beach Parkway?"

There was no answer.

I stood and walked to the one-way glass. "Maybe, Mr. Rucci, is the real leader and you're his patsy." I folded my arms. "Detective Petruca, I think we have the wrong man. I think we should pay Mr. Rucci a visit. What do you think?"

Sal checked his watch. "He opens Pinky's Powder at noon. It's eleven-forty-five. I'm sure he'd be glad to see us." Sal got up and started for the door.

"Wait. I work for Martin. I run errands for him. He has nothing to do with my discussion group."

"Bullshit." I pounded my fist on the table. "You were parading without a permit, blocking a public walkway and disrupting the flow of traffic —discuss that." I walked past Sal. "I'll be right back."

I took a ceramic mug from the cabinet in the breakroom and filled it with coffee, cream and one sugar. If Richard wasn't going to cooperate, maybe the mug would help fill in the blanks.

Richard stared at his newly acquired bracelets.

"I hope you take cream and sugar." I set the mug on the table and slid it in his direction. "I believe now that Richard has his coffee, he'd like to be a constructive participant in our conversation. Don't you think so, Detective Petruca?"

"I do."

I sat across from Richard. "How's your coffee?" I asked.

Richard wrapped his hands around the mug and took a mouthful. "It's fine."

"You're welcome." Mission accomplished—a clean set of prints and a DNA sample. "Where are you from?"

He took another mouthful. "Vermont."

"A mountain man?"

"What do you mean by that?"

"Well, the long hair and beard. Thought maybe since you grew up in the Green Mountain State you adapted a mountain man style of living and didn't leave it behind when you came to Boston."

"You're wrong, detective. I'm from Poultney. A small town near the Vermont-New York border. Most of it houses a college. Used to be a girls only school, now it's co-ed."

"Did you hang around there studying the girls?"

"What's that supposed to mean?"

"Nothing in particular—just curious. What brought you to Boston?"

"I wanted to expand my circle of life."

Sal leaned forward again. "And did you?"

"Did I what?"

"Expand your circle of life?"

"I guess you could say that. I've learned a lot more here than I ever did there."

"I bet you have."

I slid my chair out, leaned back and crossed my legs. "Now that we've covered the niceties, let's get into the core of our meeting. Those signs in the back of the Hummer, what are they all about?"

"A cause."

"Not enough information. I'd like to know more—like who are the sinners?"

"They exist everywhere."

"You're not a stupid person—at least I don't think you are. I think you're a manipulative genius, although I use the word loosely." I stood. "Here's what's going to happen. Detective Petruca and I have places to go. You and your pals are in custody for at least twenty-four hours. It could be longer. That's up to you. Right now, we've heard all the double talk and lies we want to hear." I reached over and carefully took Richard's empty mug. "The officers will be in to take you to a holding cell where you can meditate about how much you love Boston." I headed for the door. "Oh, by the way, you won't be with your pals. That way we can determine who's not telling the truth and who wants to go home. First one to talk to us, gets a break. I think you're smart enough to figure that out."

Without another word, Sal and I walked out of room four. I dropped Richard's mug off at the lab. "A nice set of fresh prints and DNA."

CHAPTER 5

"I wondered what time you guys were going to show up." The Medical Examiner was working diligently over Revere girl. "We've got no bruising, no needle marks. But then it got interesting. I swabbed her nose and bingo—cocaine. I'm sure the autopsy will find she died of cocaine overdose, just like Hull girl."

I looked at the partially covered body of Revere girl. Irving had tied her hair back so it wouldn't interfere with his work. The full frame of her face was exposed. She was beautiful—long, blonde hair, perfect facial features and a Barbie doll figure. "How old do you think she is?"

"Probably in her twenties. I can give you a better answer when the autopsy is complete."

"Was she raped?"

"She was, but the perpetrator was careful. There's no semen. Also, there was no tearing of the vagina. I don't like to say it, but it appears it was either consensual or she was raped after she was dead."

"You've got to be shittin' me." Sal cringed.

The ME pulled the sheet back up to our girl's neck. "Unfortunately, I think that's also what happened to Hull girl."

I looked at her hands that were placed at her side over the sheet. "Doc, did you check for trace under her fingernails or, for that matter, for broken nails?"

"I did, and negative on both."

"We'll need to run her fingerprints and DNA as soon as possible," I said.

"You can print her now, then I'll get a DNA test to the lab this afternoon. They owe me a favor. I should have the results tomorrow."

"I appreciate that."

"I'll have the autopsy results too, unless the cause of death isn't a cocaine overdose, then I'll order more tests. Those won't be ready tomorrow, but, at least, they'll be in the works."

"Did you get a chance to compare your reports from Hull girl and Revere girl?"

"Not yet." Irving wrote himself a note. "I'll work on them before I go home."

Sal held up his camera. "If everything comes up empty, we can run pictures through facial recognition. One way or another I hope we get a hit."

"When we get back to the station, I'll check the missing persons registry. Maybe we'll get lucky." I couldn't take my eyes off Revere girl.

Irving walked us to the door. "Did you ever get a fingerprint or DNA match on Hull girl?"

Sal answered without turning around. "Nothing."

CHAPTER 6

Pinky's Powder Lounge was ten minutes from the ME's office. We pulled into a space in front of the Light 'em up Smoke Shop next door to the lounge.

The dancing girl in the neon sign above the door was missing some of her lights. "That sign is like the old hookers Rucci hires—tired and despondent." I imagined the stench that was about to surround us. "This place should have been closed years ago."

The chalkboard inside the door listed the drink of the day as a Pink Vampire. "That's fitting for this place." Sal shuddered. "A scumbag comes in for a little guilty pleasure and gets the blood sucked out of him."

Rucci appeared from a side door. "Gentlemen, to what do I owe this pleasure?"

"Martin Rucci?" asked Sal.

"That was quick." I looked at the handful of patrons sitting in a semi-circle around the center stage. "Slow day?"

"Early. It'll pick up later."

Sal walked behind Rucci and stood at the end of the bar.

"What kind of vehicle are you driving these days?" I asked.

"Why, is there a problem?"

Detective Petruca nodded. "Could be."

"I have a Hummer."

"What color?" I asked.

"Canary yellow."

“Well, Martin, your canary yellow Hummer is parked on Revere Beach Boulevard, but don’t worry, it’s locked up.” I dangled the keys in front of him.

Rucci folded his arms over his chest and leaned on the bar next to Detective Petruca. “I have no idea what it’s doing there.”

“The person driving it said he works for you. Said he was running errands.”

“Last night, I gave the keys to Richard, my resident ‘go-for’. He was supposed to pick up some stuff for me this morning, then clock in at two.”

“You better find someone to take his shift. Right now he’s warming a bench in lockup.”

“What the fuck did he do?”

“He and his merry band of four were parading without a permit, blocking a public walkway and disrupting the flow of traffic on the Boulevard across from where a dead body was found.”

Rucci caught his face in his hands.

“The signs we found in the back of your Hummer read KILL THE SINNERS. I find that quite ironic, since sinners are your bread and butter.”

“What!” He moved away from the bar and stood straight up. “Are you implying I know something about those signs—something about a dead body?”

I threw my hands up—palms facing the ceiling. “I’m not implying anything, but I am concerned. And because of my concern, I have questions.”

Rucci didn’t say a word.

Sal motioned with his eyes to a table in the far corner, away from earshot of the bartender and cocktail waitresses.

The odor of stale smoke and lingering body stench penetrated my nostrils. “Let’s move to the table in the corner. This shouldn’t take long. Believe me, I don’t want to stay here any longer than I have to.”

The three of us moved in single file to the table—first Sal, then Rucci, then me. Sal and I sat with our backs to the wall, which didn't make Rucci happy. "Don't be so nervous. We've got it covered." I knew he never let himself be exposed to the element of surprise, but this time we gave him no choice. "Where were you last night?"

"Here."

Sal leaned his forearms on the table and stared at Rucci. "How about after you closed up? Where'd you go?"

"Home."

"If you gave Richard your Hummer, how did you get there?" I asked.

"He dropped me off."

"I hope he's going to corroborate your story. So far I've asked you real easy questions requiring simple answers. I think Richard's pea brain might be able to comprehend them and hopefully give me the same answers you just did."

Rucci's eyes shifted down.

"Is something wrong?" I tilted my head to study his face.

"Nothing is wrong. I forgot. Usually Richard drops me off when he has errands to run in the morning, but last night he left early and I got a ride home from one of my waitresses."

"Oh, I understand. The smog in here sort of clouded your brain for just a minute." I tapped my fingers in succession, each one making a noise as it hit the table.

"What's the waitress's name?" Sal looked around to see if anyone was monitoring our meeting.

Nobody said anything for a few seconds.

I leaned sideways into his line of sight. "Don't you know the names of the people who work for you?"

Rucci didn't say a word.

"This little deaf mute charade is getting old and my patience is wearing thin. A name here or a ride to the station—your choice."

"You're a prick. Her name is Tina."

"Is Tina here?" I unbuttoned my jacket.

Rucci glanced at my Glock 27 resting comfortably under my left arm. "That's her—the blonde at the drink station."

I raised my eyebrows in disbelief. "How old is she?"

"Old enough to work here."

"She's serving alcohol. If she's eighteen, then I'm ninety-two. Detective Petruca, would you please ask Miss Tina to join us."

Rucci noticeably nervous, bit his lower lip.

Tina reluctantly walked to the table where I sat babysitting Martin Rucci.

"Have a seat, Miss Tina." I motioned her to the chair beside Rucci. I didn't want her to look at him without having to turn her head. "Mr. Rucci, your boss, said you gave him a ride home last night. Is that correct?"

She looked at Rucci.

"Don't look at him. Look at me. Did you give him a ride home?"

She lowered her eyes. "I did."

"Did you drop him off or did you go into his house with him?"

"I went into his house to have a coffee."

"Where do you live?"

Tina fidgeted with the rings on her fingers.

"Where do you live?"

"With Martin," she whispered.

"I didn't hear you. Can you repeat that?" My eyes focused on Rucci.

Tina started to cry. "With Martin."

"So you didn't give Martin a ride home. He drove and you both went 'home' to his house."

She nodded.

"Tina, I have one more question for you." I handed her a napkin that was on the table. "How old are you?"

"Seventeen."

Rucci jumped up. "Shut your fuckin' mouth."

I leaped forward before Rucci could clear his chair, spun him around and cuffed him. "Call the wagon."

Sal was already on his phone to the station.

Tina sprung up from her chair and moved closer to Detective Petruca. "Please help me." She cried uncontrollably.

"Stand over by the wall, Tina, and don't move."

I heard screams from approaching sirens. Two officers ran in through the front door. A third came in from the back. I handed Rucci off to Officer Gallo.

The bartender and other waitress stood motionless.

"You two, put your hands where I can see them and come out from behind the bar." I watched as they followed my instructions. I pointed to a table in the center of the room. "Sit down." I shifted my focus on the four patrons sitting in front of the stage. "You, in the Red Sox shirt, and your three buddies, show Officer Morrow some type of identification. Once you've done that, you're free to go. Should you decide not to furnish that information, then you'll be escorted, along with Mr. Rucci, to the station." I crossed my arms over my chest. "Do I make myself clear?"

Nothing was said, the four customers nodded and reached into their pockets for a wallet or a loose driver's license.

Officer Morrow wrote down the information and ushered them to the door.

"Martin Rucci, you're under arrest for harboring a minor and for allowing a minor to serve alcoholic beverages in an establishment owned by you. You have the right to remain silent. Anything you say or do can and will be used against you in a court of law. You have the right to an attorney. If you cannot afford an attorney, one will be appointed to you. Do you understand these rights as they have been read to you?"

"Yeah, I hear you."

"Take him away." I walked over to the bartender. "You got keys to this pit?"

"I do."

"Close up the register and shut the lights. We're all going to leave at the same time, then you're going to lock the door and I'll take the keys for safekeeping." I turned to the other waitress. "What's your name and how old are you?"

She dropped her head. "Beth. I'm seventeen."

"Beth, you and Tina are coming with Detective Petruca and me to the station. We need to have a little talk."

"Yes, sir."

CHAPTER 7

It was two o'clock when we pulled into the police parking lot. I radioed the duty desk officer that we were at the back door. Sal led Tina by the arm and I followed with Beth.

Beth hesitated at the door. "Why are we here?"

"We have a few questions we need to ask. You cooperate and you won't be here long." I shrugged. "It's all up to you."

"Doesn't look like there's anyone waiting in the print room. We might as well get that out of the way." Sal guided Tina through the open door. "Tina you take that seat over there and Beth, you sit here."

"Why are we getting fingerprinted?" Beth looked at Tina, then back to me.

"We have to make sure you're not fugitives." I glanced from one girl to the other.

Beth appeared to be the spokesperson. "Yeah, sure."

Tina took a deep breath, "Detective, you might find our prints in the system."

"Shut-up, Tina."

"Why?"

"We're both runaways."

"Tina!" Beth yelled.

I stood between the two girls. "From the same hometown?"

"Yep," Tina whispered.

"Let me take a guess. You're both from Vermont—maybe a town called Poultney, near the New York border?"

Both girls sat at attention and stared at us. Without releasing eye contact, Beth asked, "How did you know?"

"Detective Petruca, please take their prints." I stopped talking and walked around the room a couple times. "Was Richard your travel companion? Did he tell you he was going to expand your circle of life?"

Sal printed the girls, then gave them a towelette to scrub off the ink.

Tina started to cry. Beth, who'd sat down next to the print table, slid her hands under her thighs and stared at the wall.

"I want you both to give me your full names and the addresses and telephone numbers you left behind. Because you're seventeen, you're considered juveniles and will be remanded to juvenile lockup until we can contact a family member to come get you."

Beth piped up. "We didn't do anything wrong."

"You did. You're runaways." I called the duty officer and requested two uniforms—one being a female—to transport Tina and Beth to juvy. "We've got a little checking to do. And, you two have a lot of thinking to do. We'll be back in a few hours." I didn't like this part of my job.

We released the girls to the uniforms.

"I don't know how long we're going to be with Rucci and my stomach is telling me it's time to eat. I'm going to walk down to Joe's and grab a dog and fries. Want to join me?"

"Right behind you."

CHAPTER 8

"I could have retired last year, living in Naples, Florida, relaxing poolside at my beach front condo. I could be eating conch fritters and sipping a dirty vodka martini with three olives. Instead, I'm stuffing a burnt dog, drowning in mustard, relish and onions, into my mouth and washing it down with a Dr. Pepper, watching weirdos through grease-coated windows." I took another bite. "Something is wrong with this picture."

"Martin Rucci under your skin?"

"I want him to be guilty—and he is, but not of the doll murders. If my sixth sense is correct, he's had sex with both Tina and Beth. That's statutory rape. If we can prove it, he'll go away for at least three and a half years—times two—in the state pen and have to register with the sex offender registry."

Sal crumpled up his food wrappers and threw them in the trash. "We should talk to the girls."

"I agree, but after we talk to them we're going to be tied up with the Dolls. We can't handle both. After we do our interviews with them, we'll meet with the chief, let him know the facts, so he can assign it to another team. We'll be around if they need us. I'd love to be the one to take Rucci down, but right now, our priorities are elsewhere."

"I'm glad we don't have to drive halfway across town to get to juvenile hall anymore. It was a wise decision for the department to open a sub-station in East Boston next to the PD." Sal checked his pocket for paper and pen.

"Afternoon, Detectives. Haven't seen you guys in a long time."

"Officer Martha Malloy, still as beautiful as ever."

"Flattery will get you nowhere, Mastro. I've been expecting you two." She smiled through the barred window and buzzed us in.

"It'll be best if we interview Tina and Beth separately. You're welcome to sit in if you'd like."

"We're short today, so I can't leave the front. You know where the room-buzzer is if you need me. Do me a favor—cover me here till I get the girls settled."

"You got it." I stood where I could see both the back hallway and part of the front lobby.

Sal stayed by the barred window.

Five minutes later Officer Malloy returned. "At the end of the hall, take a right. Beth's in three and Tina's in room two. Push the number one button on the intercom beside the door and I'll let you in. You know the drill. They're all yours."

"Thanks. See you in a few." I walked down the hall. Sal followed.

Tina looked up as we entered the room. "I wondered if you were coming back."

I nodded. "I told you we would."

Sal and I sat down across from her.

I decided to take a softened approach. "Tina, we've got questions. And, you have answers. I want you to understand the only way we can help you is if you tell the truth."

"I understand."

"You told us you live with Martin. And we know it was Richard who brought you and Beth to Boston. Did he force you to come with him?" Sal asked.

"No, we came willingly."

I studied her face. "Have you had any contact with your family since you left home?"

"I wasn't supposed to, but I called once to tell them we were okay. Martin caught me and took my cell phone away." Her eyes scanned the top of the table.

"Tina, I want you to look at me." I waited until she looked up. "Did you have sex with Martin Rucci?"

She shifted her glance from me to Sal. "Detective Mastro asked you a question and you need to answer it."

"Yes, I did," she whispered.

"Was it consensual or did he force you?" I asked without taking my eyes off her.

"Forced."

My insides were boiling. "Did you have sex with Richard?"

Tina hesitated before she spoke. "I didn't—Beth did. She hated it, but she was afraid. We were both afraid, so we did what we were told."

I walked around the table and bent down beside her. "You don't have to be afraid any more. Martin Rucci or Richard will never hurt you again."

She covered her face and started to cry.

Sal buzzed Officer Malloy to open the door. When he came back in, he handed Tina a bottle of water. "We're going to talk to Beth. You sit tight, we won't be long."

"This kills me. I hope the right person gets ahold of Rucci and Richard in prison." I took a deep breath then signaled Martha to unlock the door to room two. Unlike Tina, Beth didn't look up when we walked in. "Would you like a water?" I didn't wait for an answer, just handed her a bottle of Zephyrhills.

"Thank you."

"We just left Tina," I said.

Beth looked up, her eyes moved from Sal to me and back to Sal.

As we did with Tina, Sal and I took the two chairs across from Beth. "We've got questions. And you have answers. I want you to understand the only way we can help is if you tell the truth." I hesitated, then continued, "That's the exact same statement I made to Tina."

Sal leaned back in his chair. "Beth, did Richard force you to come to Boston with him?"

She was visibly shaking. "No."

"Why did you come?"

"I don't know."

"We know you and Tina live with Martin Rucci. Did you have sex with Martin?" I asked. "Let me rephrase that. Did you have sex with Martin or Richard?"

"What did she tell you?"

"Never mind what she told us, answer Detective Mastro's question".

She grabbed her forearms and hugged herself. Her shaking eased some. "Yes, I had sex with both of them, but not because I wanted to. I was scared. They threatened to hurt us if we didn't do what they said."

"I promise you, Martin Rucci and Richard will never touch you again. You don't have to be scared. You and Tina will spend the night here. Tomorrow you'll meet with two other officers—one will be a female. You'll need to tell them exactly what you told me. Tell them everything."

"Why won't you and Detective Petruca be here?"

"We're working another case. But let me assure you we won't be far away. We'll check in and keep on top of what's happening. Just remember to tell the truth."

"I will." Beth stood up. "Can I give you a hug?"

"Of course. They're good people here. They'll help you and Tina. Detective Petruca and I have to leave now, but Officer Malloy will be down soon to get you settled in a room."

CHAPTER 9

"Our meeting with the chief isn't going to be easy. I know he has four teenage girls." I didn't have children and it was times like this, I was glad I didn't.

"There's nothing more we can do tonight. I'm taking Becky to the North End for pasta. Wanna come?"

"I wouldn't be much company. I'm going to get me some Chinese food, a couple Sams, then sit back and enjoy reruns of Blue Bloods." I chuckled. "I'll take a rain check on the invite though."

Sal stood up and headed for the door. "You ready?"

"You get going. I've got a few things to clean up." I wanted to access the police data base and I couldn't do it at home. "I'll be right behind you."

"See you in the morning."

Once the door shut and Sal was out of sight, I fired up the computer and typed Doll murders into the search box. A list of files popped up. I opened the one labeled pictures. The Quincy girls, all except for their hair color and style, looked like twins from the back—that included their clothes. I wasn't the detective on that case. I printed a picture of Doll one and Doll two.

I went back to the original list of files, hit the one labeled reports, Doll one and made copies, then repeated the process for Doll two.

Back at the main screen, I typed Hull girl into the search box, opened the picture file and copied the picture taken by one of the responding officers, showing her face down in the sand. It was almost identical to the Quincy Dolls.

I repeated the entire process for Revere girl.

I sat back in my chair with my arms folded over my chest and stared at the computer screen.

We're definitely dealing with a serial killer.

I logged off, shut down the computer, put the reports and pictures into a folder, then headed to the China Rose Café the next street over from my condo.

CHAPTER 10

Friday

I wonder if getting a good night's sleep is a perk you earn in retirement?

It was six-fifteen—enough time to grab a coffee and donut at Dunkin's and the *Globe* at the newsstand around the corner from the station.

"You couldn't sleep either?" Sal stood two people behind me in line.

I moved back so we didn't talk over unknown ears. "Yeah. My mind wouldn't shut down."

"Have you been to the newsstand yet?"

"Nope. Planned on stopping there after I got my java fix."

"Don't waste your money." Sal held up two papers—one *Globe* and one *Daily Chatter*.

"The *Glob*e's bad enough. Why the scandal sheet so early in the morning?"

Sal pointed to the clerk behind the counter waiting to take our order.

"Two coffees—black, a sugar jelly and …" I turned to Sal. "Donut?"

"A chocolate glazed."

I pulled the papers out from under Sal's arm, took the bag of donuts and headed across the room. "I'll get the table, you wait for the coffees."

Sal set our coffees down and moved the *Globe* aside to expose *The Chatter*. "The *Globe* is the *Globe*—it can wait. Check out the feature article on the front page of *The Chatter*."

I almost knocked over my drink when I leaned forward to read it. "Vinny Balducci. I haven't seen his last name in print for years. They should credit him as Vinny 'Balls', then more people would know who wrote the piece. He sure scrambled to find a home for this one." I stared at the headline. "ANOTHER DOLL FOUND ON REVERE BEACH." I didn't look up until I finished reading. "Whoever the perp or perps are, must be sucking this in. We know we don't have any idea who's committing these murders, now he, she, or they also know we have nothing." I slammed my fist on the table. Several patrons turned in our direction. I waved them off. "Bad morning."

Sal closed the tab on his coffee cup. "Let's head over to the station."

I followed.

"What time did you leave yesterday?"

"I printed pictures and reports from files, but I can't make them sing and dance like IT can, so I called it a night just before seven. IT doesn't get here until eight. I'll get the stuff I printed and meet you in interrogation room two. Two old, tired brains might find something worth pursuing."

Sal had a pen and pad of paper waiting for me. "Figured if we did come up with something, we better write it down before we forget it." He chuckled.

"Okay, partner." I slid the beach pictures of Doll one and Doll two across the table for him to examine. "Give me your thoughts."

"Except for the hair, they look to be the same person. They are definitely posed by the same person." Sal examined them again. "And their clothes…," he held the picture closer to his face. "They're dressed the same. The colors are different, but the pattern and style are exact."

"We'll check that out on IT's big screen, but I agree." I took the pictures of Hull girl and Revere girl from the folder. "Now, look at the picture taken in Hull and the one we took yesterday."

Sal laid the four pictures out in front of him. "Looks like the Dolls. From the way they're posed to what they're wearing." He sighed. "None of this has been leaked to the press. This is not a copy-cat. We got ourselves a serial killer."

"After IT, we'll talk to the chief. He'll be in soon."

"I worked a serial murder case about twenty years ago. You remember the Beacon Hill Shadow?" Sal asked.

"I do."

"He'd hide in dark doorways, confront his victim—always a girl—rape and murder her—sometimes not in that order. There were eight murders and two attempted."

"I don't recall all the details. We were briefed, but since I didn't work it, I don't remember how he trapped his victims."

Sal leaned back in his chair and crossed his arms over his chest. "It appeared he either knew them or somehow got them to talk to him. There was never a struggle or at least not violent enough to alert a neighbor."

"Weren't the girls found in their apartments?"

"Yep."

"Clothed or not?"

"Clothed," Sal took a deep breath. "Everyone on the Hill was edgy. Residents, especially the young girls, were on high alert. His last two victims got away from him before he sweet-talked them inside. One ran to a local convenience store. The other sprayed him with mace and screamed at the top of her lungs. A neighbor a few doors down heard her and yelled at the shadow that was trying to stop her from screaming. He fled. We nicknamed him the Beacon. He ran from both encounters and was never heard from again."

"So he's still out there?"

Sal nodded. "Unfortunately."

"Did either one of the girls who lived give you any description?"

"Very little. It was so dark they couldn't provide any exact features. Not enough to sketch." Sal got quiet, then stopped and turned to face me. “Think about it—that may be why they’re still alive today.”

I looked at Sal. “If the shadow was twenty-six—today he’d be forty-six.”

“You’re grasping at straws. We have nothing to tie the Shadow murders to the Doll murders.”

“Got a better idea?”

Sal shrugged. “Not at the moment.”

I glanced at my watch. It was seven-fifty. “IT should be in now.” I threw my empty coffee cup into the basket by the door. “Have you ever worked with Lucy or Mario?”

“Not yet.”

“They’re the best in the business. I can work a computer, but they can make it do the tarantella.”

CHAPTER 11

"Morning." I approached Mario's desk. "You know Detective Petruca?"

"We've never had the pleasure of working together, but we've met." Mario reached out to shake Sal's hand.

"Looks like that's about to change."

"I heard you guys are assigned to the Hull and Revere girl murders."

"That we are."

Mario motioned for us to take the two chairs in front of his desk. "Where do you want to start?"

"Ten months ago," I said. "I need the reports and pictures from the murders of two young girls in Quincy."

"You mean the Doll murders?" Mario didn't wait for my answer before he let his fingers dance across his keyboard. "Turn your chairs around."

All the pictures taken in Quincy were displayed on a five by seven wall mounted screen.

Sal and I walked over to study the display.

"Before I went home last night, I pulled these up on the office computer, but wasn't able to enlarge them to check the details."

"Technology. I'll scroll through them slowly. There are twenty altogether—ten from the first Doll and ten from the second. Let me know when you want me to stop."

"Make one complete pass through, then we'll go back and examine them one at a time."

Sal and I were glued to the ticker-tape parade of crime scene close-ups.

"We're back to number one." Mario stopped to wait for further instructions.

The first frame was of the victim, fully dressed and carefully placed face down in the sand. She was beside a thick hedge of seagrass which made it impossible to see her from a distance.

"Sal, check the report to see who found her."

Sal flipped a few pages. "A guy walking his dog along the beach. Said he wouldn't have noticed her if the dog hadn't barked and run after a bunch of seagulls."

"Mario, I need a photo of this frame." The next couple of shots were different angles of the same scene. Frame seven popped up on the screen. "Stop here."

We walked closer to check it out.

"Does that indentation to the top right of her head look like a partial footprint?" Sal asked.

"It's something. Actually, there's the same indent on the other side of her head." I positioned myself over an imaginary body, braced myself with the inside of my shoes, then leaned down and pretended to pose Doll one. "We know she didn't walk to the beach because there aren't any footprints leading to her body, but then again, there aren't any footprints of the person who carried her there either. That person could have whisked them over as he or she walked away. Whoever put her there was careful—very careful."

Sal took notes.

"We need a print of frame seven. Then a close up of the area with the indents." I sat on the corner of Mario's desk. "Can we get a side-by-side comparison of the pictures from Doll one to Doll two?"

"Sure. Give me a second to pull up the other file."

Almost instantly it appeared on the giant screen. "You're going to want the seconds to slow down when you get older."

"Huh?"

"Never mind." I grinned. "Back to the show."

Mario moved the frames from each file around so we could make like comparisons between the two Dolls.

"There aren't any distinguishing marks at all around the second Doll. The biggest difference between the two bodies is the location where they were placed. Both were on a beach, but Doll two wasn't near the seagrass, she was closer to the parking lot, behind the cement dividing wall. She was carefully posed with her face in the sand just like Doll one, but it appeared the killer had to settle for a less picturesque setting. Maybe he didn't have time to scout out another out-in-the-open hiding place."

"Mike, take a look at the clothes." Sal pointed to two of the pictures. "Mario, can you make these two frames larger?"

"Sure."

"Earlier we determined the clothes were the same design, just different colors. These are not your run-of-the-mill, off-the-rack digs. They're designer fashions."

I was amazed at Sal's understanding of fashion. "And you know this how?"

"On good authority—my wife has a skirt just like it. I threw a fit when she told me the price. She reminded me how much my new Ping driver cost—end of discussion." Sal rolled his eyes.

"Call her? Ask the designer's name."

Sal checked his watch. "She should be home." He moved to the other side of the room to make the call.

"Mr. IT Magician, when we finish with this set, I need to see the autopsy pictures."

"No problem. When you're ready I'll make the switch."

Sal walked back to where I was standing. "Michael Kors."

"Whoa baby—and on a cop's pay?"

"Ping … Michael Kors—they kinda balanced each other out." Sal shrugged. "Believe me, it was a onetime deal. I wanted that new driver."

"Mario," I asked. "Before we check out the autopsy pics, could you pull up the Hull girl and Revere girl pictures that resemble the ones from Quincy?

"Give me a minute." The IT guru pushed a few buttons, hit enter and presto—they appeared on the screen.

"There they are, two more Michael Kors' creations. Our killer enjoys displaying his high-end handwork."

"We need copies of those." Sal pointed to the two pictures.

The photos rolled off the printer. Mario handed them to me.

"Thanks. Now can we take a look at the autopsy shots?" I hardly had the words out of my mouth, when a new photo gallery flashed across the big screen.

Mario divided the screen into four sections. The top and bottom left side were the Quincy victims. The top and bottom right were from Hull and Revere.

"That's it," I said.

"Beach shots have the same clothes—autopsy shots have the same bodies." Sal rubbed his head in puzzlement. "There's a theme, but I can't put my finger on it."

"Some sicko is befriending young, beautiful girls apparently living independently from family or friends. So far, the first three haven't shown up in the missing persons registry. That leads me to assume they aren't from the area. Maybe Mr. Suave lured them to Boston with the promise of fortune and fame." I threw my hands up. "This bastard is sending a message. What I don't know, but we've got to come up with something soon—before we find another Doll getting a sand facial." I glanced at my watch. "The chief should be in. I want to show him these photos and get his thoughts."

The printer was already spitting out copies of the autopsy photos. "Here you go, Detective Mastro. Let me know if you need anything else."

He handed me the portfolio containing the images and reports for each Doll. "You're a good man, Mario Lanza."

Outside the door Sal asked, "Why did you call him Mario Lanza?"

"It's an inside joke. Once he gets wound up, he breaks into song—and most of them are ones Mario Lanza is famous for—his favorites being *O Sole Mio* and *Funiculi, Funicula*."

CHAPTER 12

"I expected you earlier." The chief stood to greet us. "There's a pot of fresh coffee." He pointed to the back corner of his office.

Sal and I got a cup of joe, then took the two seats across from Chief Pozzi. "We've been going over some things with IT." I handed him the folder. "Photos and reports from the Quincy, Hull and Revere murders."

Nothing was said for a few minutes while the chief reviewed the contents of the folder. He grouped the pictures with their corresponding reports and put them in individual piles. The chief rested forward on his desk, frozen in position, only his eyes moving from photo to photo, then back to the original. He picked up his coffee and leaned back in his chair. "What is this person trying to orchestrate? What is he desperate for?"

Chief Francis Pozzi came up through the ranks, finally after twenty-seven years, making it to the front office. The plaque he was given when he made chief seven years ago, framed letters of commendations and awards of valor along with pictures of his wife and four children, at various ages, hung tastefully around his office.

I rested my forearms on his desk. "In my opinion, he's not a violent person. Except for the rape, the victims aren't abused. If you read the autopsy report, all four of them had wine in their stomachs. The ME also noted shrimp, cheese, grapes, cantaloupe and some type of cracker like substance was consumed just before they were murdered. Then there are the clothes they were found in. I don't believe they ever saw them. Each girl had a white jersey and the same flower patterned skirt—the only difference was each skirt was a different color." I waited for the chief to respond.

Chief Pozzi folded his arms over his chest. "This perv dressed them after he killed them?"

"Not only dressed them. The clothes were from a designer—Michael Kors," I said.

"Who the hell is Michael Kors?"

"Ask Sal, he can tell you all about it."

"That skirt goes over for two hundred dollars."

"How do you know that?"

"It's a long story and not at all relevant to the case."

"If you say so." The chief tried to hide a smirk. "Moving on."

I looked at the pictures again. "Despite the size of the girls, they were dead weight. They weren't dropped off. They were carried, gently placed and posed on the beaches where they were found. The person who did this either had help or was strong enough to do it himself."

"Serial killers don't have partners. They want to take the credit themselves. They want total control." Sal took a deep breath. "I did a lot of research when I worked the Beacon Hill Shadow case. There's sick people out there."

"What's our next move?" Chief Pozzi glanced at the photograph of his four daughters.

"Gossip travels at warp speed, so we have to be careful what gets out to the public. If somebody like Vinny Balls gets ahold of the designer clothes breakthrough, he'll run with it. Our killer knows we're not stupid. That we've already discovered the likeness in the wardrobe. He knows it, but seeing it in print is a whole different ballgame. I want to keep things under wraps as long as we can. You never know what might set him off."

Sal looked from me to the chief. "The challenge of the kill."

"Exactly. You two work on a game plan and get back to me." The chief's phone rang. "Hold on." He put his hand over the receiver. "I've got to take this call."

CHAPTER 13

"I hate profiling, but we have no choice." I kept walking down the hall. "This should have started after Hull girl. We need to find this person before he kills again."

There were only a of couple guys at their desks in the detective bureau, but we still decided to resume our conversation in one of the interrogation rooms. "We need a plan or at least something to go on before we involve anyone else." I stopped at the coffee station on the way to room two.

"Grab me one. I'll meet you in a few." Sal moved back out in the hallway to make a call. "Becky, where did you buy your Kors skirt?" Sal nodded. "Thanks. Talk to you later." He slipped his cell back into his pocket and joined me. "My wife bought her favorite skirt at the Michael Kors boutique in Copley Place. I know it doesn't mean our killer was a customer, but it's a start."

"You're right, but does a department store like Macy's also sell Kors?"

"I'll find out." Sal googled it. "Yep, they do."

"A mail order would leave too much of a trail. Boston is filled with high end stores. Probably half of them carry Kors, so we've got some leg work ahead."

Sal took notes. "We should start by targeting locations in the Quincy and East Boston areas, since that's where our girls were found."

"Agreed, but here's another thought. Would our killer use a store so close to the scene?"

"Depends on what scene you're talking about. We actually have two—the one where the girls were killed, which I'm assuming is the same in all four murders, and the ones where the girls were found."

There was a knock on the window. A detective pointed to me and held up the universal hand signal for a telephone call. I nodded. "Be right back."

"You've got a call from Detective Scully, Quincy PD."

I took it at my desk. "Yes, Detective Petruca and myself are working on it as we speak." I opened my desk calendar. "We'll be here." I hung up and walked back to room two. We're meeting here with Detectives Scully and McGinnis from Quincy PD at one-thirty."

"Since that doesn't give us time to check any of the retail stores, let's continue with our game plan. Now that we've determined the four murders are connected, collaboration between the two departments is a given."

"Murdering these girls plays into the serial killer's fantasies—the targeted victims and designer clothing. The autopsy reports, and the list of stomach contents, indicates our serial killer either enjoys or dreams of a high-end lifestyle." I opted for enjoyed, but chose to keep that to myself for the time being.

"I don't understand why these girls haven't been reported missing. They don't look like they live on the streets."

"Yeah, but look at it this way—maybe they did live on the streets and our Mr. Suave lured them in with the promise of a complete change in lifestyle. There's no doubt they were chosen carefully." I leaned forward. "Did you ever see the movie *Pretty Woman*? Richard Gere, a highly successful, ruthless businessman, hired Julia Roberts, a beautiful street-smart prostitute as a companion during a business trip to LA. The movie ended with Gere and Roberts falling in love. In our case, the girls ended up dead. Think about it, they all fit the Julia Roberts profile and nobody is looking for them—dead prostitutes who were introduced to the 'good' life before they died."

"You do have an imagination." Sal scratched his head. "That's what it might take to solve these murders."

"Quincy guys won't be here for an hour. Let's head over to Lulu's. It's clam chowder day. Can I interest you?"

"You can and you did. Let's go."

There were still a couple of unoccupied tables at Lulu's. We took the one furthest from the door.

"You're quiet. Who's talking to you in that head of yours?"

Sal took a deep breath. "Just thinking about Tina and Beth. Two young girls promised a better life. What did they get?"

"Shit—that's what they got. The only positive thing is that they're still alive. If that's what you call it."

Lulu brought us our chowder and a couple packages of oyster crackers. "Hey, what's happenin' with the girl they found on the beach a couple days ago? You guys workin' the case?"

"Who filled you in?" I asked.

"I read it in *The Daily Chatter*."

"Figures," Sal said under his breath.

"It's my paper of choice." She gave me a look, then walked away.

"Something has to click—and soon."

Sal wiped some chowder from his chin. "She might be a ditz, but she sure makes a mean chowder. It's just as good as Legal Seafood."

There were people lined up at the door waiting for tables. "Time to get back to the station." I signaled the cashier to put our bill on my tab. "Next time it's on you."

The two Quincy detectives pulled into the lot as we got to the door. "We might as well wait for them." I checked my watch. "You're early."

"Traffic was light—took half as long as normal."

I reached out to greet Detectives Scully and McGinnis.

Sal followed my lead. "You lucked out."

"It doesn't happen often," Scully said. "I've worked between Quincy and Boston for almost thirty years. We used to car pool or take the T. This new generation has to have their car steps away from them—for why I can't imagine." He chuckled. "Now that I've got that off my chest, let's get started."

I stopped at the duty desk. "Tricia, Detectives Scully and McGinnis will be with Sal and me in room two if you need us."

She nodded and wrote it in the log.

"I'm going to grab a coffee from the breakroom. You guys want one? Somebody usually makes a fresh pot around noon."

"Sounds good."

It was time to settle in and get down to business. "I need to stop by my office to pick up the case folders." I looked at Sal. "Why don't you guys head to two and I'll meet you there in a couple minutes."

CHAPTER 14

Scully took his Doll pictures out and laid them on the table, then pulled out a stack of reports from a manila envelope. "You've probably got some of the same ones."

"I do. I had our IT department print them up for me this morning, but I'm sure you must have some that aren't in the general files."

"Yeah, we have some. They make me sick every time I look at them. They're not gory. They're senseless. The thought of such young lives taken away turns my stomach." McGinnis looked away and took a drink of his coffee.

I took the pictures of Hull and Revere girls out of my folder and slid them across the table one at a time. "This one is the girl from the beach in Hull." I waited for Scully to briefly examine it, then slid the other one over. "Revere Beach girl."

Scully gave the first photo to Detective McGinnis then studied the second one. "We do have a serial killer on our hands."

"We do." I leaned back in my chair.

"Take a look at their clothes." Sal gave them time to comply. "They all have the same white jerseys. The skirts too, except for the color. And, both pieces of clothing are compliments of creator, Michael Kors."

"Who?" McGinnis asked.

"A high-end designer—those outfits cost megabucks." I moved on. "I checked the autopsy reports from your Dolls and compared them to our beach girls. The ME listed the last things they ate and drank. It wasn't your run of the mill pizza, peanut butter pretzel puffs and taco dip washed down with beer. All four of these girls were very well fed and I'm sure the trace of wine cost more than a bottle of *Boone's Farm*.

"Do you think they had an ongoing relationship with the killer?" asked Scully.

I sighed. "I don't, but that's only my opinion and murders aren't solved on opinion."

Sal spoke up. "There's no doubt, the killer is no slouch. He plays a flirty game of mixed doubles and once the game is over, his partner is eliminated."

I stood and walked over to the window to look down to Revere Beach Parkway. "He likes the game, but needs a new challenge every time he plays. The girls are pawns on a chessboard. They look alike, but their moves are different. It's that difference that keeps him interested."

McGinnis intertwined his fingers to create a shelf to lean on. "This is about to get crazy."

"I'm telling you the facts as I see them." Just as I came back to the table, my cell rang. "Detective Mastro here." It was the medical examiner. I held up my finger. "Okay, hold on. I've got Detective Petruca and Detectives Scully and McGinnis from Quincy with me. I'm putting you on speaker."

"Good afternoon detectives. I just got off the phone with the Crime Lab. They confirmed my suspicions. The cause of death for the girl found on Revere Beach was a cocaine overdose. You'll have my official report within the hour."

"I appreciate it. Talk to you later," I ended the call. "There, you have it. All four died of a cocaine overdose."

Detective Scully stood up and threw his hands in the air. "We got fuckin' nothing to go on. Either our murderer enjoys a high standard of living or he wants us to think he does. We need to find this mother before he kills again."

"Up until now, the two Quincy murders were linked together, the Hull murder was a stand-alone, as was the Revere Beach murder. They were individually reported in the papers as separate incidents. That was until Vinny Balls wrote a story for *The Daily Chatter*. He didn't have to say the murders were related, all that shithead had to do was mention them all in the same article. The public will draw their own conclusions." My chair squeaked as I rocked back and forth. "Our murderer is part of that public. When he reads between the lines, the letters S E R I A L will flash like a neon sign. He's either going to get his jollies off and strike again or he's going to go into seclusion until this becomes a cold case."

The room went quiet until Sal broke the silence. "I think he fancies himself the mind master in his game of superiority. I think he's already planning his next move. Only this time he knows we're watching. So the game plan could change."

"What game plan?" McGinnis asked.

"What, is the operative word. First, I'm sure we can all agree the four murders in question were done by the same person." I waited for everyone to answer. "The times of death ranged from nine to ten hours before they were found. They were all found on area beaches by early morning joggers or dog walkers."

"There's a couple of late night restaurants, bars and clubs relatively close to the Hull and Revere Beach locations, so our killer would have to take that into consideration before dumping the body." Sal hesitated then continued. "Dumping isn't the right word. He carefully placed them. That required extra time."

"We'll check along Ocean Street and Revere Beach Boulevard to see if there are any surveillance cameras. A couple years back we had a string of robberies in the area. I know several of the businesses and a handful of residential properties had them installed." With my finger, I traced the route on a map of the area.

"Scully and I will do the same on the Wollaston Beach road." Detective McGinnis continued to make notes. "High-end cars,

SUV's or vans—maybe tinted windows—sometime between two and five a.m. Sound right?"

Sal nodded. "It's a start."

I looked at Sal. "We're also going to mingle with the homeless population that comes out to dumpster dive after the paying population retires. A couple bucks will start them talking. If something sounds interesting, a couple more keeps the juke box playing."

"Same goes for our informants," said Scully. "There's also a couple stores around Quincy that might carry that Kors line of clothes. We'll check sales with them."

I handed the Quincy detectives my card. "My cell's on the back. Call me if you find anything of interest. I'll do the same. We'll conference tomorrow. Let's say here at three o'clock."

CHAPTER 15

"Time to get answers." I picked up the file of reports and pictures and put it into my briefcase. "We can scan the businesses for surveillance cameras this afternoon. Maybe we'll get lucky."

"What about the dumpster divers?"

"We can canvass the homeless camps around the beach. It'll be a hit or miss. I know at least one of the residents behind St. Mark's should be around. There's a guy living there—or at least was living there—who might be able to help us out. I've worked with him before. He usually rests in the afternoon so, at night he can move with the swiftness of the cat to get in and out of alleys and back lots of the restaurants and clubs without being caught."

"We should also plan on an impromptu meeting with more of our night crawlers after the witching hour."

"First things first—we'll visit the homeless camp, then check out some of the establishments for cameras." I picked up my phone and dialed IT's extension. "Mario, can you work your magic and come up with a list of businesses with a Revere Beach Boulevard address that reported break-ins within the last couple years?"

There was no hesitation. "Sure."

"Thanks, we'll pick it up in about ten minutes."

Sal punched a number into his cell, then mouthed Becky. "Hi Babe, I'm working late tonight. Not sure what time I'll be home. Call you later." He snapped his phone back in its holder. "I think she told me she was doing a girls-day-out. Makes it easier when I can leave a message and don't have to do a lot of explaining."

CHAPTER 16

At three o'clock, we drove down the Boulevard and pulled into the rear parking lot of St. Mark's Catholic Church. It wasn't Sunday and, apparently, there weren't any programs going on. The only two cars on the property were in front of the office door.

The property behind the church was covered with heavy foliage making it perfect to conceal tents, cardboard boxes covered with tarps or make-shift lean-tos. "Most of the homeless that live here are harmless. The church knows they're squatting on church property, but as long as they don't cause problems, the church looks the other way. In fact, they've been known to give them food, and in the winter, if they can't find room in one of the shelters, they've opened their hall for the night." I took a deep breath. "Ready."

"Let's do it."

"Best way to go is down that path." I pointed to a narrow opening in the far corner of the lot. I took the pictures of our girls from my briefcase and got out of the car.

Sal was waiting. "Poor bastards. I know some of them choose to be homeless, but there are some here as a result of the economy."

"Follow me." I felt for my Glock. "I don't anticipate trouble, but the climate in these places can change as fast as a coin flip."

It was quiet. From a quick visual sweep of the camp, most of the tent flaps were down, the lean-tos had flimsy plastic-bag-doors moving gently in the breeze and the cardboard box openings were facing away from the path.

We stopped at the first tent. I rapped my key on one of the spines holding the tattered structure up. There was no response. I rapped again. "Anyone in there?" I moved aside.

"Go away," came a gruff male voice.

"Boston PD—we need to talk to you."

"Go away," he said again.

"Here's your choice. Either you come out here now or I grab hold of this tent and we drag you out." I switched my briefcase to my left hand just in case I had to grab my tool of persuasion.

I concentrated on the tent I was standing beside, while Sal perused the rest of the camp. "There's a couple people stirring ahead. One appears to be a female. She crawled out of the lean-to on the left. Somebody else stuck their head out from the tent across from the lean-to, then quickly pulled it back. A man I think." Sal shifted his watch. A guy unzipped the front flap of his shelter and sat crossed-legged with a small child on his lap.

"I'm going to count to ten, then I own your tent. Your choice." I got to seven and grabbed one of the spines.

"Wait, wait. I'm coming out."

I stepped back and slid my hand inside my jacket. "Good choice. Come out slowly. All we want to do is ask a few questions."

A scrawny, shirtless, shoeless man edged out, on his knees, his hands over his head. "Please don't hurt me. Don't hurt none of us. We're good people. We didn't do nothing. The church lets us stay here as long as there ain't no trouble. We don't make no trouble."

"Like I said, we just want to ask you some questions." I looked down the path. By now, several more people had gathered. They kept their distance, which was fine by me. "Stand up and walk down to where your friends are."

He followed my directions. Sal and I walked behind him, still keeping an open eye for anyone who might decide to join us from behind or try to blindside us.

I held out my shield. "My name is Detective Mastro from the Revere PD. My partner is Detective Petruca."

“Detective Mike Mastro.” The voice came from a figure in the shadows about twenty feet down the path. “It’s me, Pete Fortunado.”

Sal stayed at the beginning of the camp and I walked in Pete’s direction. He moved from the shadows into a clearing. The sun doubled as a spotlight. I held out my hand. He reached forward to shake it.

“You’re still here,” I said.

“Yeah. I’ve had a few odd jobs here and there, but when you’re down on your luck it ain’t easy to move back up. I’m doin’ okay though. These are my friends. Nobody hassles us here. We’re lucky.” He moved his hands in a semi-circle and looked around at the other residents.

“Glad to hear you’re all right. I need a favor. Can you assure these people we’re not here to cause problems. We need their help.”

“I can,” he said. “Hey, everyone, this is my friend. He wants to talk to us. Find something to sit on and we’ll listen to what he has to say.”

I positioned myself with my back to a tree. “Yesterday the body of a woman believed to be in her early twenties was found face down in the sand on the beach side of the seawall. She was about ten feet away from the bath house across from the Do-Drop-In.” I stopped to observe any changes in expressions. There were none. “I realize the Do-Drop-In Lounge is a ways down the street, but I also know it’s where you all do a lot of dumpster diving after the bars and restaurants close.”

Sal shifted his position and did an updated survey of the camp.

I took two of the Revere girl pictures from my briefcase and handed them to Pete. “Take a look at these, then pass them around.”

Pete studied them. I watched his face. It didn’t reflect any recognition. He handed them to the girl standing beside him and instructed her to take a look, then pass them along.

"Here's what I need from you." I addressed the group. "Right now, the girl that was on the beach is listed as a Jane Doe. She has a name and a family. We'd like to reunite them."

One member of the group raised his hand. "Do you think she was one of us? I mean a homeless person. We live in fear for our women. Bad people prey on them—promise them a new life, then abuse them. They're vulnerable—especially the young ones—like this girl." He looked down at the picture of the girl's face. "Can I see the other picture?"

Sal handed him the one of Revere girl lying face down in the sand.

I watched.

"She was dressed nice."

I acknowledged his observation. "Very nice."

"We're a small group. She's never been here." He reached over the head of the little boy and passed the pictures to the person standing beside him.

The girl beside Pete spoke up. "Detective, I have a question?" She was very soft spoken and appeared somewhat timid. "Was she one of the girls from the article in *The Chatter* this morning?"

"She was."

A paled look came over her face. "So that means there were three more just like her."

"Unfortunately, it does."

Pete paced slowly back and forth along the path. After a couple minutes of silent contemplation, he stopped in front of me. "I'm afraid to ask the next question, but I have no choice." He looked around. "This is our home—as humble as it may seem—we are a family. Our family is far more vulnerable to a crime like this than a family living two streets over in a locked and sometimes alarmed house." He hesitated, then lifted his head and looked straight into my eyes. "Is this the work of a serial killer?"

Vinny Balls—that fuckin' bastard. "I can't truthfully answer you. It could be, but then again it could be isolated incidents being made to look that way. That's why I need your help."

The same man who raised his hand before, raised it again. "What do you need us to do?"

"Detective Petruca and I are going to canvass the area. We don't live here. You do. You are the eyes and the ears of the night more than the day. Our Revere girl was carried from a vehicle, lifted over the seawall and gently placed on the sand in the position you viewed in the picture. It's been determined this happened sometime between two and four a.m."

"We'll do what we can."

"I don't want you or anyone in your camp to tell people what you're doing. If you're talking to someone from another camp, just bring it up in conversation by referring to *The Chatter's* newspaper article. At this point, we're not going to interview any other homeless people. Detective Petruca and I will give each of you a card with our contact information. Don't hesitate to call if you have something or need us." I stopped to wait for a response.

Pete agreed and the rest of the group nodded.

We personally handed each person, except the child, one of our cards hoping the personal exchange would instill a level of trust.

"Before we leave, I have one more question. Has anybody noticed a vehicle, possibly a high-end one, riding up and down the Boulevard over the past week? It could be day or night. It might be one that would stand out—not necessarily because of the color, but because of its size. Something like a Lincoln Expedition or Navigator or a Mercedes SUV, maybe with tinted windows," I said.

There was no response.

I tried to analyze their faces to figure out what they were thinking. Nothing. I turned to Sal and gave him the high sign that we were about to leave, then turned back to the group. " Keep your eyes open, but remember, don't talk too much."

Pete walked to the parking lot with us. "We'll do what we can." He reached to shake my hand.

I took a hundred dollars in small bills from my pocket and handed them to Pete. "Later."

Chapter 17

I put the Revere girl pictures away and took out the list Mario gave us. There were ten businesses noted. "Most of the break-ins were on the Eliot Circle end of the Boulevard. The only two past the bath house were in the four-hundred block." I handed Sal the list, then pulled to the front of the parking lot.

"A year and a half ago, St. Mark's was broken into. Since we're here, let's check the perimeter for cameras."

We parked beside the two cars we'd seen when we arrived forty-five minutes earlier as we cut through the parking lot to the homeless camp. I reached around and lifted my Konica from behind my seat, then got out of the car, and pointed to the eaves above the office door. "Looks like they took precautions. Let's hope this wasn't the only one they had installed."

Sal made a note, then thumbed through the attached blurbs Mario had copied from the files. "According to the report, the Church was hit hard. It was a night job. The thieves stole money from the safe, religious figures, several gold crosses, and four gold chalices, spray-painted the insides of six stained glass windows and tried to carve something into the front pews."

"I remember that. I wasn't the one who did the investigating, but I do know the PD couldn't determine what they were trying to inscribe. It didn't appear to match any known gang-related symbol or one from a radical religious group. If I'm not mistaken, the Church didn't have an alarm system and the perps went in through the front door."

"According to the report, that's what happened."

We rounded the corner to the front of the Church.

"Bingo." Sal made a note.

I took a picture. "These cameras might be able to give us some useful information. Looks like they're set up to scan the entire front. That includes part of the parking lots on either side of the Church, the street frontage and the immediate area surrounding the front entrance."

The only other camera we found was in the rear—over a door that I assumed was primarily used for maintenance entrance and egress. Even though it couldn't provide us with any pertinent information, I took a picture of it anyway. We walked back to our unmarked, put our reports and the camera into the back seat, then headed inside the Church.

The door opened into a long, wide hallway with eight knobbed and two restroom push doors. The second knobbed door on the right was open. We knocked on the jamb. Before I could introduce ourselves, a quiet female voice invited us in.

"Good afternoon, gentlemen." A smartly dressed, middle-aged woman got up from behind a desk and extended her hand to us. "How may I help you?"

"I'm Detective Mastro and this is Detective Petruca." I held out my shield for her to examine. "We're investigating a murder that may or may not have happened in the area. The victim was found not far from here on the beach side of the seawall, near the bath house across from the Do-Drop-In Lounge."

Her expression turned to concern. "That place breeds trouble. Sounds like she was a patron."

"No ma'am. We don't believe so."

"I'm not a ma'am. My name is Martha McDonald. Please call me Martha."

I stepped back and let Sal take over. "We know that approximately a year-and-a-half ago you had a break-in that caused a lot of damage. We know that this whole area was hit, and the one or ones who did it were never apprehended."

"Oh, make no mistake about it. There were more than one, maybe even more than two. The destruction here was horrific. And, to a church—a place of God. I know I'm not supposed to say it, but I hope they burn in hell." She made the sign of the cross. "Please sit down." She directed us to the two chairs in front of the desk as she made her way behind it.

"We walked around the outside of the building to see if St. Mark's installed surveillance cameras."

Martha spoke up before I could continue. "Right after it happened, Father Mackey requested and was granted permission from the Diocese to have them installed. We're very solvent, so we were able to get top-of-the line equipment. We even have cameras with backup capability."

"Martha, you just made my day. We need to take a look at the data created from your system over the last five weeks. Are you able to help us with that or do we have to make a formal request?" I asked.

"I'll be right back." Without any explanation she left her office.

"We'll probably have to have the blessing of the Cardinal," I said before I realized there was somebody standing behind me.

"No, that won't be necessary."

I felt my face flush. "Caught red-handed."

We stood to greet Father Mackey. "Detective Mastro, it's been a while."

Sal saw my expression go from 'oops I got caught by Father' to genuine puzzlement.

"Since I've had the pleasure to meet Detective Mastro before, I'm going to assume you're Detective Petruca."

"Yes, Sir, I am."

"Please have a seat." Father Mackey sat where Martha had been. Martha opened a folding chair and sat slightly away from her desk to the left of the Father. "Martha said I should talk to you. That it's important. You wouldn't be here if it wasn't important. So, here I am, ready to listen."

I studied Father Mackey's face.

"You don't remember me do you?"

"I do and I don't." I felt like a ten-year-old getting the third degree because I skipped catechism.

"Last year I headed the Red Mass at St. Stephen's on Clark Street. You were there with Chief Pozzi. After Mass, a group of us went for coffee and an invigorating discussion about the *Boston Globe*."

"I remember now." The discussion was about the filming of an upcoming movie that involved the Boston Diocese. I tried to recall my input into the conversation.

"Don't think too hard. You were fine." He tittered.

"Thank you, Father."

He leaned back in Martha's chair and folded his hands over a very comfortably formed belly. "Now, with those formalities out of the way, what is it you need from me today?"

I repeated the same bits of information I'd already given to Martha, then continued, "We believe our killer staked out the area before he chose it to be Revere girl's final resting place. He studied the patterns of area establishments and the foot and automobile traffic along the Boulevard. He planned it very carefully. He obviously didn't want to get caught, but he did want his victim found. He knew the tides. He knew the layout. He knew, for him, the time of year was right for this location."

Father Markey put his hand up to stop me. "Is this the same victim that Vinny Balducci wrote about in *The Chatter*?"

"It is."

"He didn't leave much to the imagination. You didn't have to read between the lines to know he was linking the cases from Hull, Quincy and Revere together. He implied they were done by the same person. So, let me ask you, do we have a serial killer running around Boston?"

"You mince no words, Father." I took a deep breath before answering. "Your concern is a valid one, but it hasn't been officially labeled serial. Once we can rule that in or out of our investigation, I'll let you know. I'm sure your parishioners will look to you for direction." I rested an elbow on the desk and took the pose of the Thinker. "I can tell you that we believe our latest victim was not killed in the neighborhood. We are working on the assumption she was killed elsewhere and brought here. I can't give you specific details, though."

"I understand."

"The reason we want to look at your church surveillance data is to study passing vehicles." I sighed. "That's about all I can say right now."

"Do you want me to make copies?"

"That would let us examine them closely. It's easy to miss things on a first go-round."

"Give me the dates and about an hour and I'll have them for you."

"You don't know how much we appreciate your help."

I gave Father Markey the dates. He checked the calendar on Martha's desk, then nodded an acknowledgment. We all stood at the same time. I wanted to pump fist Sal, but bit my tongue instead to conceal my enthusiasm.

I took Martha's one hand in my two. "Thank you."

CHAPTER 18

Sal checked St. Mark's off the break-in list. "I've been a cop for twenty-six years—twenty-two of them on Beacon Hill and the last four in Revere. It never ceases to amaze me how different one city can be. That's why I love Boston."

"Four years here and three of them with me. How lucky can you get?"

We pulled away from the church, but stopped before hitting the Boulevard again. I put the car in park. "What are some of the other names on the list?"

"Jack Satter House, Kelly's, Bianchi's Pizza, Renzo's, Santorini's and the Do-Drop-In Lounge."

"The Jack Satter house is senior citizen apartments. Is there a report attached for that one?"

"Yeah. Says that four computers and two televisions were taken from the back offices."

"What time did the break-in occur?

"The time of incident was listed between midnight and two a.m. There's a footnote. One of the employees thought it might be an inside job. She said there'd been problems with management and people were fired. No reasons given or anything else said. There might be more in their complete file, but it sounds like whoever broke into the Satter House used the timing of the other break-ins as a cover."

"I agree. We can look into it further if we need to. Let's take a ride by, though, to see if they installed cameras." I made a left onto the Boulevard. In less than a mile, we made another left into the Satter House parking lot. The glass front doors were completely exposed. There weren't any surveillance cameras mounted above or around them. We drove around the building. There were two glass doors and three solid ones. They were all about six feet in from the parking lot, each having a walkway leading to them.

"No cameras." Sal made a note and checked them off the break-in list.

"At this time, there's no need to head any further north. It's heavily populated with mostly houses and just a scattering of businesses." I made a U-turn. "Kelly's is on the list. You hungry?"

"Always."

"They've got good food. I'm getting a clam roll with French fries and onion rings." I pulled out onto the Boulevard, then immediately turned right into Kelly's lot. We parked and headed toward the door. "Smile, you're on candid camera."

Sal looked up and flashed his pearly whites.

I opened the door and we went inside. "Benny, Benny, Benny—how the hell are you?"

"You old bastard—you still sportin' that badge?"

"Yeah, one of these days you can visit me in Florida."

"Make it soon, will ya? I'm gettin' tired of smilin' and bein' nice."

"You don't know how to be any other way." I turned to Sal. "Benny, want you to meet my partner, Sal Petruca. I'm educating him on all the fineries in the North End and the ones worth mentioning in the East side. He started out on Beacon Hill, then decided he wanted to be a real cop, so here he is." I slapped Sal on the back.

Benny wiped his hands on his apron and stepped around from behind the counter. "Glad to meet ya." He took Sal's hand. "Don't know how you stand this guy though."

"It isn't easy, but I'm learning."

"You got good clams today—you know, the ones with the big bellies?"

"Got 'em in this morning. That what you want?"

"Yep, a clam roll with all the fixins'."

"Make that two," Sal said.

"Get yourself a table and I'll bring the stuff to you."

I grabbed a Diet Coke from the cooler. "Want one?"

"Yeah."

We had our choice of tables.

"Did you read the report attached to his break-in?"

"They broke in through a back door and took a computer, money from the safe and a TV. It appeared they stayed in the office."

I looked around. "They didn't want to risk getting seen. Look at this place, all glass."

"You going to ask about the camera?"

"I am, when he brings our food. After we leave here, we'll pick up the Church DVD, then I figure we can hit a few more places then head back to the station. I want to look at the church data before we call it a day. If we can get a few more DVDs, maybe we'll get lucky and find someone who likes to cruise the Boulevard. It's a long shot, but I like long shots. It's the obvious that turns out to be nothing. It's like when I used to play the dogs at Wonderland. The favorites never paid much, but those long-shots, when they came in, they paid." I looked at Sal. "You hear what I'm sayin'."

"Loud and clear," said Sal. "I told Becky I didn't know what time I'd be home, so I'll stay and watch the DVDs with you."

"Sounds good. I want to go to Renzo's, Santorini's and the Do-Drop-In. Walter Adams is a cop out of downtown. We went through the academy together. I heard he's getting ready to retire. He bought the bar ten, twelve years ago. He bills it as a sports bar, but it's a dive. He doesn't care. It's a cash cow."

Sal checked Mario's report. "The Do-Drop-In Lounge is on the break-in list."

"I know. It had to be a fuckin' asshole or holes that went into his place. I heard they stole more than he reported. He keeps some serious cash in his safe. Plus, he sells lottery tickets. They took those too. The lottery money wasn't in the safe. Adams had a 'secret' hiding place for that. They either knew where it was or got lucky. They got that too. Adams likes his tea. I figure one night he got cocked and talked too much or didn't feel like opening the safe and went into his 'secret' place for some money. Somebody noticed and the next morning everything was gone."

"Do you think he put up cameras?"

"I'm sure he had them before the burglary, but whether or not they were working is another story. We'll soon find out."

We stopped talking when Benny brought over our food. "So, Mike, what brings you to the Boulevard?"

"If you read *The Chatter*, I'm sure you've figured it out."

"I saw it. I was surprised to see Vinny Balls is still around. He's crossed so many people, I thought somebody might've put him in a box." Benny pulled up a chair.

I nodded. "Question for you. After you had that break-in last year did you put up a surveillance camera?"

"Yeah, three of them. There's one over the back door. It scans the rear lot. There's also one on the left corner of the building. It covers the outside seating area, the side parking lot and the Boulevard where you turn onto my property, and the one you saw over the front door."

"Can you see both sides of the Boulevard?"

"Absolutely." He leaned forward on his forearms. "Why do you ask?"

"Can your system make a hard copy?"

"Sure."

"I need to see footage from the camera that scans the Boulevard. I need it from a month ago until now."

"No problem. When do you want it?"

"Yesterday." I waggled my clam roll. "Still the best around."

Benny turned to his employee working behind the counter. "Oscar can handle the front. Give me a half hour? I'll go back and start now."

"Thanks, we'll wait."

Benny disappeared through a door next to the prep counter.

"You appear to be an icon around here."

"Been around these parts for years. Grew up not far from here. Revere Beach was always a hangout."

Twenty minutes after Benny left, he returned and slid a take-out bag onto the table. Inside were two plastic cases—one with a generic DVD and one CD with a Frank Sinatra's *Ol' Blue Eyes is Back* still sealed. I thanked him. "Those were the days my friend, those were the days."

Benny wouldn't let us pay. "Keep me in the loop. Catch the funkin' bum." He shook a finger and pointed out the window. "We don't need scum like that messin' up our Boulevard."

CHAPTER 19

Father Mackey told us to give him an hour—an hour and a half had passed. "Before we see if Adams is at the Lounge, we'll swing by St. Mark's. The DVD should be ready. I'll run in."

Sal studied the reports while he waited in the unmarked.

I was back in two minutes. "Two down."

"Do you know if there was a rash of break-ins in other sections of the city around this same time as the Boulevard ones?"

"I never checked. It's Boston. There's always something going on somewhere. Face it, we're only here because of our Doll." My cell rang. "Mastro." It was Irving. I put my cell on speaker.

"I've just finished the complete autopsy on your Revere girl. There's something you should see." He hesitated. "Are you near my lab?"

"Sal and I are on the Boulevard. We could be there in twenty minutes as long as we don't get held up in traffic."

"It's important. I'll be waiting."

"On our way."

"What was that all about?"

"The ME wants us to stop by. Says there's something we should see. I know Irving and he'd never call us in unless he had somethin' we needed to see." I tried to imagine what he had. "It's Friday night, I know Adams will still be around. We'll meet with Irving, then make the return trip."

There were only two cars in the ME's lot when we pulled in. I pushed the buzzer for the intercom. "Detectives Mastro and Petruca." The lock clicked open and we went in.

Irving was outside his lab. "Gentlemen, please come in." We followed him to the table where Revere girl was laid out. "Earlier today, when I was working on our girl, I found she has a very small tattoo on her right buttock. I didn't call you then because I didn't think it was relatable to the case. After I finished my examination of Revere girl, I pulled the reports on Hull girl. I didn't do the complete exam, my assistant did, so I didn't realize she also had a tattoo and in the same location. I have a call into Quincy. As soon as they get back to me, I'll let you know." Irving's assistant helped turn the Revere girl over. The ME tugged at the skin on her buttock to stretch the tiny tattoo. "This is what I was talking about. It's not your ordinary run-of-the-mill design. It's custom."

Sal and I leaned forward. "Interesting," I said. "It looks like our girls both, for some reason, liked football. Maybe a different side of the game though."

"It's a capital D followed by a picket fence. Defense."

"I know what it is."

Sal took a deep breath. "We should run it by the gang unit to see if they've seen one before." "Given the ages of the girls, it may be some kind of secret society thing."

"And their purpose?"

"Who the hell knows? Maybe some bookies are paying them to cozy up to players to throw a game. Or film them having sex and blackmail them to work the point spread."

"I'm betting Quincy will verify there's ass art on the first two Dolls. These girls played a dangerous game of something with someone one too many times." I moved away from Revere girl. "Irving could you get me a couple pictures of her artwork. And make sure you put a copy in the file."

"I have another scenario to consider. You know how bands have groupies that follow them all over the country, these girls could be football groupies. They probably didn't know each other. There's lots of money in football. These girls were young, beautiful, maybe adventurous and, apparently, estranged from family and friends since nobody stepped forward to claim them."

"Not a bad theory."

"I want to keep our new found artwork under wraps for the time being. We'll show it to the Chief and to the Quincy detectives, but no one else." I turned toward Irving and his assistant for a response.

The ME looked to the young man standing beside him. "You heard what the detective said. Don't discuss this with anyone."

CHAPTER 20

It was four-thirty when we pulled up in front of the Do-Drop-In Lounge—the kind of place that was a pit stop for the regulars between work and home. Friday nights were more of a destination spot. Adams' car was parked under a floodlight two spaces down from the front door.

"Cop by day, bar owner by night. And, in this place, there's a lot the 'cop' turns his back on. See the pizza place next door? There's an inside window between them. I think Adams owns part, if not all, of that place too."

"Quite the entrepreneur."

"Quite," I said. "Got the picture of Revere girl?"

"On the back seat. I'll take it in."

Three more cars pulled into the lot in the short time we'd been sitting there. "This place is a gold mine, but I couldn't deal with the bullshit. When you meet Adams you'll understand how he does. Even if he wasn't the owner, this is the kind of place where he'd hang around."

Stale smoke hit us in the face as we walked in. The place hadn't changed in years. Narrow, dimly lit booths lined the wall opposite the bar—two of them were already occupied. Small round Formica topped tables, each surrounded with four wooden chairs filled the rest of the room. Poorly framed pictures of bikers hung uneven on the far wall with an array of dew rags pinned to a molding over them. A dart board with a sign advertising the Tuesday night dart league hung in an alcove to the left of the biker art. The only item of real value hung behind the bar—an official Red Sox shirt autographed by members of the 1967 Dream Team.

I pointed to the specially encased piece of memorabilia. "Do you remember the 1967 Red Sox season?"

"I wasn't born."

I chose to ignore him. "For my fifth birthday my dad told me I wasn't going to school. Instead we went to a game at Fenway Park. The Sox played the Yankees and Lonborg pitched. The Sox won. My first big game, I'll never forget it."

Adams' back was to us. He was busy checking his liquor cabinets for inventory and didn't see us come in.

"Hey Adams, you dirty dog," I slid onto one of the bar stools. "Busy figuring out how much you make a bottle?"

He spun around. "I'd recognize that voice anywhere. What the hell brings you to the Boulevard." Adams put his hand up to keep me from speaking. "I know, I know—the chick they found dead on the beach yesterday morning." He laid his inventory sheets on the counter behind him. "Got any clues?"

"Working on it." I turned to Sal. "Meet Detective Petruca."

Adams held a hand out to Sal. "How long you been working with this asshole?"

"Four years in the Revere, three with Mike."

"Aren't you the lucky one." Adams picked up a couple glasses. "Can I buy you a drink?"

"Not today." I wouldn't drink out of one of his glasses any day.

"So, why are you here harassing me?"

"I need your help."

Adams phony laugh was loud enough that the five patrons at the end of the bar turned to see what was so funny.

He'll never change. "Get serious."

Sal took the picture of Revere girl from the folder. "Does she look familiar?"

"In this place they all look alike. If that girl, dressed in those clothes, walked in here she'd stand out. Look around, what would she want from my clientele?"

"You've got a point there."

"Second question. I know you have cameras inside. I'm not sure if you're using them to make your own porn movies or what."

Adams wasn't amused.

"Calm down buddy—just kidding. I know you got hit real bad about a year ago in the Boulevard string of break-ins. And, I also know you wouldn't sit back and not do anything about it, so I'm assuming you put several surveillance cameras outside."

"You can bet your ass I did. If those fuckin' bastards ever think of repeating their little stunt, I'll find them and they'll never wake up on the green-side again."

"Do the cameras out front scan the Boulevard too?"

"Damn right they do."

"That's where we need your help. We want to check out the automobile traffic up and down the Boulevard from about a month ago until yesterday. Do you think you could make us a copy of your data for that period?"

"I can." Adams nodded. "I'm not busy and it won't take me long. I put in a real good system. You'll be impressed. Give me fifteen, twenty minutes and I'll have it for you." He walked through a door at the end of the bar.

"Sounds like you've been here before."

"I have. I used to hang with Adams. We were known to visit the Lounge before he bought it." I shrugged.

"Are we stopping anywhere before we head back to the station?"

"No, we need to review the DVDs. Even the slightest inclination of a suspicious vehicle might trigger concern. There's a sick bastard messin' around with our city and, if I can help it, he's going down."

Sal knew, that at this moment, it was better to listen than to speak.

"Tomorrow we should be hittin' the stores for Mr. Kors fashions. I can't imagine the purchase of the same style skirts by the same high-end designer in same size and same pattern only in different colors would go unnoticed."

Sal rested his arms on the bar. "I don't have a good feeling. We need something to break real soon or I think we're going to have another Doll on our hands."

"I think you're right." I didn't see Adams come out of his office, so when he put his hand on my shoulder, my automatic reaction was to turn and grab the person behind me.

He backed up quickly, then handed me the discs. "Touchy, touchy."

I slid them into my pocket and stood up. "Thanks, man. It's been a long couple days. I'll let you know what I find." I waved without looking back.

CHAPTER 21

I paused the DVD player. "I'm going to make a pot of Joe. Want some?"

"Yeah. My senses need a kick in the ass."

Sal was rereading the break-in reports when I came back to the office carrying two cups of fresh coffee. "Did anything change?"

"I wish."

"I need to get ahold of Mario. Somewhere in my desk is his cell number." One of these days I'm going to get organized. I sorted through a stack of business cards, then a pile of post-it notes fastened together with an oversized paper clip. "Here it is." I punched in his number. He answered on the second ring.

"Mario, it's Mastro. Detective Petruca and I are at the office with a few DVDs we picked up from St. Mark's and a couple of the businesses on your Boulevard break-in list. We've looked at them three times and are about to view them once more. We haven't come up with anything."

There was a short silence before Mario began talking. "I can take…"

"Wait, I'm putting you on speaker. Can you repeat that for Sal?"

"I can take the DVDs you got today and enhance them. We'll get so close it'll look like you're standing right next to the image—be it a person or a vehicle. Sometimes, depending on the angle when the camera recorded the image, I can move it around. Since you're talking about moving objects, it might not be completely clear, but it might be enough to get something identifiable."

"Can you come in tomorrow morning?"

"What time do you want me there?"

I held up five, then three more fingers.

Sal nodded.

"Eight o'clock okay?"

"See you then, detectives."

"I told you he's the guru of the IT department."

"What time are we meeting with the Chief?"

"Around noon. Depending on what time we finish with Mario, we might have a couple hours to embellish our knowledge of the female fashion industry. I'll scan the internet tonight and get names of boutiques or clothing stores that sell Mr. Kors pants—I mean skirts. We can hit a few close by."

"It's almost nine o'clock. I'm going to call it a day. There's nothing more we can do until after we meet with Mario." Sal took his cell from its holder and punched in his home number. "Hi, have you eaten? Jammies already? Then how 'bout I call Pagliuca's and order a pepperoni and mushroom pizza?"

I folded my arms over my chest. Those were the kind of moments I missed.

"Yeah, sure, I'll ask Jimmy to make one of his special antipastos for two. Have the wine ready." Sal chuckled and hit the end button.

"Honey, have the wine ready." I mocked. "Get the hell out of here before I get sick."

"Tomorrow."

An hour later I sat in front of my home computer eating peanut-butter cheese crackers, washing them down with an icy Sam's Cold Snap and looking at women's fashions. At ten o'clock, I changed my venue. I put my feminine side to bed, moved to the living room and switched on *Blue Bloods.*

CHAPTER 22

Saturday

I swung by Dunkin's and picked up a box of joe and a dozen donuts for the office. I'm not usually in the office on a Saturday, but this case was a priority. Sal wasn't in yet. When I turned, I noticed Mario parked beside the back door to the station. *Good man.*

My hands were full, but I managed to push the button to get buzzed in. I gawked at the camera above the door, then, heard the click signalizing recognition. "Thank you."

I wrapped on the window that looked into Mario's outer waiting room and held up the box of donuts. It didn't take him two seconds to get to the door.

"I got here fifteen minutes ago myself. I wanted everything set up so we could get this show on the road."

"Don't just stand there. Take one of these before I drop them."

Mario cleared a spot on the table next to his desk and set the box of joe on one side and the donuts beside it. "You got the DVDs with you?"

"Right here. Let's have a donut and give Sal another minute." I headed to the breakroom to get some cups and napkins. Sal was rounding the corner at the end of the hall when I got back.

"I thought I'd be early." Sal looked in at Mario, who was busy tweaking his equipment, then back to me.

"Just got here myself. Coffee?"

Sal jerked his head to some side. "Does a bear shit in the woods? Of course I want coffee."

"Hey guys, I'm ready to run the DVD labeled Kelly's." Mario grabbed a donut and poured himself a cup of joe, then walked behind the three-by-four foot table-top computer control panel."

I backed up and slid my ass on the corner of his desk. "Ready when you are."

"Mike, this is how the common people would view this scene. There are cars, people and, across the street by the beach, a couple dogs. It's your everyday activity on the Boulevard when you looked at them on your home DVD player."

I didn't say anything, just nodded.

"I'm going to bring the action down to a crawl, run the whole thing once, then we can go back and analyze it."

The three of us didn't take our eyes off the screen.

"Mario, I concentrated on the vehicles. There are a couple I want to take a closer look at. I'll let you know when you come to them."

"There," I came up off his desk.

Mario froze the frame.

"That appears to be a Lincoln Expedition. Back it up so I can see in the driver's side window."

Sal looked at me. "It's tinted."

"Can you zoom in any closer?"

"I can." Mario moved his hand across the control panel. "It is tinted, but the silhouette appears to be a male." He hit print. "Sal, grab the picture from the printer beside you."

Sal grabbed the pictures from the printer. "It is a male. His features are defined. The face is elongated, his nose could hold a fist full of dimes and he could use a haircut. I'd say he was Caucasian."

"Start the crawl again." My eyes were focused on the slow moving movie. "Stop. Check that one out." I moved closer to the screen. "It's not an SUV, but it's a Mercedes 550. Big car, much lower to the ground and easier to lift a person out of. We need a close-up."

"Just like the Lincoln, only one occupant and definitely a man."

"The driver's wearing a baseball cap and, lucky for us, in reverse. Zoom in. We need to figure out the logo." I knew I'd seen it before, but was drawing a blank.

The printer spit an image into the tray.

Sal folded his arms across his chest. "He's wearing a Boston Bean Club hat."

I studied the image on the big screen. "This guy's shoulders stretch from one side of the seat to the other and at least four inches above the top. The headrest appears to be pulled up as high as it can go. He's a big guy."

Sal nodded. "Strong enough to easily lift one of the Dolls."

"Hold that thought. I want to look closer at the license plate. It's recessed in, but I think I can get part of it." Mario slid his hand across the control panel again. "It's rough, but it looks like a Jimmy Fund Red Sox plate."

It was distorted, but I could see what Mario was talking about. "You're right. It's definitely a JF plate. And, the first number is either a 0 or a 9."

Sal was on his feet. His hands out of his pockets. " It's a start."

"We've still got more footage to look at."

Mario zoomed out to clear up the remaining images. He stopped at a Lexus. "Check this one out."

"I don't think so. It's a female driving and it looks like there are a couple kids in the back. You can flag it in case we need to come back after we check out the other DVDs." I warmed up my coffee.

"Whoa. Check the car heading toward the city. It's a Cadillac Escalade. It's the side closest to Kelly's. It should be clearer," said Mario.

"The car might be closer to Kelly's, but we don't have a clear picture of the driver. We have a clear picture of a passenger." Sal checked out the image on the screen. "It's a female, but that's all we can determine. She's looking at the driver. She's small, but I don't think small enough to be a child." I turned toward Mario. "It's a little late to ask, but did you date and time stamp the images of the vehicles we've looked at?"

"Way ahead of you detective. It's on the pictures we printed out. Do you want to keep going on this DVD?"

"Take the disc from St. Mark's, find the same time period. We've tagged three vehicles heading away from the city and one heading in. Run the church disc to see if any of the four vehicles are visible."

It didn't take any time for Mario to have the church disc up and running.

"Slow it down a bit in case we see new vehicles we need to flag. Remember there's a street beside Kelly's. Since the Cadillac is the only car heading south past Kelly's, it could have turned off the Boulevard before it reached the church. On the other hand, new cars of interest could have pulled onto the Boulevard." My eyes followed the moving images.

"There's the Lincoln." Sal stepped closer to study the screen. "We got two different images from Kelly's because of the camera locations. Since the church only has one camera installed to scan the main entrance, I'm guessing the best shot we've got is straight into the driver's side."

"Give me a minute." Mario played with the control panel moving the Lincoln back and forth. He froze the image. "Take another look." An electronic pointer appeared on the screen, with Mario controlling its movement from eight feet away. "Definitely the same vehicle and, with the slight change in angle, I can tell you the first number on the plate after the JF is a zero." He moved the pointer to solidify his statement, then zoomed in as far as he could before it fuzzed out. "I know this isn't very clear, but it's the best I can do."

"Just fine, my man, just fine. The second number is a seven. Do you see that?"

"I do."

Mario nodded. "The church camera is much higher quality than Kelly's. Also, there's no question, the driver is a white male."

I felt good about our find.

Mario handed Sal a sharpie. "I'm printing out more pictures. Write church on the back of these."

Sal moved over by the printer, lifted the three new images and followed Mario's instructions for identification.

Mario's new control panel was amazing—something like you'd see on *Hawaii Five-0* or *CSI Cyber*. Between the panel and picture window sized screen, the Revere PD was finally part of the twenty-first century.

"I don't see the Mercedes, but there's the Lexus." I pointed to the vision creeping along the screen.

"The Mercedes must have turned off. Forget the Lexus."

I agreed. "If the Cadillac is still on the Boulevard, we'll take a closer look at it."

The Escalade inched into the picture. Mario froze the screen before it came into full view. "I can get a partial plate." He zoomed in and studied the image in front of us. "Detective P, can you write this down—BO, then, maybe an L or an I—or could be a B,H, or any letter that has a straight left side."

"You thinking a vanity plate?"

"I'd say so." Mario pulled a stool up behind him and sat down, then resumed the forward movement of the Escalade.

"Stop here." I checked the occupants. The driver was definitely a male and the passenger a female. We had a clear shot of her face. "Can you get any closer without distorting the features?"

"I'll try."

"Perfect". I turned to Sal. "Give me your take on Miss X."

"It's clear she's not a child." He folded his arms over his chest. "She fits the category of the Dolls."

"Exactly."

Mario sent the image to the printer.

"We're meeting with the chief in ten minutes. I'll bring the images we have to keep him in the loop. While we're gone run the disc from the Do-Drop-In covering the same time period, then before you take it out fast forward to one a.m. The ME examined Revere girl at eight a.m. and said she had been dead for about nine or ten hours. That would make the time of death approximately between ten and eleven p.m. Our murderer wouldn't risk getting rid of her body during busy bar hours. On the other hand, I don't believe he'd wait until he was the only moving object on the street." I closed my eyes and tried to envision the scene.

"Remember she was placed, not dumped. And she wasn't mangled. Not the right word, but you know what I mean. Even if somebody saw them, they probably wouldn't bat an eyelash—just a couple lovin' it up on the beach."

"Exactly."

"I'm ready to run the Do-Drop-In footage." Mario waited for my instructions.

"Check it out the same way we did Kelly's and St. Mark's. If you've got time, backup a few days and check to see if our tagged vehicles were cruisin' the Boulevard. Be sure and note any new ones of interest. Be back within an hour." My mind was moving in umpteen directions with none of them crossing paths.

CHAPTER 23

The chief was engrossed in the Doll file when we walked into his office. “Have a seat.” Without looking up, he motioned to the same two chairs we occupied several times the last couple days. “In my thirty-four years on the job, I’ve never been involved in a case quite like this. I read it over, and over again, as though it was the beginning of a best-selling thriller. The problem being, the author died before he completed it. Now, we gotta finish the story and nail the guilty bastard.”

There was no need to rehash what the three of us already knew, so I went right into our *morning with Mario* finds. “We’ve been scrutinizing discs from security cameras located three different places along the Boulevard—Kelly’s, St. Mark’s and the Do-Drop-In. As we speak, Mario is working on the ones from The-Do-Drop.”

“Humph, Walter Adams.” Chief Pozzi shuffled some papers on this desk. “It was near the bath house across from his fine upstanding establishment where Revere girl was found. As long as he’s on the job, he holds a golden ticket. In my opinion, he’s a black mark on the department. I’ll be glad when he retires and I can hold him responsible for his shady … never mind.” He leaned forward on his desk. “Tell me what you’ve got.”

I wouldn’t give copies of the pictures to the chief until we knew exactly what we were going to use them for. “Not much at this point. We’re in the process of observing the traffic along the Boulevard from a week before our victim was discovered. She was left in the sand. We’re targeting up-scale and large vehicles that may have been used to transport her. There are a couple we intend to take a closer look at, but at this point we have nothing concrete." That wasn't the answer the chief was looking for.

"We're meeting with the Quincy detectives at two. They're doing the same as we are. I talked to Scully last night. He said they found a few businesses and a residence with surveillance cameras. That gives us a couple more hours to continue the review of our discs before we compare observations." I waited for the chief to chime in. He didn't. "Sal and I should get back to IT."

"Call me at home after your meeting with Quincy."

"Will do." Sal and I got up and headed back to the second floor. Mario was waiting.

"That was quick."

"Yeah, but we had nothing new to report." Sal settled back against Mario's desk. "Let's resume the movie trailer."

The digital readout on the top of the wall screen read twelve forty-five. "It's going to be a long day. I'm calling Tony's for pizza."

Sal and Mario agreed.

"Now back to business." I slipped my cell into its case and moved closer to the screen.

"The first one of the three discs from Adams is the back parking lot. It's got nothin'. The other two scan the front parking lot and the sections of the Boulevard approximately twenty feet north and south." Mario inserted the first disc.

I put my hand up to stop him from pressing play. "The discs are supposed to cover a five week period. How far did you go back?"

"I ran through the first two weeks and nothing popped out. Disc two, that included the next two weeks, were more interesting. Then we have footage that covers the past week. This may provide frames of concern. I've noted them. That's what I'm going to show you first. Afterwards, we can go back further if you think it's necessary."

"It's your show."

Sal nodded in agreement.

"The frame number is in the top right-hand corner. I printed out the ones I feel are the most informative." Mario handed Sal and me copies. "I've put images of each vehicle of interest from our three locations up on the screen so you can compare them."

I studied the car, trying to detect anything defining. "That's got to be our Lincoln Navigator."

Sal shook his head. "Still can't get any more info on the plate."

Mario's desk phone rang. "Yeah, okay, I'll be right down." He hung up the receiver. "Pizza's here. There's Diet Coke in the fridge and paper plates and napkins in the closet next to the fridge."

"A well-equipped office." I handed Mario a twenty-dollar bill.

Five minutes later, he was back. "Your change."

"Thanks."

The others ate as I flipped to the next printed image. "It's our Mercedes. He didn't show on the church disc, so he probably turned left onto Shirley, then right onto Ocean. He could have reconnected back with the Boulevard just before Kelley's. By doing that, he avoided passing the State Police Barracks."

Sal spoke with his mouth full. "Doesn't the barracks have a camera?"

"They do, but it only covers their back parking lot and just outside their main entrance. There aren't any on the beach side. That's why I didn't try to get footage from them."

I moved on to the next image. "It's our Cadillac."

Mario shook his head. "Nothing more on that one."

I paused my soda near my lips. "Is that it?"

"Yes and no. No other big or expensive vehicles cruising the Boulevard stood out. I'll take a another look to make sure I didn't miss anything. Two of our spotlight vehicles traveled both north and south at least a dozen times, and one only a few times over the course of the last five weeks."

I put my third slice back in the box and sat forward. "Which ones were the frequent flyers?"

"The Lincoln and the Mercedes were right at home on the Boulevard, all different times of the day. I didn't see the Cadillac at all."

Sal shook his head. "We're looking for a freaking needle in a haystack."

"I'll follow-up on all three." I folded up my plate, threw it in the trash and poured myself more Coke. "McGinnis and Scully should be here within the hour. We'll compare notes. Hopefully, they've got clear images from the surveillance cameras in their areas. We're working against the clock."

"Remember I told you I did a lot of research into serial killers when I worked Beacon Hill?" Sal looked back at the now empty screen. "It's the shits trying to crawl into the mind of a serial killer. He kills in a fit of passion, another for the thrill of it, or because of a deep-rooted problem he lived through, usually as a child. In my opinion, the worst serial killers make their subjects characters in a well-thought out fantasy. The control and obedience they demand may never be achieved with the victim or victims. It's the obedience factor that scares me the most. That's the one I believe we're dealing with."

"We need to find him before he kills again. I also think if he has any idea we're on to him, he won't wait another six months. He'll make a move soon or he'll re-locate." My cell rang.

Mario and Sal sifted through the printed images again while I took my call.

"McGinnis and Scully are on their way." I turned toward Mario. "Are you here all day?"

"I am. Like I said, I'm going to run through those discs again. It's easier to do when there's nobody around. If you need me or you want to bring the Quincy dicks down, feel free to do so."

"Since you're going over the discs again, check back two weeks. I want to know if our spotlighted vehicles made an appearance."

CHAPTER 24

Sal and I were waiting by the back door when Scully and McGinnis pulled into the lot.

"Right on time," I said.

"Traffic wasn't bad."

"I hope you've got something good to share in that briefcase."

"You should find it very interesting."

I held the door open. Sal went first, followed by the Quincy guys. While we walked, I offered a plan. "My suggestion is we compare information you've found with what we've compiled. The objective being, we find one or more similarities of interest. We'll start in the conference room, make notes, then head down to IT to view the discs."

Scully and McGinnis sat across from us. We had our information sorted into piles: ME reports, pictures, notes corresponding to pictures and our to-date investigative reports.

Detective Scully spoke up. "We're ready when you are."

"I know the ME tried to reach you regarding a tattoo he found on our last Doll. Did you talk to him?"

"I did," McGinnis offered. "I have the reports with me." He flipped through the pile between him and Scully. "Irving told us your Revere girl had a tattoo that appeared to be somehow related to football. He checked the files for Hull girl, she had the same one in the same location."

"How about the Quincy girls?" I waited for a response.

"Both of them, same tattoo, but in different spots."

Sal leaned forward. "It's obvious these girls are connected, but how? We ran it by the gang unit, but they'd never seen one like it before."

"I'm not surprised. These girls didn't seem the type that would hang with street gangs. They were involved with someone who fashioned himself as a prominent member of the upper class. In my opinion, he was. It's those people who believe they are exempt from the law and can get away with murder." I took a deep breath.

McGinnis stared at the tattoos inked on the dolls. "Money, connections and well-rehearsed lies."

"That's what I believe we have here," I said. "So, what's your take on the tattoo?"

Scully leaned back in his chair, his arms over his chest. "I scoured the internet trying to find anything at all resembling the D Fence inference. Nothing. These girls are linked somehow. I'll bet my life on it. Football also plays into it."

The tattoo scenario would need more time, but we needed to move on. I set the pile of pictures in front of me. "Did you have any luck with the surveillance cameras?"

Scully laid the Quincy pictures on the table facing Sal and me. I took one look, then jumped up, at the same time flipping through our stack of pictures. "The Mercedes." I matched our pictures of the 550 with theirs. They had five, we had three. "What's the time period for these?"

"Approximately a week before the murders."

"Did you bring the discs or just the pictures?"

"I've got the discs." Scully picked up a nine-by-twelve interoffice envelope and unwound the tie. "Between the two places the Quincy girls were found, there were five businesses that had cameras. Two of them didn't help because they'd been installed since the killings."

"We don't need them." I looked at the other pictures. "One of them showed a Cadillac Escalade." I squinted. "There's a female driving."

Sal disgustedly tossed the Quincy pictures of the Mercedes back onto the table. "None of these show even a partial of the license plate."

I stood up. "Maybe Mario can run the discs and enhance the pictures enough to make out at least one number or letter." I picked up all the pictures and the envelope with the discs, and headed for the door.

Sal motioned for Scully and McGinnis to follow. "We've got an IT guru who works wonders."

McGinnis paused with his hand on the door. "Are your pictures all from Revere Beach?"

I nodded. "They are. If we determine the 550 is likely the same vehicle, we'll check Hull for cameras."

Mario was still checking Boulevard footage for additional sighting of our spotlight vehicles when the four of us walked into IT. "Mario, this is Detective Scully and Detective McGinnis from the Quincy PD. They need help getting into the twenty-first century." I handed Mario the discs. "He got his new toys last year."

"How far do you want me to go back?"

I turned toward the Quincy detectives. "What was the date of the Quincy Doll murders?"

"May 14, 2015." Scully raised his eyebrows." It's embedded in my brain. We checked the discs from a week before through the day after."

Mario already had one of the Quincy discs playing on the big screen. He stopped and backed it up. "Unfortunately, in this shot we can't see the entire car closest to the water because the passing red pick-up walls it off. But, it's a black Mercedes. We can't see the driver and the camera angle doesn't allow us to see any of the plate."

"Mario knows exactly what we're looking for, so rather than the four of us stand here watching Mr. IT perform his magic, we should hit the streets to introduce ourselves to Mr. Kors." I didn't wait for a response. “If you come up with something give me a call. Otherwise, we’ll meet Monday morning, here at eleven o’clock. Sal and I will work our end, update the reports and come up with possible scenarios to consider.”

“We have copies of the reports and discs we brought today. You keep those. With Mario’s magnifying glass, I’m sure there are things we missed.” Scully shrugged. “This case could help our department get out of the dark ages.”

Sal walked Quincy to the lobby.

Mario resumed scanning the discs. “Mike, I’ve seen a couple vehicles of interest on the Quincy discs. I don’t recall seeing them on ours, but I want to go back and do some comparisons. I plan on staying all day. Don’t take this the wrong way, but I work better without somebody looking over my shoulder. I’ll document everything and let you know what I find.”

“Mario Lanza, start singing.” I patted him on the back and went to meet Sal.

CHAPTER 25

"It's four o'clock. Most of the little boutiques close at six and aren't open tomorrow, so we should start with them." I'd already checked times for the ones in question.

Sal got behind the wheel. "Where to first?"

"Newbury Street, *The Purple Plume*, two store fronts down from Gloucester."

"Traffic hour is starting. Do you have any problem using the wig-wags?"

"Not at all."

"The second place, *Maggie's Closet*, is a block down on the opposite side of the street."

"On our way."

We weren't in suits, so we fit in better with the local clientele. Providing a time frame for the sale wasn't as easy as it was with the vehicles. Obviously, our killer made his multiple skirt purchase at least eleven months ago, before he killed the Quincy girls. Who knows, he could have made it two years ago in anticipation. Since we had nothing concrete to go on, we had to investigate every minuscule hint that might unlock a key piece of evidence.

"May I help you?"

I took my shield from my pocket and showed it to the young lady standing in front of me. "We'd like to talk to the manager. Is she or he available?"

"I'll get her for you."

A minute later an older woman, probably in her mid sixties, walked through an open doorway behind the sales counter. "My salesgirl, Veronica, said you'd like to talk to me. How can I help you?"

"I'm Detective Mastro and this is my partner, Detective Petruca. We're assigned to the Revere Police Department." I looked around the store. "We understand you sell the Michael Kors line of clothes."

"We do. There was no need to ask for me, Veronica could have helped you."

Typical Newbury Street attitude.

"We're not here to make a purchase. We're here to ask you some questions about a possible customer who may have purchased Michael Kors items from you."

"If you look around, we are a high-end boutique. Michael Kors is a high-end designer. We have lots of customers who purchase his designs."

"Here's the scoop. We're investigating a murder, actually several murders and we have a few questions to ask you." I kept my eyes focused on hers. "I'm sorry. I didn't catch your name."

Her demeanor changed. She extended her hand to shake ours. "I'm Catherine Butler, the manager/owner of *The Purple Plume*. In fairness to me, I get lots of badges looking for discounts."

I raised my eyebrows. "There are some that give us all a bad name. We're a couple of the good ones."

"Let's talk in my office." She turned and we followed.

We were out of there in ten minutes. She offered us no unusual information and, in turn, I didn't supply her with anything that could feed into a daily gossip circle.

A half hour later, we stood in front of *Maggie's Closet*. "Here we go." I pulled the door open and went inside. We showed our badges and I introduced ourselves.

"Hello detectives, I'm Maggie Smith, the owner of *Maggie's Closet.* "It will be easier to talk in the backroom, slash my office.

With what I pay for rent on Newbury Street, I have to utilize all available space for merchandise."

The only normal office furniture was hidden behind a standing room divider sporting images of Boston. Maggie took the chair behind her desk and offered us the two folding chairs opposite her. "What can I do for you?"

Sal scooted the small chair back for more legroom. "Michael Kors."

"Don't know the man personally, but he does help me pay for the privilege of operating on Newbury Street."

"We're working a case that involves one of his designs."

Maggie leaned forward on her desk—the smile gone from her face.

"It's possible someone, we presume a male, made a purchase of at least four skirts all of the same style, pattern, and possibly, size. The only difference was the colors. We believe they were all bought at the same time. Also, there could have been more than four." Sal sat back and glanced at me.

"We don't have a definite time period in which this possible purchase may have taken place. At this point we're investigating several. We know it was at least eleven months ago."

"I will tell you this. High-end designers don't let their designs get stale. If one of his skirts was purchased eleven months ago, you probably wouldn't find another one of the same print, even in a different color, two months later. Especially Michael Kors. His stuff moves quickly."

I didn't show our last entrepreneur the Doll pictures, but I had the feeling Maggie Smith might be able to help us.

Sal handed me the folder. I opened it, but held it up so that I was the only one who could see its contents. I carefully pulled out the picture of Revere girl and slid it across desk.

She froze. Finally she spoke, "That is a Michael Kors skirt." She turned to her right and opened the bottom drawer of a well-worn, battleship-gray file cabinet.

I watched as she isolated a section of green Pendaflex hanging folders, then, scanned some manila ones. About halfway through, she stopped, pulled one out and laid it on her desk. "Here's your skirt." She handed me the picture. "It was popular. And, as you can see, it came in eight different colors."

I didn't want to hear that. "Can you make me a copy?"

Sal examined the catalog page. "Can you tell us when these first hit the market and approximately how long they were available?"

"Give me a minute." Maggie went back to her filing cabinet. She thumbed through several folders, then pulled out another one. "If I'm going to carry one of his designs, I always get it in as soon as they're available. They were released on April 13, 2015. I ordered them on April 17th and received them on April 29th. I bought two of each, in sizes six and eight. That's the size of the person who'd wear this design."

"Is that how it works for most stores that carry designer clothes?" Sal asked.

"Boutique stores like mine, yes sir. As far as the big box stores, I'm not sure."

"By big box, you mean places like Macys and Bloomingdales?"

"Exactly." She looked at the Revere girl picture again. "Can you tell me more?"

"Some." I had to choose my words carefully. "We're not investigating just one homicide. We're investigating four. I don't suspect you read *The Daily Chatter*?"

"Only if I'm waiting in line to pay for my groceries."

"Then, you didn't see an article regarding the murders of four girls estimated to be in their early twenties. The first two were found almost ten months ago in Quincy, the third six months ago in Hull, and the fourth was last Thursday on Revere Beach. They were all the same size. The girls were dressed in a Michael Kors white jersey and a patterned skirt also by Kors—the pattern was the same, the colors were different. Hence, the probe into the Michael Kors skirts." I took the other three pictures from the folder and handed them to Maggie.

"There are four colors represented here and this skirt came in eight. Are you telling me there could be four more murders in the planning?"

"We have no information to indicate that." I tried to change the subject. "Do you have any records of your customer's purchases?"

"Not unless they used a credit card."

I took a deep breath. "Is there any way you could go back to April, 2015, and check for us?"

"I can, but it will take a while. I close at six and I have a prior engagement tonight. Tomorrow I'm not open, but I'll come in and go through my records."

"I'd appreciate that." I handed her my card. "One of those numbers will reach me. The handwritten one on the back is my cell. I'll be working all day tomorrow. After you check, please give me a call."

"I will."

"One more thing. I need you to keep our conversation between the three of us. The information I gave you is not for public knowledge. If it gets leaked to the press, it could jeopardize our entire investigation."

"I understand. You don't have to worry. My grandfather was a cop. My father is a detective in Rochester, New York, and my brother is a lieutenant in the Syracuse, New York Police Department." I'm well-seasoned. "Talk to you tomorrow."

A customer was waiting to talk to Maggie when Sal and I left her office.

"Tomorrow, then." We headed out the door.

"Our next stop, Copley Place. They have a dedicated Michael Kors store. After we leave Copley, we'll check The Shops at the Prudential Center. They don't have a Kors store, but Lord and Taylor carries the line. All the Lord and Taylor information is probably in their main office. I felt confident talking to Maggie Smith, but we have to be more discreet in the next two places."

"We probably have to get warrants for the Kors company store and Lord and Taylor's records." Sal shrugged. "Could be a long process."

"We'll check them out, then, make a decision."

"My wife said she bought her skirt at Macy's in Downtown Crossing. They're open tomorrow. We can hit them then."

"We're actually closer to the Pru. Pull in behind where the Duck Tours park." I took the police vehicle placard out of the glovebox and put it on the dash in front of Sal. "I'll let the duck desk know we'll be less than an hour." We were steps from the desk when my cell rang. "Mastro." I mouthed Mario's name. "Interesting. We're at the Pru. We'll be back to the station within the hour."

"What's that all about?"

"He's linked bits and pieces from the Quincy discs with the Revere discs and he thinks we should take a look at them."

CHAPTER 26

The IT room smelled like Dunkin's right after they'd made a fresh pot.

"Perfume to my nose. Does the coffee mean we're in for a long night?" Sal poured himself a cup.

Mario's eyes were glued to the screen. "It could."

"What did you find that couldn't wait?" I joined Sal with a cup of joe.

"I went back an additional two weeks on all the discs. I didn't come up with any additional vehicles of interest. However, our Mercedes 550 and our Cadillac Escalade appeared on several of the Quincy discs. The angles aren't as good as they are on the ones from Revere, but I'm positive the vehicles are one in the same. I'll show you."

I couldn't be as sure as Mario about the likeness of the two vehicles in question. Nothing that could tie them together was visible to me. "Mario, when you went further back in Revere, did you see the 550 and the Escalade cruisin' the Boulevard?"

"I did. The images were about the same as the ones you already saw."

"Did you check the days following the murders?" I asked.

"Yes. The Escalade was around, but not the 550."

Sal nodded. "What it says is that one or both of those vehicles may have found the Boulevard a desirable ending to a chapter in an ongoing fantasy."

Mario walked us through a whiteboard of vehicles' images he'd put together. "I noted dates, times and locations when each one was spotted."

"I said it before and I'll say it again, serial killers don't have partners. They're control freaks. They don't want to share their glory with anyone. There was only one case I found that involved two doctors. They collaborated with each other, but when it came to the actual killings, they worked alone."

"So, you think the sightings of the two vehicles around where the Quincy and Revere girls were found was purely coincidental?"

"Could be." Sal sat back on the corner of the desk. "We need to find some footage from Hull. If both the 550 or the Escalade are spotted there, then maybe I'll reconsider."

"Mario, can you check the same time period as you did for Quincy and Revere for break-ins in Hull."

"I already did. None near the beach where Hull girl was found."

I glanced at the digital printout on the top of the screen, it was six-twenty-seven. "It's time to call it a day. The only thing we can do tomorrow is ride around Hull and Nantasket Beach and visually check for cameras." I turned to Sal and Mario. "You two take Sunday off and we'll regroup Monday morning. Before we close up for the day, I want to leave you with something to think about. Our killer isn't stupid. He could have checked establishments for surveillance cameras, like we did. None of the cameras we know about recorded footage in the exact spots where he stopped to dump the girls."

"That's because the spots were out of range." Sal folded his arms over his chest. "And, he knew it."

CHAPTER 27

It was a few minutes before eight when I sat down with my notes, a bottle of Pinot Noir and a couple of Bracioles surrounded by a serving of al dente penne pasta swimming in a pool of tomato vodka sauce. Living in the North End had its advantages.

I read my notes over several times. Our killer was definitely playing a game, but with whom? The girls were unsuspecting minions easy enough to eliminate. But, the challenge of not getting caught was what he got off on. His game wasn't with the girls, it was with us. That fuckin' bastard was toying with us. I poured myself another glass of wine.

Who are these girls? Where are they from? Why isn't anybody looking for them?

The tattoo. I was sure it held the key to unlock the beginning of the end for our killer. I started my to-do lists for tomorrow and Monday. The killer had lured us in. I felt another article from Vinny Balls would trigger the need for our killer to strike again, and soon. My gut told me this sick bastard was already planning or had planned his next move. We had to plan ours.

There was a tattoo guy on Washington Street—been there for years. I heard his artwork left something to be desired. If our Dolls are local and got their D Fence logo somewhere in the area, he should know. Since his business was just up from Macy's, I can check on Mr. Kors skirts at the same time.

So many of the businesses on Hull Shore Drive were closed for the season and wouldn't open until May. The only ones open were

The Red Parrot, Paragon Grill, Nantasket Beach Resort on Hull Shore and a couple more on Nantasket Ave. Those streets formed one big loop. If our guy was cruisin' and one of those establishments had a camera, we'll spot him.

I was on my third glass of wine when my cell rang. Maggie's name flashed in bold green letters. "Hello." I put her on speaker.

"I know it's late, but I didn't think you'd mind."

"Course not. "What's up?"

"Your visit got me thinking. I cut my evening short, came back to my store and looked back in my files. A friend of mine, Sophie Glover, owns a small boutique similar to mine in Cambridge, at Harvard Square."

I could hear her rustling papers.

"Here it is. She called me a week after I got my Kors order in and asked if I'd ordered any of the skirts in question. I told her I did. She told me she only ordered four out of the eight colors in the three sizes she thought would be the most popular, but a customer came into the store and wanted to buy one of each color, all the same size. I had the ones she didn't, so I worked with her. We do it all the time. To you it was probably a strange request, but in this business, nothing is strange."

"So you did a store to store transaction with your friend?"

"Yes."

"How's her record keeping?"

"I don't know. I didn't call her. You told me to keep our conversation under wraps. She's open tomorrow. I can introduce you to her."

"I'll pick you up, say two o'clock."

"Do you want me to meet you at my store?"

"It's up to you."

"I live at 109 Commonwealth Avenue."

"See you there, same time."

CHAPTER 28

Sunday

I wasn't picking Maggie up until two o'clock. That gave me time to drive the Hull route to check for surveillance cameras. In March, a Sunday morning ride down Hull Shore Drive was like riding through a ghost town minus the tumbling tumbleweed. Come June until September, half the cars cruisin' are just getting home from who knows where.

I pulled into The Red Parrot's parking lot. It was just me and the janitorial service van taking up space. I walked the entire front of the restaurant, but didn't find anything remotely resembling a video security system. Don't need one, why install one. It was the same situation at the Paragon Grill. Even though Hull's Kitchen was closed for the season, I figured if I found a camera, I could contact the owners about getting a copy of the surveillance disc. Not to worry, they didn't have a video security system. Since the level of crime in this area was so low, I wasn't surprised at the lack of security systems.

The last place on my check list was Nantasket Beach Resort. This was the first place my ex and I shared a night of mad, passionate love making. The sex was good, but like our relationship, it disappeared faster than it appeared.

The Resort had a video surveillance system over the main entrance and smaller cameras over two secondary entrances. The angles clearly indicated the shadowing was to identify persons entering and/or leaving the establishment and not any foot or vehicle traffic on Hull Shore Drive.

I checked the Hull ride off my to-do list and headed back to the city. Sometimes cop work ends with progress spelled dead-end.

Maggie was leaning against a black wrought iron fence that separated the front of 109 Commonwealth Avenue from the sidewalk. I didn't see any parking spaces, so I slowed, flashed the wig-wags to let her know it was me, then came to a stop just long enough for her to jump into the front seat.

"Love the location, but the parking around here is horrible. I use the T to travel around Boston. Any other means of transportation isn't worth the aggravation."

"Good afternoon to you, too." Even though I was a cop, her attempt to cover up her nervousness of jumping into a car with a complete stranger was amusing. Fortunately, it was Sunday so the traffic on Commonwealth was light. Still, there were the few who chose to ignore the wig-wags and let me know their cars came equipped with an annoying horn. "Ready to head to Cambridge?"

"Sorry. I've been thinking about why I'm sitting here in your car. You didn't come into my boutique yesterday to talk about a random break-in on Newbury Street. You and Detective Petruca are investigating a murder or murders. It hit me a little hard."

I pulled away, made a U-turn and headed west on Comm Ave., took a right onto Massachusetts Avenue, left onto Beacon, then right onto Storrow Drive. "Who parted the waters for us—no traffic and no red lights. Now you can play the role of an obnoxious GPS lady and direct me to your friend's store."

Maggie scowled. "You do have a way with words."

"So I've been told." I knew if I caught a glimpse of her face, I might laugh, so I kept my eyes focused on the road in front of me.

"Sophie's store is on Mass Ave. two blocks from the Harvard Book Store. Parking is iffy. Sundays are usually busy on the Square."

"What's the name of her store?"

"*Sophie's Sophisticates.*"

"Slow down, I see a parking spot just before the corner." Maggie craned her neck to make sure it was available. "Never mind. There's a no parking sign beside it."

I pulled into the space, reached for the placard lodged between the console and the passenger seat and put it on the dashboard in front of me. "Sometimes the job has privileges. After all, we're here on official police business." I shrugged.

A bell sounded when Maggie opened the door. Sophie glanced in our direction, nodded, then, without missing a beat, went back to assisting her customer. Another employee, who was in the process of checking out an elderly woman in a wheelchair, told us to feel free to look around and somebody would be right with us. Instead, Maggie and I found a bench, usually reserved for a waiting companion, and sat down.

"I've never just come in, sat and looked around. I thought my store was small, but hers is smaller. I don't know if I could handle smaller."

Sophie finished up with her customer, sent her to the girl behind the register to check out and walked over to where we were sitting. "Maggie, why didn't you call? It's been slow today, so I sent one of my girls home early. If I knew you were coming, she could have stayed and we could have gone for coffee." She leaned forward, gave Maggie a hug, then turned and gave me the once-over. "Who's your friend?"

"Mike Mastro." I held my hand out.

Maggie looked around the store. "Before you get another customer, can we step into your office. Detective Mastro wants to talk to you."

Sophie lifted her shoulders and turned her palms toward the ceiling. "Detective?"

"Yes—with the Revere Police Department."

Maggie nodded. "Your office."

"Follow me." Sophie stopped at the counter to speak to the girl behind the register. "If you need me, I'll be in the back."

Sophie's office wasn't any bigger than Maggie's, but she had a door we could close. She offered us a seat as she sat down behind her desk. "Now that we're not within ear-shot of my customers, of which I have none at the moment, what can I possibly do to help the Revere Police Department?"

"I should have called you first, but it wasn't my place to be a front runner for Detective Mastro."

Sophie leaned forward on her desk. Her eyes widened. "Now you've spiked my curiosity."

I took over the conversation. "Do you ever read *The Chatter*?"

"Not if I can help it." She grinned. "Maybe when I get my hair done or while I'm getting a pedicure, I might take a peek."

"Friday morning the body of a young woman was found on Revere Beach. The facts surrounding her death matched three other deaths within the last ten months. They all involved women believed to be in their early twenties, all with Barbie doll figures and all died in the same manner."

Sophie's face lowered. She studied the surface of her desk for something to say. "I do read the *Globe*. Is the Revere Beach death related to the Doll murders in Quincy?"

I nodded. "We believe it is."

"Was the Revere girl raped like the Quincy girls?" She looked at Maggie. "Tragic and scary, but I don't understand why you're here talking to me about it."

Maggie, in a nervous moment, brushed her hair back behind her ears. "That's why I didn't call you ahead of time. I knew you'd have questions I couldn't answer. Let Detective Mastro explain what's going on. Then, between us, maybe we can furnish information that will help get this bastard off the streets."

"Sophie leaned back and covered her face with her hands. It was quiet, nobody said a word. When she put her hands down, tears had formed in her eyes. "Before we go any further, there's something I should share. There's no easy way to start."

Maggie glanced at me. When I didn't respond, she turned back toward Sophie.

"After I graduated from college, I worked in a small boutique on Beacon Street in Brookline. Maggie you remember that place, don't you?"

"I do. You were there for quite a while. In fact, didn't you leave there to open *Sophie's Sophisticates.*"

"I did." Sophie took a deep breath before she continued. "One night, after I closed the store in Brookline, I took the T to Park Street—like I did every day. I used to take the T everywhere. I had a car, but it was garaged at my parent's house in Newton. I only used it when I wanted to get away on a mini-vacation and those were few and far between after I paid my Beacon Hill rent."

"You lived on Beacon Hill?" I wanted to write things down, but didn't want to make Sophie uncomfortable, so I committed what she said to memory.

"I had a studio on Walnut Street. It was the in-place to live."

"You said 'was'. Does that mean you don't live there anymore?" I asked.

Sophie wove her hands together in a death-gripping prayer grasp. "I left there twenty years ago and haven't been back to Beacon Hill since. I was an intended victim of the Beacon Hill rapist, but I was one of the lucky ones. I got away."

CHAPTER 29

A silence filled the room.

Maggie was the first to speak. "Sophie, I'm sorry. I didn't know."

"Until now, the only ones who know are my parents. I went home to Newton for a few months, then got an apartment in Cambridge and opened my store. The Beacon Hill incident is a part of my life I've tried to forget. Now, out of the blue, it's back to haunt me."

"Your case isn't why we're here. At this point, we don't have any evidence connecting the Beacon Hill Shadow with the Doll murders. We're following a lead, and we believe you and Maggie are involved."

Sophie wrinkled her face. "Involved?"

"Bad word choice. Let me explain." I took a picture of Revere girl from my briefcase. "Do you recognize the skirt?"

Sophie studied it intently.

I handed her a picture of Hull girl, then one of each of the Quincy girls.

"Those are Michael Kors skirts."

"Exactly." I glanced at Maggie and nodded.

Maggie leaned forward on the desk. "Remember back about eleven, or so, months ago you had a customer who wanted to buy this skirt in the eight different colors it came in, all in the same size?"

"I had four of the colors in stock. I called you to see if you had the other four." A puzzled look replaced the flat expression on Sophie's face. "Are you telling me the guy who bought those skirts is the one murdering the Dolls?" Her voice trailed off. "Why me? Am I a magnet for deranged degenerates?"

I reached across the desk and laid my hands on hers. "Not at all. From several pieces of evidence we've obtained, my partner and I are running on the assumption our murderer/rapist enjoys the niceties of life. It was your upscale boutique, not you, that fit into his plan. There's no reason to think he'll revisit *Sophie's Sophisticates.*"

"I went back in my files and found the date the skirts transaction took place." Maggie took a piece of paper from her purse and handed it to Sophie.

She looked at me. "I'm assuming you want me to look through my files to see if I have anything that could attach the skirts to a name. My filing system leaves something to be desired, but if you give me until tomorrow, I'll find it. Large bottom line sales on high-end designer clothes isn't unusual—especially in Harvard Square and on Newbury Street."

There was a rehearsed knock on the door.

"That's my signal I'm needed out front." She stood and walked around to the front of her desk. "Detective, I'll get in touch with you tomorrow." She leaned forward and gave Maggie a hug. "Later."

I handed Sophie one of my cards with all my contact information, then Maggie and I left Sophie with a customer.

"I hope she's going to be okay."

I put my arm around Maggie. "She's going to be fine. She's lived a long time with her self-inflicted guilt. Rapists have a way of transmitting their blameworthiness to their victim. That's what they do."

"The retelling of her story and idea she may be able to help you put away a rapist could be a way for her to get the lost part of her life back." Maggie was quiet. "I'll be there for her."

I pushed the remote button to unlock the car doors.

"Thanks, Mike."

She reached for the door handle at the same time I did. "I've got this, my lady."

Maggie slid into the passenger seat.

I walked around the back of the car, so I could take another look down Mass Ave. The light gray sign trimmed with a dark purple border, introducing *Sophie's Sophisticates,* swayed gently in the afternoon air. I took a deep breath and got into the driver's seat.

"Detective Petruca worked out of the Beacon Hill Division when the Beacon Hill rapist was working the streets. He told me about the last two victims and that the perpetrator never got caught. He'll be very interested in our visit with Sophie."

Maggie sat quiet. She stared out the window.

"You don't need to be alone right now. I haven't had anything but coffee today. Will you join me for an early dinner? Your choice, Abe and Louie's or Pagliuca's in the North End." I turned my head in Maggie's direction. "And, I won't take no for an answer."

"You're a smooth talker, Detective Mike Mastro. How about Pagliuca's?"

"Good choice."

We arrived between the lunch and dinner crowd, so we took a table by the window overlooking Parmenter Street. Maggie ordered a glass of Cabernet Sauvignon. I had the same.

"I have no doubt Sophie will stay late tonight to go through her files. You hit a sour chord that's orchestrated her life for a long time. I had no idea what happened to her. Thinking back, though, before she opened her store, I'd try to get her to go to concerts on the Common. She'd always have some excuse. I had no reason to second guess her. Now I understand. When she lived on the Hill and worked on Beacon St., she'd cut across the Common to get to her apartment." Maggie stopped to take a sip. "I can't imagine. I just can't imagine."

I caught our waitress' attention and ordered a house special antipasto for two. "Hope you've got a good stroke."

Maggie wrinkled her nose. "A what?"

"Umm, I meant to say, appetite." I shrugged. "Forgot you weren't one of the guys."

"You better stop. The hole's getting deeper."

I leaned down and pretended to slide something under the table. "I hid the shovel so I can't dig anymore."

She gave me an 'I'm not sure what to make of you look'.

"You'll get used to me."

A couple, sitting two tables away, turned to see what was so funny.

"Saved by the salad." I ordered two more glasses of wine.

CHAPTER 30

Monday

Sal had his coffee poured and was reading the *Globe* when I walked into the breakroom. "You're early." I took a mug off the shelf and headed toward the Mr. Coffee.

He looked at his watch. "I think it's the other way around. You're later than usual."

"While you got some rest over the weekend, I was pounding the pavement. You're going to want to hear what I came up with." I took a donut from the open box of Entenmann's. "Ready?"

"Right behind you."

I wanted privacy so, instead of staying in the break-room or going to the detective bureau, I motioned Sal to follow me to interrogation room two. We sat at the table facing each other.

"We've got a situation, actually two situations. One we're both familiar with and one you're familiar with." I took a deep breath, then, continued. "I spent yesterday with Maggie Smith, from *Maggie's Closet*."

"I know who she is. I was with you when you met her."

"Just listen. Maggie called me Saturday night. She cut her evening plans short and went back to her store to do more file checking. She hit pay dirt. A friend of hers owns a boutique on Mass Ave. in Cambridge, two blocks from The Harvard Book Store. Back about eleven months ago, this friend called her about the Michael Kors skirts in question. Said she had a customer who wanted to purchase eight of them—one of each color, all the same size. Maggie had the ones her friend needed, so they did a between store transaction. Neither one of them thought anything of it. It was a sale for her friend and a good one at that." I snickered. "You know how much they cost."

"Smart ass."

"Yesterday, Maggie and I drove out to talk to her friend, Sophie. Her record keeping isn't nearly as organized as Maggie's, so she wasn't able to readily put her finger on the customer sale's transaction. She's going to try to do that today and call me when, or if, she finds something. The name of her boutique is *Sophie's Sophisticates*."

Sal reached up and rubbed the back of his neck. "Why is that name screaming at me? What's Sophie's last name?"

"Glover, Sophie Glover."

Sal jumped up and paced in front of the table. His voice elevated. "You've got to be shittin' me. It can't be. I know her."

"I'm afraid you do."

"She was the last intended victim of the Beacon Hill rapist." Sal sat back down. "Let me clarify that. She was a victim, but got away from him before he was able to get into her apartment. She talked about opening her own store away from downtown and calling it *Sophie's Sophisticates.* I lost touch when she moved away. I didn't know she'd opened a business in Cambridge."

"Maggie went to college with Sophie. They've been friends for over twenty years, but she was just as shocked as I was when Sophie confided in us."

"The case was never solved, so it was never closed and sent to archives. I can check, but I'm sure they still have it filed with the cold cases at the station. Every once in a while when I was still working the Hill, I'd read it over just to keep parts of it fresh in my mind."

"I'd like to read the files."

CHAPTER 31

The Monday morning traffic from Revere to Beacon Hill PD was backed up more than usual. "Most commuters this time of the morning take the T. Something must be happening at the State House. I don't miss this at all. Traffic division will have a field day writing parking violations. We'll have a better chance of finding a parking space if you go down New Chardon Street then turn left onto Bowker."

"I haven't been here for years. Parking hasn't changed. Still sucks." I took one of the two spaces left in the area marked for police vehicles.

"Since I don't have a pass card anymore, they're going to ask to see our IDs and badges." Sal pushed the button on the keypad beside the door.

A raspy-voiced female answered. "Can I help you?"

Sal stepped forward. "Detectives Sal Petruca and Mike Mastro requesting permission to enter."

"Detective Petruca, Officer Flemming here. They're getting real strict, so I need you to hold your IDs and badges up to the screen beside the keypad. You'll see a flash."

"All this new technology and still stuck in the dark ages."

"That about says it all."

The door buzzed and we went inside.

At the end of a short corridor, a middle-aged, attractive uniformed female officer sat behind a desk. She immediately got up, gave Sal a hug and offered her hand to me. "Good to see you Detective P."

"Mike, meet Officer Penny Flemming. We started together twenty-two years ago, then I up and left her for you."

"Want him back?" I cocked my head. "Kidding."

"I know you didn't stop by to shoot the shit. What's happening?"

"I need to check a cold case that happened twenty years ago. Is Chief Wilkins in? Before I head down to records, I want to talk to him."

"He got in about an hour ago. Let me check to see if he's available." Officer Flemming dialed the chief's extension.

Sal and I walked away from the desk while she made the call.

"He's waiting." She buzzed us into the secure corridor leading to the chief's office.

"Thanks. Catch you on the way out."

The chief stood as we walked into his office. "Chief, I'd like you to meet Detective Mastro from Revere PD."

We exchanged handshakes, then took a seat.

"Officer Flemming said you wanted to read over one of our cold cases. Which one are you referring too?"

"The Beacon Hill Shadow." I slid my chair closer to the desk. "Sal tells me he worked the case and, while doing so, did a lot of research on serial killers."

"That was an ugly one." The chief glanced at Sal. "We busted our balls—thought we turned over every stone. Obviously, the one key piece of evidence is still hidden. We worked it up until about five years ago, then classified it a cold case. Rape is hard enough to work alone, but when you mix it with multiple murders in the same area, over a short period of time, it becomes almost impossible. Whoever the Beacon Hill Shadow was—no, is—still walks the streets—somewhere."

The room went quiet for a minute, but felt like an hour. I wanted to say amen.

“Why do you want to look at the file?”

“Sal and I are working the Revere Beach murder. We have reason to believe it’s linked to a murder two months ago in Hull and, ten months ago in Quincy. We are confident it’s the work of the same person.”

“What’s it got to do with the Beacon Hill rapist?”

“Each of these girls was raped. Very carefully raped. Sal’s already told me the Beacon Hill rapes and murders bordered on the side of violence.”

“That’s right.”

“Sal thinks I’m crazy, but I want to make sure your serial killer didn’t decide to come out of hiding to start all over again.” It was too early in the investigation to mention Sophie’s name or the Michael Kors skirts.

“I tend to agree with Sal, but I have no objection giving you guys a copy of the reports.” The chief reached for his phone. “I’ll call records and have them get copies made. It shouldn’t take more than a half hour. Keep me posted. And, if you need this department’s help in any way, don’t hesitate to ask.”

CHAPTER 32

We made record time getting back to Revere. "Quincy's supposed to be here at eleven. We've got an hour and a half. I'll check in with Mario, then, meet you in room two to start scrutinizing the Beacon Hill files." I handed Sal the package of paperwork and pictures.

He gave me a two finger salute and continued down the corridor.

Mario was on the phone, so I whispered, "I'll talk to you later and left his office." I passed the breakroom on the way to meet up with Sal. There wasn't anyone around so I grabbed two cups of joe and hustled down to room two.

"Smart man. I need something to motivate the senses."

"What?"

"Never mind." He slid the first case and a pad of paper across the table. "Start at the beginning. Remember, there were eight murders and two attempted murders. The latter is where Sophie comes into the picture."

"You said you did research on serial killers. Was that on your own or part of the department investigation?"

"Both. I have it in my notes in a lock box at home. I'll bring it in tomorrow. I looked up old cases and tried to find similarities. I'm not a profiler, so without knowing exactly what to look for, I came up blank. It was extremely frustrating."

"I forgot to let the duty officer know about McGinnis and Scully." The wall phone rang, just as I reached forward to pick it up to make my call. "Yeah, we're in two. Send them down." I waited outside the door until I saw them round the corner, then stepped back into the room. "They're on their way."

We piled the paperwork from Beacon Hill and put it back into the folder.

"Good morning." I checked my watch. "Seems like it should be later."

Sal and I moved beside each other and Quincy sat across from us.

"There are days when I hate this job." Detective McGinnis took a small pile of files from his briefcase. "I love being a cop, but dealing with demented people like this makes me sick."

I ran my hand across the back of my neck. "If we can take this asshole off the streets, I can retire with piece of mind." "Know what I mean?"

"Scully and I checked twelve stores in the area for Michael Kors. There were only three. And of the three, only one carried any kind of inventory. We cropped the pictures of the girls and showed the owner just the skirts. He didn't recognize them at all."

I nodded. "We may have found the source of the skirts. I'm waiting for more information before I can be sure the boutique in question was the one that sold our perp his Dolls' signature attire. I should know for sure later today." I decided to keep Sophie's name anonymous.

Sal changed the subject. "We're going to check with some of the tattoo parlors around the area. Somebody has to know something about the D Fence tattoo. Since the ME didn't say anything about them being fresh, I assume the girls had them for a while. If that be the case, we can work on several different scenarios. First, they could, at one time, have been a member of the same sorority, although this is probably the least likely, unless it's not local. By that I mean, it could be as far away as California. Second, they could be groupies who follow a particular football team. Again, you'd think if it was a particular team, the tattoo would be the team logo. Third, they could be fly-by-night escorts for a big-boy sports club. And fourth, they might have been well acquainted with Mr. Scumbag and he had each one personally tattooed. Could have been a way of branding his herd."

"I'm sure if we think about it, we could come up with more tattoo scenarios. Sal and I will head down to Washington Street, then spread out from there. Why don't you guys hit the Hull and Quincy areas. If you come up with anything interesting, call me right away."

McGinnis and Scully let themselves out.

Before we left, Sal picked up the picture of the Cadillac that showed a female in the driver's seat. "I wish we could see her face. If this is our vehicle, the person driving could have been one of the girls. The deadly encounter might not have been a one night stand."

CHAPTER 33

The highest concentration of tattoo parlors Sal and I planned on visiting were in the Washington Street area. After leaving the fifth hole-in-the-wall with no more information than what we had when we went in, we stopped at Starbucks to grab a coffee.

"I would never let any one of those people stick needles full of ink under my skin."

"Do you have any tattoos?"

"And mess up this beautiful body. Absolutely not." I took a drink of coffee. "My ex-wife had a picture of a slot machine tattooed on her ass. Before my time. She'd tell me to slap the machine and I might get lucky. I guess I didn't slap it enough. I very rarely got lucky."

"Too much information."

I took out my list and crossed off the names of the five establishments we visited. "There are a couple more places close by, we can walk."

Sal rested his elbows on the table and went into his thinker mode. "I know you haven't had a chance to go through the Beacon Hill Shadow file. We did have DNA, but when we ran it through the Crime Lab there was no match."

"Meaning your guy had no priors that required him to produce a sample." I shrugged. "In our current case, our perp was careful not to leave any trace. Our girls were not traumatized or abused. I think they were very well taken care of. In my opinion, the scumbag wrote a script and, without knowing, the girls followed it to a tee.

Once he had them savoring the finer things in life, he was done with them and he'd move in for the kill."

"To quote serial killer Ted Bundy—'*We serial killers are your sons, we are your husbands, we are everywhere. And there will be more of your children dead tomorrow.*'

I took a deep breath. "Our girls were certainly somebody's children." I finished my coffee. "You ready to meet some more skin artists?"

Sal stood up and stuffed his napkin into his cup. "I'm ready."

Inking for Pleasure was the first one we came to. The small print advertised erotic tattooing. I raised my eyebrows and turned toward Sal. "You first."

Samples of the artist's work were displayed along both sides of the short hallway leading to a small reception room. Sal rang the school bell that hung on the wall next to the counter.

A male voice answered the ring. "Don't be shy. Look around. I'll be right out."

Two minutes later, a middle aged man with salt and pepper hair pulled back into a ponytail and tattoos wherever you could see, all except his face, came out from a backroom to greet us. "Gentlemen, did you see something that interests you?"

I pulled back the right side of my jacket to reveal my badge.

He put down the cloth he was wiping his hands with and reached forward to shake my hand. "I'm Tony Cataleno, the owner. How can I help you officers?"

"That's Detectives, Mastro and Petruca." I motioned for Sal to continue.

Sal handed the proprietor a picture of the Doll's tattoos. "Is this some of your handiwork?"

"No. What you see on the walls is the mild version of my artistry. My masterpieces are displayed in the back. Would you like to see them?"

I crossed my arms over my chest. "Maybe another time. Right now our interest is the tattoo in the picture you're holding. Since normal sports aren't your forte, do you know whose work this might be?"

Tony moved closer to the desk lamp and studied the D Fence picture. "Nope. I wish I could help you, but I've never seen this before. Most of the parlors in this area, ink tattoos that aren't so cut and dried. We're artists. The body is our canvas. That's not to say they couldn't help you find the person who inks graphic designs." He took one more look, then handed our picture back to Sal. "You never said why you're looking for the person or person who inked this."

"I might want to get one," I said as I turned and walked out the door.

There were three more tattoo parlors within a two block radius. Hurt Me Tattoos and Hello Gorgeous Body Art were a waste of time. Gottie's House of Style took a copy of our picture and said he would ask around. I gave him my card.

We walked back to the cruiser and continued on the tattoo parlor circuit. I left my card with several people we talked to, but held little hope I'd hear back from any one of them.

There were only two things we knew for sure. We had four dead girls with knock-off similarities and a serial killer.

"We're getting nothing, unless you've got a better idea, I say we go back to the station and outline our next plan of action."

Sal fastened his seatbelt. "If you swing by my house, I'll get that lock box."

"Works for me."

Sal's wife, Becky, wasn't home, so we didn't have to engage in idle talk. My thought process was focused on getting into the mind of a serial killer and nothing else.

We were halfway back to the station before Sal broke the silence. "I'm pissed. That bastard isn't smarter than we are. What are we missing?"

CHAPTER 34

Hallway traffic at the station was light and those we did encounter just exchanged 'good afternoons'. Sal and I headed straight for room two.

I slammed my fist on the table. "That fuckin' bastard. While we're trying to smoke him out, he's working his next victim." I paced the room. "It's not going to happen. Where the hell are these girls coming from? And, why isn't anyone missing them?"

Sal opened his lock box and took out a couple of manila envelopes. One of them had the Sam Bundy quote boldly written in red magic marker across the front. "My reminder."

"Your sons, your husbands." I felt like vomiting. "We could have been sitting next to him this morning when we had coffee. He knows who we are, but we don't know who he is. I don't like that."

"There are conflicting definitions of a serial killer. Our killer overlaps each one of them. The Quincy girls were murdered ten months ago. Hull was two months ago. Now Revere. He's left a cooling off period between them, but it appears it's less than what some authorities considered when they penned their serial killer characteristics. Yet, other experts have noted lesser time in between. If our killer decides to overlap into the hybrid category of 'spree-serial killer', he could strike again without a cooling off period or a return to normalcy."

I sat down, leaned back and locked my hands behind my neck. "Going on that assumption, we could find ourselves with another dead Doll."

"Exactly."

My eyes scanned the ceiling from one corner of the room to the other and back again. "I'd love to feed Vinny Balls a story. Our killer could be waiting for a written update on the progress of the Revere Police Department. On the other hand, it could work against us and set our killer off, then we'd possibly have another unknown beauty moving to the morgue."

"The other side of that argument is he could put a cork in it for a while—like the Beacon Hill Shadow."

I sighed. "Yeah, but the Shadow's last victim got away."

"All the reason someone like him is ready to come back into the picture."

"You still thinking the Shadow has something to do with our serial killer?"

"Could be." I leaned forward. "Did you ever canvass the Hill for suspects?"

"You mean amongst residents?"

"Yeah." I nodded. "The age you've assigned him fits the demographic of the area and also the ages of his victims. You had his DNA, but there was no match. Do you remember the case back in 2002 on Cape Cod where a forty-six year old woman was raped and stabbed to death?"

"I read the papers like everyone else and listened to the breakroom talk, but I didn't know any more than the public."

"The State Police made an unusual request. They asked all the men who lived in or were in the lower cape area during the time period of the murder to take a DNA test. Most of them obliged. If you did that for the Shadow, and if he lived in the area you may have caught your rapist."

"You're pulling stuff out of your ass. It would have been a voluntary DNA sample, so unless the Shadow was stupid beyond belief, the whole scenario would be moot. Besides, what's that got to do with our scumbag?"

I hesitated, then spoke. "If they're one in the same, we wouldn't be investigating the Doll murders."

The room went quiet.

Sal picked up his cup. "I'm getting another coffee. You?"

"Sure." I needed a few minutes to compose my thoughts. We had to move on, but I didn't want Sal to think I felt his investigative skills were substandard.

My cell rang as Sal came through the door with our coffees.

There was no name, just a number on my screen. "Detective Mastro?"

"This is Sophie Glover. I found my receipt for the Kor's sale. My fax machine isn't working, but if you give me your fax number, I can go up to the bookstore and send you a copy?"

I looked at Sal. "We're about to leave the station. We'll stop and pick one up."

"See you when you get here."

"Thanks," I ended the call.

"Where are we going?"

"To Cambridge—*Sophie's Sophisticates*. That was Sophie. She's got a copy of the sales receipt for the eight skirts." I took a deep breath. "When I was there with Maggie, I didn't mention your name."

"So, she doesn't know I'm your partner?"

CHAPTER 35

I parked in the same 'no parking spot' I'd parked in yesterday, just down from *Sophie's Sophisticates*. Sal put the police ID card on the dash and we proceeded to the boutique. A bell jingled announcing our arrival.

I didn't remember hearing that when Maggie and I came in or when we left.

The same girl that was there yesterday was straightening out clothes on a sales rack. Before she could ask if she could help, Sophie came out of the backroom. "Good afternoon. Amy, I'm going to be in the office if you need me."

Sophie led and we followed. She and I took the same seats as yesterday and Sal took the remaining one.

"Sophie, I'd like you to meet my partner."

Before I could introduce Sal, she held up her hand to stop me. "I know you, don't I?"

Sal nodded. "From a long time ago. How are you?"

"Surviving." She looked at me. "I'm sure Officer Petruca filled you in."

"Actually it's Detective now. He did."

"Let me give you the rest of the story. What he didn't know is, if it wasn't for him, I probably wouldn't be here." She didn't look at Sal while she talked. "He helped me through a very difficult time. I was afraid and ashamed to talk to anyone. The stigma attached to rape is that 'she asked for it'. I know Officer, I mean Detective Petruca didn't believe that theory. What he doesn't know is there were times when he was like a big brother. We'd meet every once-in-while for coffee. I could talk to him and he listened. Not that all siblings listen, but he did."

Sal beamed.

"I never had a chance to say thank you." She came around the desk and gave Sal a hug, then went back to her chair.

"You're making me blush."

We all smiled.

I spoke up. "In this job, the criticism outweighs the praise." I looked at Sal. "I got me a good partner."

Sophie took a piece of paper from under her desk calendar. "Here's the copy of the sales receipt. It was a cash sale, so I have no name or credit card information." She leaned forward on the desk. "I did a lot of thinking after you and Maggie left. I stood outside my office staring at the front door trying to visualize anything that could help describe this man."

"How about his face or hair color or build? Maybe his voice—soft spoken or loud and demanding or a lisp? Any characteristics, like a limp? Since he came in looking for Michael Kors skirts, was he dressed in comparable male designer clothes?" I thought about the bell over the door. "A bell over the door rang when we came in. I don't remember hearing it yesterday."

"You didn't. I had it tied up. A couple people hit their head ...." She stopped abruptly. "The man you're hunting—he hit his head on it. When he came in and when he left."

"Sophie, are you sure?" Sal's face was like a stone.

"I am. It's an annoying sound. I don't like it, but with only a couple employees and me, it lets us know when someone comes in or leaves."

I turned toward Sal. "How tall was the Shadow?"

He didn't have a chance to answer.

Sophie's body tightened. "What? You thinking this guy and the Beacon Hill Shadow are one in the same?" Her expression tightened. "Let me tell you. They are not. I'd swear on a stack of bibles. I'm five feet three inches tall. The asshole that came after me was four, maybe five inches taller than me. The guy who came into my store last May was well over six feet." She stopped for a minute, then continued, "Let me do some more thinking. I saw the Shadow's face, but it was dark so I couldn't give the police sketch artist enough of a description for a composite. He also had a cap on, so I couldn't even tell them what color his hair was. Fear blocks out lots of things. That night, fear was the only thing I felt. Did you know fear has features? It does. Don't ask me to describe them, I can't, but when I was being assaulted fear was staring at me.

"This time you weren't being assaulted. I need you to think back—dig deep."

"He wasn't only tall, he also had a nice body. Tessa, one of my employees, remarked about it. He was well-spoken and a man of few words."

"Did he have an accent?" I asked.

"You asked me that before. Nothing noticeable. At least nothing I can remember."

Sal studied Sophie. "Anything else?"

"He was on a mission. He looked around, then asked about the Michael Kors' skirts. He didn't ask if they came in different colors. He knew. He asked if I had all eight colors in stock. I didn't. He asked if I could get them. That's when I called Maggie."

I looked at Sal then back at Sophie. "Did he look at anything else in the store?"

"White jerseys, also Kors. He bought eight. I had twelve in stock."

I stood up and took a few steps away from the desk. "So you called Maggie. He waited while you called?"

"Yes. He knew I had four of the colors in stock and I told him I could have the others the next day at two o'clcok." She took a deep breath. "He agreed, so I called Maggie back and told her to courier them over to me."

"So he came back the next day?" Sal leaned forward on the desk.

"He did."

I shrugged. "This didn't seem like an odd request?"

"No. You have to remember where we are. Harvard University is all around us. MIT, Boston University, Boston College…do I need to go on. We're also in Cambridge." Sophie motioned toward the cash register. "Money is no object. Then you have Boston—theaters, high society, penthouse parties. It's not my business to know where my clothes end up. I never question why people purchase what they do."

"Your employee, Tessa, when is she due in?"

Sophie turned to check the schedule beside her desk. "Tomorrow at ten. Do you want me to ask her what she remembers about that customer?"

"It's better if we talk to her. I'd appreciate it if you keep our conversation between us." I stood and headed toward the door, then turned back with one more question. "After we talk to Tessa, I may have you each meet with our sketch artist."

She nodded. "Works for me. I'll see you in the morning. Detective Petruca, it was good to see you again."

"Same here."

Sophie stayed in her office. We showed ourselves out.

I stopped at the bottom of the steps and did a quick survey of the surrounding buildings. Our guy paid two visits to *Sophie's Sophisticates*. "Let's take a walk.

CHAPTER 36

There it was—above the Mass Ave. entrance to Harvard Book Store—a state of the art surveillance camera. I wasn't surprised. This wasn't Revere Beach. This was an upscale section of Cambridge. "Bingo."

Sal and I went inside and waited until the clerk at the register finished with a customer.

I moved my jacket aside to reveal my shield. "Is the manager available?"

"Um. I think so. Ah, let me call his office. Like, is there anything I can do for you?"

I nodded in the direction of the phone. "Make the call."

Sal perused the store while I waited for an answer from the clerk.

"He'll be right down."

"Thank you. We'll wait at the end of the counter for him."

"Haven't been here for years. Forgot how big this place was."

"And, this is only one of the rooms." I'd just finished my response when I saw a middle-aged man, dressed casually in navy chinos and a long-sleeved navy and white stripe shirt with the cuffs rolled up to the elbows, stepping hastily in our direction. He certainly looked the part of a Harvard preppy—whether or not he'd been a student across the street didn't make any difference. He played the part to fit in.

He reached his hand out. "I'm Leon Staples, the manager. Matt, my cashier, said you wanted to speak with me."

I returned the handshake and introduced myself and Sal. I looked around. "Is there anywhere less crowded where we can talk?"

"My office. Follow me."

Once inside, he gestured us to have a seat at a mini-conference table. He took a chair across from us.

"We're canvassing a four-block strip to see what businesses have surveillance cameras focused on the Avenue. You appear to have one installed above the main entrance."

"We do. I've worked here for fifteen years and we've always had one. The original camera was there before my time. About two years ago, they had state-of-the-art ones installed on both the front and side doors. We've had a little trouble with robberies, so it was a precaution. We have a lot of inventory, along with money."

Sal sat back and let me ask the questions. "I'm assuming they have back-up video?"

"They do. It's also the same system that monitors the inside of the building, so I'm positive it's always recording. I know we have a special cabinet the owner, Paul Rimes, stores the discs in."

"You're saying everything is on discs?"

"I think so."

"If I furnish you with dates, are you authorized to release copies of footage recorded on the Mass Ave. camera."

"I'm sure that won't be a problem. This is a first, so of course, I have to check."

This interview was progressing at a snail's pace. I was getting weary of his attempt to portray a level of importance.

"Mr. Staples, or can I call you Leon?" My attempt to relate to him on a casual basis caught him by surprise.

"Leon's fine."

"Okay, Leon. We're involved in an investigation of which I can't share any details. I'll furnish you with two dates. You will furnish me with a copy of your camera footage from the Mass Ave. location for those dates. If you have to call Mr. Rimes, my partner and I will sit here, in case he has any questions." I sat back and folded my arms across my chest.

Sal didn't say a word.

Leon made the call. After listening to him try to explain what we wanted, I held out my hand for the phone. I gave Mr. Rimes the same information I'd given Leon, and without question, Mr. Rimes authorized him to give us whatever we needed. We accompanied Leon to Mr. Rime's office and watched while he found the footage covering the front of the store and several feet on either side of the entrance for the dates in question.

Leon put the disc into a plastic holder and handed it to me. "I hope this helps in your investigation."

"I'm sure it will." I slipped the case into my pocket, then Sal and I followed him out of the office. "Leon, I have a question."

A puzzled look came over the manager's face.

"Earlier you said checking footage on the surveillance camera was a first for you. You made it look like a very familiar process. Does Mr. Rimes know you're spying on his employees or maybe even him?"

Leon's breathing hastened. He went to speak, but nothing came out.

"We'll show ourselves to the door."

There were a few more businesses on the bookstore side of Sophie's. Only two had cameras and neither one was working. The owners had been lucky. We walked back past *Sophie's Sophisticates,* and stopped in front of TD Bank. Their ATM was on the side of the building, but their main entrance was on the same street as Sophie's and the bookstore. There were three surveillance cameras across the front—one over the door and one on each corner.

Sal stood with his hands in his pockets, switching his glance back and forth from the bank to the street. "We could get lucky. The angles of these cameras not only cover the immediate area in front of the bank, they get the complete picture across the street. Stand here and watch them. They're moving very slowly taking everything in. If we can match one of our cars from Revere Beach

Boulevard to a car passing by here, we might have something more to go on."

"Getting the footage from these cameras might not be as easy as the bookstore. Ready?"

The branch manager wasn't available. Her assistant expected her back by two-thirty.

We walked outside. "We've got an hour. Grafton Street Pub and Grill is on the other side of the bookstore. We'll grab lunch, then head back to the bank."

Sal agreed.

We found a couple stools at the bar. I ordered calamari with a diet coke. Sal got a Grafton burger with fries.

"They're known for craft beers. I could go for one, but diet coke is my on duty beer. I'm going to give Judge Polito's office a call. I know his assistant. I'm sure we're going to need a court order to see the bank footage. If I give her a heads up, we can swing over to the courthouse, pick it up and get back here before the bank closes."

"Cuttin' it close."

"At least it'll be in the works. I would have bet my paycheck we'd find lots more cameras." I gave Sal money and went outside to call the courthouse.

He met me on the sidewalk. "The college probably has some on campus, but those aren't going to help us either."

I checked my watch. "It's twenty minutes past two. Might as well get going."

The manager was back and, as I suspected, the bank required a court order. I told her we had one in the works and we'd see her before closing.

I hit redial and got Judge Polito's office. "Adrienne, it's Mike again. I'm going to need that court order. We're in Harvard Square. We should be able to make it there in a half hour."

Sal shot me a puzzled look. "No goodbye?"

"She's the one who hung up."

CHAPTER 37

"Wait in the car. I'm not going to negotiate parking."

"Yeah, yeah."

I double-stepped the stairs to Judge Polito's office. "Yo, Adrienne."

"Cut the shit, Mike." She handed me an envelope. "The judge said he'd talk to you later."

"Thanks babe. Tell him I owe him one." I leaned over and gave her a kiss on the cheek.

Sal was startled when I opened the passenger door. "That was quick."

"Coffee and donuts every once in a while help." I wanted to get back to the bank as fast as I could, but traffic was starting to pick up, so I flipped on the wig-wags.

I pulled into the side lot. Sal and I walked around to the front and went inside.

The manager was surprised. "I didn't think you'd be back today. Did you get the court order?"

I nodded and handed her the envelope.

"This will take about a half hour."

"Thank you. We'll be back at four."

Sal pointed at the benches across the street on either side of the entrance to the Harvard campus.

I pushed the crosswalk button. "As good a place as any to observe the rich and wannabe famous. Who knows, maybe some of that bottled-up smarts will seep out to us common folk."

No sooner did we sit down, a white Mercedes Metris pulled up to the curb, blocking any view we had of the business landscape across the street. Kensington Academy was tastefully lettered on the front passenger door. A matronly woman, who I presumed to be a chaperone, stepped off, followed by six girls, properly clad in matching uniforms. Once everyone was accounted for, the van drove off.

"My wife has a friend whose daughter goes there." Sal rubbed his fingers together. "Mega-bucks."

"Kennsington's been around for a long time. Those girls must be Harvard 'preschoolers' taking a tour of the campus."

"The friend's daughter hates it, but her parents insist she stick it out. I guess her grandfather has lots of money, went to Harvard and now wants his granddaughter to follow in his footsteps. He's paying. The girl's a regular kid. The girl's mother told Becky that some of her classmates come from as far away as California. She even has a couple from somewhere in England and one from Italy. The sad part is they never see their family. The daughter said some of them do more partying than studying, and when they're done at Kensington, they'll head to college—Harvard being one of them. Whether or not they graduate doesn't seem to make a difference. One girl told the daughter she probably will never see her family again—unless she becomes rich and famous."

"Sad—no sick—world out there." When the bus faded out of sight, I turned to watch the girls walk to where they might spend their next four years.

"Kensington's one of the few all girls' schools left—at least around this area. What's the name of the all-male one the next county over?"

"Whitman Boarding. If I remember correctly, to go there you have to live there. Whereas, the girls at Kensington can commute, even though most of them live in dorms on campus." I leaned back on the bench and stretched my legs out in front of me. "It must have been twenty-five or so years ago, Kensington had a problem. Seems as though a couple of the jocks from Whitman partied too much after a football game and ended up in one of the Kensington dorms. It was a night of wham, bam, thank you ma'am, until one of the girls cried rape."

"I'm surprised it only happened once."

"Trust me, it happened a lot more than once. The original rape charge went away. We monitored the area for a while, but the schools were on private property and not our jurisdiction, unless we were called and we weren't. End of story." I checked my watch. "Time to see our branch manager."

CHAPTER 38

Back at the station, Mario was still at his desk.

I knocked and waited for the okay to head in. Music played softly in the background. "Got a minute?" I asked.

"Yep. Got something new?"

Sal handed him the discs we got from Harvard Book Store and TD Bank. "We're still checking cars, but this time we're also checking people—one to be exact."

"Do you have a description or, to use an overworked cliché, are we still looking for a needle in a haystack?"

"Little of both. The cars are the same ones as before. The person is what we're most interested in. He's your needle."

"He's—so we're looking for a male. That should narrow it down somewhat." Mario shrugged. "Although, these days you never know."

"True. We know our unknown is around six foot two or three. He's supposed to be a good looking guy, sharp dresser, but we don't have any facial features or hair color. Got the looks and the body. Normally, he'd stand out, but since these discs are from Harvard Square, he'll most likely blend in. He visited a store call *Sophie's Sophisticates,* a few doors down from the bookstore one way, and TD Bank the other way. He was there two days in a row. You know the parking in the area—virtually none unless you have a resident permit."

"I'll run them now."

"We'll be in room two." I thanked Mario.

On the way to room two, Sal and I stopped in the breakroom to grab a coffee. There was only a bottom full left in the pot. "I'll brew some if you'll have one."

Sal nodded. "I could use the caffeine."

We waited until there was enough to fill two cups, then headed to room two.

I blew on my coffee and took a sip. "This is what we've got. Three cars, one of which may or may not belong to our killer. A person, male—over six feet tall, good looking and built."

"Don't forget the well-spoken with no noticeable accent."

"When we talk to Tessa tomorrow morning, we'll be able to determine if Sophie's memory is correct. Assuming it is, this person should show up on the discs we gave Mario. Even if our guy crossed the street, he'd have to pass one place or the other to get to a crosswalk. And, to get to the municipal parking lot behind the bank, he'd have to pass by the bank's front door. The ideal situation is to get a full face picture on one of these cameras. You can run facial recognition without a full face, but it has to have some distinguishing features. And, if the killer has no record, it's ninety-nine percent his mug isn't in any of the data bases, but it's a tool in our toolbox."

"Our best facial recognition is going to come from Sophie and Tessa." The phone rang. Sal answered. "We'll be right down."

CHAPTER 39

"Detectives, you might have stumbled onto something." Mario's magic screen displayed two rows of four—eight different views. "This first group is from Wednesday." He moved the electronic pointer to the top left-hand window. "The time stamp on the bank's camera is three-seventeen. During the week, mid-afternoon … not busy." He paused the screen. "Note the guy in what appears to be a leather bomber jacket. By the way, I checked the weather for that day. It was forty-three degrees. This picture only shows the lower part of his face, but the jacket has a logo on the back just below the collar."

Sal and I moved closer to the screen as Mario enhanced the image.

"You've got to be shittin' me." I stared at an icon of the same D Fence likeness tattooed on our dead Dolls.

Sal moved to the next picture. "It appears he's walking away from Sophie's boutique."

"He is. He turned left, so his car must be parked behind the bank. The fourth picture, and any ones after, don't show our guy anywhere in front of the bank. The bottom row is pictures from the bookstore disc. He walked by Harvard Book Store, toward Sophie's. He kept his head down, but you can still see part of his nose, and check out the dimple on his chin. According to the time stamp, he came from the bookstore side, went to Sophie's, then left and walked in the opposite direction."

I didn't take my eyes off the images. "These are all from Wednesday?"

"Yep."

"Sal, make a note. In the second picture he's standing beside a light pole. Tomorrow morning we take a measurement to determine approximately how tall he really is. Since these are black and white, we can't establish hair color. I'll need prints of all eight."

Mario sent them to the printer, then swapped the first images with eight new ones. "These are Thursday's. Like the Wednesday discs, I started checking at nine o'clock. I know Sophie opens her store at ten, but he could have been hanging around waiting for her. He wasn't."

"Probably because she told him to come back around two."

Mario gave me a sideways look, then continued. "That's why the first picture in the top row is the first time I put eyes on him. It's time-stamped one-thirty. It's him approaching Sophie's store from the direction of the bookstore. Now look at the first one in row two. This is from the bank camera. The first one is time-stamped one-thirty-five. When he got to the street past the bank's front entrance, he turned around and walked back."

Sal continued making notes. "That means he paced the two blocks before he went to the boutique. Note that he's got the same jacket on."

"The next time he appears is twenty minutes later, carrying two shopping bags and heading toward the bookstore. The camera range doesn't show if he took a right or, because Mass Ave. starts to curve to the right, if he continued walking." Without me asking, Mario sent the second set of pictures to the printer.

I let out a weighty breath. "He didn't look up in the last set of pictures and he's not looking up now, but we can still catch some of the lower part of his face. This is the first concrete clue we have and it sucks."

Sal took the pictures from the printer and handed them to me. He looked at his watch. “There’s nothing else we can do tonight. I promised Becky I’d be home for supper. I’d like to keep that promise.”

I went back to my office and slid the prints into my briefcase, along with Sal’s notes and any other reports that were on my desk, then headed to the parking lot. The chill in the air penetrated my jacket and found my bones. The weatherman had predicted a five day cold spell. For once he was right. I started the car and turned on the heater. After a couple minutes, I left the lot. I didn’t even feel like stopping for Chinese food. I just wanted to get home.

CHAPTER 40

I dropped a couple pieces of bread into the toaster, got out the jar of peanut butter and cracked open my last Sam Adams Cold Snap. The quiet in my condo was interrupted when my cell rang. The number on the display didn't register with me.

I answered cautiously. "Hello."

"Mike?"

"Maggie."

"I just got off the phone with Sophie. She said you and Sal were at the boutique today."

"We were. She found the receipts. We talked. I tried to jog her memory."

"Anything?"

I figured the girls would be talking back and forth and I didn't want them discussing the case. "We're working on a few things."

"Is there anything else I can do for you?"

"As a matter of fact, there is."

"And."

I looked around my condo. "I can't cook, but sure can open a mean bottle of wine and I know a great place for Chinese take-out. Pick you up at *Maggie's Closet* tomorrow at six?"

"Make that six-thirty and you're on."

"It's a date." I choked on my words. It's been a long time since I had an actual date.

"You okay?"

"Beer went down the wrong way—that's all."

There was a giggle from the other end. "I'll be waiting."

The line went dead. A woman of few words. I might be able to handle that.

Now back to my 'gourmet dinner' and the contents of my briefcase. I read over some of the reports again, but my concentration was on the pictures Mario pulled off the security camera discs. A couple of years back, I bought a magnifying glass with a light. This will be the perfect test of its usefulness. I set myself up back in the kitchen to pull something of interest from our subject's images.

The D Fence logo was definitely the same as the girls' tattoos. That will be a question for Maggie. The logo might be associated with some line of clothing. She deals with high-end shit. If he's wearing designer clothes, she'll know. I turned my focus to what I could see of his face. I couldn't see his eyes and could only see the bottom of his face. He appeared clean shaven—an observation that could change overnight, but in the two day's images we had, it didn't. I could see part of his nose—nothing distinguishing about it. Unless his jacket had padded shoulders, his build suggested he worked out—lending credence to his ability to lift the girls into his car, then out of it to their final destinations.

I moved the magnifying glass to his hands—no gloves. Right now fingerprints would be a moot point since his visit to Sophie's was eleven months ago and anything he touched would be compromised by anyone else entering or leaving her store. I didn't see it in the bank's images, but in the ones from the bookstore, he had a ring on his third finger right hand. It was from a school or sports related. It almost filled the space from his knuckle to the first bend. I zoomed in as close as I could. The light from the magnifying glass was trying to identify an emblem. I couldn't be sure, but it looked like the D Fence. Above the emblem was a date. I could read the nineteen, but couldn't see the last two numbers. Judging from its size and assuming it was sports related, our guy was no wimp. I googled the D Fence logo. Almost every college had one.

CHAPTER 41

Tuesday

I'd been at my desk for an hour when Sal walked in carrying two cups of coffee and a bag of donuts from Dunkin's.

I looked up. "You're a welcome sight."

"Who you shittin''? The coffee and donuts are the only things you see."

I held my hand over my mouth and mumbled, "You could be right."

"From the looks of the piles of paperwork and pictures, you've been here a while."

"Yep. I spent part of the night at my kitchen table trying to get inside this guy's head. It backfired. He got inside mine." I braced myself on the desk and stood. "We're missing something and he knows it."

Sal handed me my coffee.

I paced as I drank. "Here's my take. The son-of-a-bitch comes from money. I don't know why, but I think big money. The girls from Kensington and what you said about Becky's friend's daughter sparked food for thought. If Harvard gives Kensington preppies tours trying to lure in the family money, then there's no doubt most, if not all, of the local boarding and/or private high schools are extended the same invitation."

"Are you saying our perp is local? Maybe a Harvard graduate? Maybe he took that tour twenty something years ago."

"It's a possibility we have to consider." I sat down and took a glazed donut from the bag. "Last night I went over the pictures for the hundredth time. I'm sure he knew about the cameras. I have no doubt he was familiar with the area. We've already determined his persona fits. He knew it too."

Sal bent forward and rested his chin in his hands. "His 'fit-in' wasn't rehearsed."

"I don't think it was."

"What about the girls?"

"That's where I'm drawing a fuckin' blank. Our perp's got balls bigger than the one that drops from the roof of One Times Square on New Year's Eve—only times two. I spent the better part of last night on the computer looking up serial killers."

Sal nodded. "And you reread Bundy's story more than once."

"I did."

"Yeah. Me too."

"No doubt Bundy was a sick bastard, and our perp didn't engage in his methods, but that's not what spiked my curiosity." I took another bite of donut and washed it down with coffee. "It was the man himself that caught my eye. In all the accounts I read, he was regarded as handsome and charismatic. This is what the authorities believed won the trust of his young female victims. They also established the fact that he approached many of them in public places, gaining their trust, then luring them to more secluded locations. The difference is, Bundy butchered his victims and our perp isn't a cannibal."

Sal waited for me to finish. "The other thing that stood out was Bundy's education. He was no dummy."

"And, in my opinion, neither is our perp." I took a deep breath. "After we talk to Sophie and Tessa, I want to visit the library at Harvard. I'm sure they have copies of old yearbooks. It's a shot in the dark, but nevertheless it's a shot. Two things I want to check. First, our perp, then, our girls. We have pictures of them and know approximate ages."

"You do realize Harvard graduates thousands every year."

"I do, but we might get lucky. We'll check the sports sections for players and cheerleaders first. It's a long-shot, but it could yield a big payoff."

Sal crumpled the donut bag and stuffed it in his empty cup. "I'm going to hit the head, then grab another coffee. Want one?"

"Yeah."

While Sal was gone, I flipped through some of the notes I made last night. We'd pretty much covered the Bundy stuff for now. There was one more aspect I wanted to run by Sal before we headed to Cambridge. I was deep in thought, and didn't realize Sal was back, until he set my coffee on the desk.

"Hey, big guy, where's that mind of yours off to now?"

"Last night, after the bout with Bundy, I had another brainstorm. We've got a possible on our perp's vehicle and, like I said before, he's familiar with the area—the reason … he may live in the area."

"I agree. Have you got the pictures Mario printed of the vehicles?"

"I do."

"When we looked at the surveillance camera discs, we assumed our perp parked behind the bank on Wednesday and around the back of the bookstore on Thursday. We didn't take into consideration that he might have permanent parking somewhere because he either works or lives in the area."

"I'm hesitant on this theory, because it would be hard for him to move a body without anyone seeing him. Then again, being in a college town, a lot of stuff happens and people look the other way not wanting to get involved. A party with drugs or drinking, a passed-out girl—whatever. It might not be an unusual scene. Our boy could have a condo in the square and a house in a more rural area." I shrugged and held my hands in the air. "Anything, at this point, is worth investigating."

Sal checked his watch. “Drink up. It’s eight-thirty. We told Sophie we’d be at her place at ten. If we’re going to do any poking around, we need to roll.”

I stood and downed the rest of my coffee. “Let’s go.”

CHAPTER 42

What sounded like a good idea when I ran it past Sal, turned to shit. We drove down the street behind the bookstore and the bank. Most of the residential buildings were dorms that belonged to Harvard. There were, what appeared to be, independent condos, but judging from the age of the people hanging around them, they also housed students. The Harvard Lampoon building took up a sizable space on Bow Street. I hadn't been in this area for years and was amazed to see how many small stores and restaurants had sprung up. The Malkin Athletic Club was still going strong, as was *The Owl Club*.

I slowed to check out the vehicles parked on the street by The Owl. "You have to be a member of the who's who in Boston to join this place. It's an all-male club. From what I understand, it doesn't fall under Harvard's rules and regulations. It's privately owned, so who knows what goes on behind the walls. I remember when Ted Kennedy gave up his membership because of something to do with not allowing women to join. All politics. Maybe our perp belongs."

"Pull over. There are cars parked in the driveway beside the place. You wait here. I'll do a quick check." Sal didn't give me a chance to answer, he got out and walked back to the side of *The Owl Club*.

I watched in my rear view mirror as he disappeared from sight. Five minutes later he emerged.

"Anything?"

"All high-end vehicles. A couple Lincolns, a Mercedes SUV, two Cadillac Escalades and a Ferrari. None appear to be a match, but to be sure, I took pictures anyway. I also wrote down the license plate numbers."

"Enough of this. Time to see Sophie."

I brushed the bell over the door with my hand as we walked into *Sophie's Sophisticates.* I looked at Sal. "Our perp was more than six-two."

Tessa looked up from the register at the same time Sophie came out of her office.

"Detectives, I'd like you to meet Tessa."

We reached out to shake her hand, at the same time introducing ourselves.

"Tessa's been with me for almost five years. Knows the business inside and out and also knows most of our regulars on a first name basis." Sophie smiled. "That's an important attribute in this line of work."

I nodded. "Tessa, do you know why we're here?"

She sported a puzzled look. "No. Sophie said you were coming, but told me you'd explain why when you got here."

"It's about one of your customers. Not one of your regulars. He's only been in twice that we know of, and that was eleven months ago. I'm going to try to jog your memory. He came in and asked about some Michael Kors skirts. You didn't have enough in stock, so Sophie called another store to see if they had them. They did. She made arrangements for four to be couriered here the next day." I tried to read her facial expressions. "Does any of this sound familiar to you?"

"Actually, it does. I remember it because the guy was tall—like you. He signaled his arrival and departure both days with the new bell we'd just hung the day before. The other thing is, he was really good looking and had a great body. Our customers are mostly females." Tessa held her hand up and waved it across the store. "If you asked me to remember a female buyer, unless she was a regular, I probably couldn't give you a description. This guy stood out."

"I want to set you up with the police department sketch artist." I looked at Sophie. "I want you both to see him, but not together. I also don't want you to talk about our person of interest after we leave. You'll need to individually try to remember features or distinguishing marks that might help us identify him."

Sal took a pad of paper from his pocket. "Give me a couple times within the next two days you can take an hour or so off to come to the station, and I'll call to see if our officer is available."

Sophie took a hard-covered journal from under the counter. "Tessa gets off today at three and, it would be best if I can do it before I come to work tomorrow morning."

"Be right back." Sal walked to the far corner of the store to make the call.

Tessa's voice was faint. "Detective Mastro, can you tell me what this is about?"

"We're trying to find this person. Right now, that's all I can tell you."

Sal finished his call and came back to join us. "He'll be at the station until five and tomorrow he'll be in at eight."

"We're going to be in the area for most of the day." I looked at Tessa. "We can pick you up at three and take you to the station, then give you a ride home, or wherever you want to go."

She shrugged. "I'll be ready."

We all turned when the bell over the door rang. It was a UPS delivery man carrying several boxes. "Mornin' Tessa. Be right back, I've got two more."

"A regular." She smiled.

Sal leaned forward. "Sophie, if you give me your address, I'll pick you up at eight and drive you down to the station."

Let me get one of my cards, I'll write it on the back." She left and went into the office. A minute later she returned. "See you then."

CHAPTER 43

"We know our perp is Mr. Suave. It appears he knows the area well. We're guesstimating an age of late thirties or early forties. And, judging from the surveillance camera images we can surmise he's in good physical condition. We know he's got some tie to sports, most likely football, because of the D Fence logo and tattoos. Since Tessa doesn't finish work until three, we've got some time to kill. Let's follow up on my hunch and visit the Harvard library."

The librarian at the information desk made a call to the caretaker in the section of the library where the yearbooks are kept, then pointed us in the right direction.

"This place is huge. You need a road map to get around," I said.

Sal stood still and let his head pivot around the area. "Good place to hide out for a while."

"I don't think *Marion the Librarian* misses much. When we get those composite sketches done, we'll show them to her. In the meantime, we'll use Mario's images to see if we can find a possible match."

The guy in the yearbook room greeted us as we came through the door.

I looked around. "Are these all yearbooks?"

"They are. Dating back to 1636. Of course those are in special cabinets. What years are you interested in?"

"We'll start with 1993 until 2000. I'll let you know if we need more."

He pointed to a mini conference table away from the windows looking out onto the rest of the library. "If you gentlemen have seats over there, I'll bring the books to you."

"Thank you," I said.

The librarian returned with the eight yearbooks I'd requested and set them on the table between us. I took 1993 through 1996 and gave Sal the other four. "These dates put our perp between thirty-seven and forty-four. Start with the sports section."

We moved our respective piles to one side so I could put Mario's pictures from the surveillance cameras between us, where we could readily view them. I'd slipped my magnifying glass into my pocket when I left my condo, so I took it out and laid it beside the perp's partials.

Sal picked it up. "Now I really feel like Sherlock's pal, Dr.Watson."

I opened the first yearbook and spoke without looking up. "The fuckin' asshole we're looking for is a smooth stalker. A chameleon that can change his persona to suit his liking. I haven't figured out how, but the tables are going to turn and he's the one who's going to be stalked. He's killed four times and he's not done yet."

The sports section of the yearbook featured several, what I assumed to be, top athletes in each category. I scrutinized the camera images, trying to match our partial features with those in the professional shots. Nothing.

I was on the fourth book, when Sal turned to me. "Not working. I've only got one to go."

I snapped. "You got a better idea?"

"Short of giving Vinny Balls a much orchestrated story—no."

I ripped a piece of paper from my pad and marked the page I was on. "We've got to come up with something. The Vinny Balls bullshit might flush the peckerhead out, but it could also backfire to the point where we'd have another Doll on our hands. Let's finish this up, then head back to the station."

Sal had started with the 2000 yearbook and worked backwards. He was halfway through the '97 sports pages when he picked up the magnifying glass and focused on the team football picture—counted to the spot of one of the players, then matched the image to the names. "Matthew Morrison," he said.

"Who's Matthew Morrison?"

Sal handed me the pictures Mario had printed, along with the yearbook, open to the pictures of the 1997 football team. "Top row, sixth from the left—holding his helmet under his right arm."

"Everybody else's helmets are on the left."

"That's the one. Look at the spotlighted photos—the last one in the line-up." He pointed as he talked. "One in the same. Now, look at Mario's prints. I see similarities."

I used the magnifying glass to zoom into any and all the details from our prints and the professional pictures. "Does that look like a dimple to you?"

Sal nodded. "There are too many similarities to ignore. It also puts him in our age range."

I walked over to talk to the librarian. "Does the library allow the yearbooks to leave the building?"

"Not really. I've been here for forty-one years. The only time I saw it happen was because of a request from the president."

"Is there any way we could borrow a few of the books?"

"Can I ask why?"

"You can ask, but unfortunately all I can tell you is one or more of these yearbooks could provide valuable information in an investigation we're working."

"Since this room is my responsibility, I'll authorize you to take the books. Which ones do you want?"

I figured it was going to take an act of congress for the books to leave the library—"1993, '94, '95, '96 and '97."

"That's one of the yearbooks the president wanted—1997 to be exact."

I looked at Sal. "Was there a reason he wanted to see that particular book?"

"Every once in a while, Harvard has a good football team. That year was an 'every once in a while' one. We had a great team. I used to go to all the games."

I didn't need his reminiscing, although some of his ramblings may be helpful. "What did a good football team and the 1997 yearbook have in common?"

"The star of the team was in a horrific automobile accident. He was a senior. That was his graduating yearbook. He and the girl driving were pronounced dead at the scene. The newspaper said there were drugs involved, but I don't remember the exact details."

The librarian picked up the books I'd requested and put them into a bag.

"I'll see that you get these back within a couple weeks." I didn't want to give him the option to change the length of loan, so I changed the subject. "I'm impressed by the efficiency of your operation. Harvard is very lucky to have such a dedicated employee."

Sal reiterated my praise as we walked out the door leading to the library lobby.

CHAPTER 44

Tessa was waiting for us when we pulled up in front of the boutique. I checked my watch. We were ten minutes early.

Sal got out of the car and opened the back passenger door.

"This afternoon was slow, so I was able to leave a little earlier than usual."

I glanced at her in my rearview mirror.

She was looking around the back of the car. "This looks like the backseat of my dad's Impala."

I gripped her innocence. "A marked cruiser's a little different. The handles to open the door have been removed, there's a cage between the front and back seats and they're usually not as clean as the unmarks."

"You said you'd give me a ride home, right? I'm not sure about taking the T from Revere."

Sal twisted in his seat to answer her. "No problem. You'll work with the sketch artist for about an hour. He'll draw the face as he asks you questions about the person who came into the store and bought the Michael Kors skirts."

"I've been doing a lot of thinking about what he looked like."

"You and Sophie didn't talk about it, did you?" I asked.

"You said not to, so we didn't. We want to help you find the guy you're looking for. I don't know what he did, but it must have been something bad enough for you to go to all this trouble."

"You'll know in due time. We appreciate your help."

Tessa nodded and watched out the side window as we wove our way through traffic.

We were about ten minutes from the station when my cell phone rang. I didn't recognize the number, "Detective Mastro."

"Detective, it's Pete Fortunado. Can you meet with me?"

"Where are you?"

"Across from The Do-Drop, next to the bath house on the Boulevard."

"We'll be there in a half hour."

Sal shrugged his shoulders.

I rolled my eyes in Tessa's direction. "The gentleman that lives behind the church on the Boulevard."

"Okay."

I pulled up in front of the station and we escorted Tessa in. I introduced her to Officer Motley at the front desk. She's here to meet with Wayne."

CHAPTER 45

Pete, and, I assumed, one of his homeless neighbors I didn't recognize, were sitting on the seawall next to the bath house when we pulled up. "Hey, buddy, what's up?"

"I'd like you to meet my friend, Sammy. He's lived with us in the compound for about six months."

I shook his hand.

"Pete tells me I might have information you could use regarding something that happened last week."

I half sat on the wall next to Pete. "Depends on what it is."

"Pete said you were asking questions about fancy cars. There are lots of fancy cars that ride up and down the Boulevard all the time."

Sal took a deep breath. "We know that. Do you have something unusual to tell us about one of them?"

"Umm. Well, I didn't think too much about it until I was talking to Pete."

I was starting to get a little impatient. "Okay Sammy. Pete called me to meet him. We're here. Now why are we here?"

"Well, I used to work on cars, so I know my fancy expensive ones. Last Thursday there was a guy in a Black Mercedes 550 that pulled up just past the bath house. It was about three in the morning. I'd gotten some food from the Do-Drop-In dumpster and was sitting against the side of the bathhouse—right there." He pointed to a three-by-five spot that was cut into the main frame of the building. "In the summer, they put trash barrels there. It's not well lit. Any light from the street doesn't shine in there, so I can sit and eat my food without being bothered."

I took a furtive glance at my watch to make sure I'd be back in time to get Tessa. "What did this guy look like?"

"I couldn't see him real clear like, but he was a white guy, and a big one at that. Someone I didn't want to tangle with. I remember his jacket. It was one of those leather bomber ones. In better times, I had one just like it. He jumped over the sea wall onto the beach, did a three-sixty of the area, then started walking around. At first he didn't see me. I sat real quiet. Some folks aren't kind to us who are less fortunate than them. He walked a little more, then sat on the wall just like you're doing. That's when he saw me."

"Did he say anything?"

"Not at first. I was scared, so I didn't say anything to him either. He just stared at me. When I started to get up, he stood. When I started to walk to the street, he blocked me, then handed me a twenty dollar bill and told me to get the hell out of there. I did just what he told me to do."

"So, you don't know if he was alone or had a passenger?"

"Didn't see anyone else, but his door was closed and there was no light on inside the car."

"Where did you go after that?"

"Back home behind the church."

I stood. "Okay, thanks for the help."

"Wait, I haven't told you the rest of the story."

I looked at Pete. "There's more?"

Sal stood like a statue and listened.

"Sammy, tell the detectives what else you told me."

Sammy got nervous and started to rock slightly, then reached into his pocket and pulled out a watch. He handed it to me. It was a Rolex.

"Where did you get this?"

"The next night I came back to eat my dinner. When I stepped over the wall and started to walk to the bathhouse, I kicked something. It was that watch. I found it. It was mine. Right?" Sammy looked at Sal and me. "I didn't stay around. I put it in my pocket and left. I was across the street when I saw the Mercedes pull up, park in the same place and watched the same guy get out. I hid near The Do-Drop. He looked around the bathhouse, then, walked around kicking sand and bending down. He kept repeating it. He didn't look happy. I was sure he was looking for his watch, and I had it. I haven't been back there since."

I dropped the watch in an evidence bag. "I'm going to have to take this, but I'll see that you get it back."

Sammy nodded. "I'd appreciate that."

Sal stepped forward. "One more question. Have you seen him since you found the watch?"

"The first time I saw him, there was a lady found dead on the beach about four hours later. Then the next night was when he came back looking for something. I didn't want to find out if he was the killer—if you know what I mean. I still get my food from The Do-Drop, but now I go sit near the church to eat."

I crossed my arms over my chest. "Why didn't you come forward sooner?"

"Cause I was afraid. It took all the courage I could find to talk to Pete. He's the one who assured me you could be trusted."

I gave Sammy an affirmative nod, then reached out to shake his hand. "Stay safe. We'll get back to you." I turned to Pete. "Thank you my friend. We'll talk."

We dropped the evidence bag containing the Rolex at the crime lab before returning to the station. I explained they'd probably come up with several DNA samples. "If we get lucky, they'll find a match in the State Police or national DNA data banks."

Tessa was still in Wayne's office finishing up when we returned to the station. Her back was towards the window, so she couldn't see us watching the 'artist' detailing his work. I marveled at his ability to make a face come to life from bits and pieces relayed to him by a witness. He saw us and motioned us in.

Tessa turned as we walked through the door. "The more Wayne drew, the more I remembered."

"Have a seat. We're almost done. I want her to take a final look to see if there's anything we need to change or add." He moved the sketch so it was directly in front of Tessa. "I wish all my clients were this easy to work with."

The three of us sat back and watched as she studied Wayne's artwork.

"There is one more thing. He had a dimple on his chin. I remember remarking to Sophie about it."

Wayne picked up his pencil. "Show me where."

Tessa pointed to a spot directly in the middle.

"How big was it?"

"Not as big as cheek dimples, but noticeable."

Wayne performed his 'pencil' magic, then showed Tessa the results.

"That's it," she gushed.

Sal and I looked at the sketch, then at each other.

CHAPTER 46

It was six-thirty when I got to *Maggie's Closet*. I was on time—a trait I wasn't known for. Before I could get out of the car, Maggie was already at the passenger door.

"Slow afternoon?" I asked.

"Sales wise, yes. Otherwise, no."

"I won't ask. Ready for some Chinese food and a bottle of wine?" I tried to make small talk without sounding like an idiot. "First dates can be awkward. What do you like? I'll call it in so it'll be ready."

Maggie waited until I got off the phone. "What's for dessert?"

I wasn't sure what she was referring to so I lightened the conversation. "Since I live in the North End, how about a cappuccino and a cannoli at Mike's Pastry?"

"Good rebound. I'd like that."

We swung by the China Rose, picked up our order and headed to my condo on Battery Street.

I pulled to the curb. "You must be good luck, I rarely get a spot right in front."

I grabbed the food bag and walked around the car to meet Maggie as she lifted her purse from the backseat.

My eyes lit up at the size of her purse. "Don't get your hopes up, it's not an overnight bag."

We walked the two floors up to a waiting bottle of Beringer Merlot.

Maggie looked around. "Nice place."

"Been here for almost twenty-three years. I was working out of the North End Precinct when they made this building into condos. Back then I could afford one. Now they're going for mega-bucks."

I liked Maggie. She was easy to talk to and, judging from the few times I've been in her company, comfortable to be with. I got the wine glasses out and the bottle of Beringer, then went to work with my new electric cork screw.

"I'm impressed. Got to get me one of those."

"My secret's out. I'm a connoisseur of fine wine and an aficionado of wine toys." I poured. We toasted. "Did you talk to Sophie?"

"I did and I didn't. She called around eleven. I had a few customers, so I couldn't talk. I was going to give her a call back, but never got around to it."

"Tessa, one of the girls who works for her, went to the police station today to meet with our sketch artist. Sophie is going tomorrow morning."

"I know Tessa. How'd she do?"

"The features she provided our artist made for an interesting sketch. After Sophie's session we'll compare them."

"Are you any closer to finding the killer?"

I didn't want to be evasive, but I also didn't want to say too much. "I think we're moving in the right direction."

"I'm not going to get any inside information, am I?"

"Smart lady."

Maggie turned away. "Okay, where's the plates?"

I pointed to the cabinet over the dishwasher. While Maggie was setting the table, I slipped a disc into the Bose. Billy Joel's *New York State of Mind* played softly as we ate from the paper serving bowls and drank from Walmart wine glasses.

"I promised you dessert. Feel like taking a walk?"

"For a good cappuccino and a cannoli, I'd walk anywhere."

Even though it was a nice night, Mike's Pastry wasn't busy. We sat at a little table in the corner by the window, and waited for Lena to come over to take our order.

"No see you much lately, Michael. Where you be?" She looked at Maggie. "He a good man, but he need more meatball and pasta."

Maggie laughed quietly. "We'll see what we can do about that."

Lena nodded and left to get our order.

"When you asked about the case before, I forgot, there is something I want to run by you. Do you know what the D Fence symbol looks like in football?"

"Of course I do."

"Why of course?"

"Because there's a designer who uses that logo—very expensive clothes."

"Do they make leather bomber jackets?"

"I believe they do. I don't carry the line, but I've gotten literature on it."

"Are they a local company?"

"I'm not sure. Now you're going to have to tell me why you're asking."

"The person we're looking for was wearing a jacket with the D Fence logo on the back, up near the collar." I hesitated, then, continued. "And, our dead girls all had a D Fence tattoo on their body."

Maggie sat quiet.

Lena brought our order, but didn't stop to talk.

Maggie took a sip of her cappuccino. "I'll try to get you information on the jacket first thing in the morning."

I nodded.

After a few moments of silence, she said, "How can you be a cop?"

"My ex-wife asked me the same question. It's hard to explain. I hate bad guys and love good guys. You either like the job or you don't. There's no in between."

"Let's change the subject."

"I agree." We started back to my condo. "Can I interest you in an after dinner drink?"

Maggie checked her watch. "I'd like that."

I put my arms around her. "You okay?"

She looked up at me. "I am now."

CHAPTER 47

Wednesday

The alarm clock on my night table reminded me it was time to start a new workday. I hit the snooze alarm and rolled over, took Maggie in my arms and gave her a kiss that I didn't want to end. "You look much better in my tee shirt than I do." I kissed her again. "Was I a good cop or a bad cop?"

"Detective Mastro, you were definitely a good cop."

The reoccurring buzz coming from over my shoulder, again prompted me to get up. "I'll check on breakfast while you take a shower. There's clean towels in the bathroom closet."

"No peeking." She got up and meandered down the hall to the bathroom, turning several times to see if I was watching.

"Promises, promises. If you're not careful, we're in the shower together."

When I heard the door shut, I got up and took the mugs and K-cups from the pantry. There wasn't anything beyond that I could offer. I had cereal, but no milk, and the bread was just barely fit to feed the pigeons on the Common.

I didn't realize Maggie had finished in the bathroom until I walked back down the hall to the bedroom. "That was quick." She was standing in the middle of the room with just her bra and panties on. "I'm definitely walking back to the kitchen."

Two minutes later she walked up behind me and kissed my back.

“Us bachelors-type people don’t keep much in the line of healthy food around. I checked and there’s nothing I can offer you except a cup of coffee.”

“That works just fine.” She looked around. “Do you get the paper?”

“It’s outside the front door.”

“Go take your shower and I’ll get it.”

Where did this person come from?

It was the quickest fluff and buff job I’d done in years. I knew I had just enough time to get her to her store or her apartment, but not both. I walked to the kitchen—tie in hand and jacket over my arm. “I’ve got to be at the station by eight. I can take you to the store or your apartment.”

“The store would be closer. I have a change of clothes there, and if I didn’t, I’d take something off the rack.”

“Okay then, Miss Maggie Smith, let’s get this show on the road.”

The traffic getting to Newbury Street wasn’t bad. I pulled in front of *Maggie’s Closet* to let her off. “I’ll give you a call later. Don’t forget D Fence.”

CHAPTER 48

Sal was waiting for me in the hall outside the squad room. "The chief wants to meet with us in his office after the morning briefing."

"I knew this was coming. The fourth victim, in what's been deemed a serial killing spree, was found six days ago, and we're only baby steps into finding the perp."

"Remember, the Beacon Hill Rapist was never found. Believe me, we have more traces on the Doll murders than I ever had on the Beacon Hill one. The chief just wants to be kept abreast of what we're doing. I'm going to sit back and let you do the talking. We've been analyzing and theorizing back and forth. If I listen, something we're overlooking might jump out."

"You've got a point there."

The morning briefing was short. Captain Bosworth reminded the uniforms to keep their eyes and ears open for any information that could help in the investigation of the Doll murders. It was obvious his concentration was on our case.

Fifteen minutes later we were sitting across from the chief at his desk. "There's fresh coffee." He took a drink of his as Sal and I got us a cup. "It's been six days. I know you've been working with Mario, but other than that, what's the word from the street?"

"It's pretty tight mouthed." I paused." We're working on a few leads."

The chief stopped me. "A few leads. Unless they're really good, concrete ones, I don't want to hear the words 'a few'."

"We've discovered the D Fence tattoo found on the girls also appeared as a logo on the back of a leather bomber jacket worn by a person of interest. I'm in the process of getting the name of the company who uses this logo. I understand it's a high-end designer. The designer jacket fits with the Michael Kors attire the girls wore. Also, yesterday, on a hunch, Sal and I visited the Harvard University library. The library is located directly across the street from the boutique where we believe our perp bought the girls' clothing. We determined he was familiar with the area, hence the hunch he may have attended Harvard. From images and descriptions, of which I'll touch on, we've put him between thirty and forty years old. Anyway, we scoured yearbooks encompassing the dates that covered the age range." I stopped to gather my thoughts as to how much I wanted to say at the moment.

"Is there more I need to know?"

"The information I just gave you happened yesterday. We have two possible witnesses from the boutique working with Wayne. One of the girls was here yesterday afternoon and the other one is with him as we speak. We're also working with a homeless person who lives in the compound behind St. Mark's. He says he saw someone acting suspicious hanging around the bathhouse. It was around three in the morning. Our victim was found at seven. We're checking on that. Our homeless person also found a Rolex watch in the same area the guy was checking out. We delivered it to the crime lab for DNA testing." I didn't want to mention the ideas of working with Vinny Balls on a preapproved newspaper article. The chief didn't trust him any more than I did—probably less. "That's what we've got to date."

"Today's Wednesday. I want a full report on my desk by the end of the day on Friday." He stood. "Good day, detectives."

I didn't want people hanging over us while we were scrutinizing the books. I checked with the duty desk—room two was empty. "If anyone is looking for us that's where we'll be."

We grabbed coffees and a couple chocolate glazed donuts from the breakroom, took the bag of yearbooks and headed for room two.

Sal opened the 1997 book to the sports page. He again noted the name of the player of interest, Matthew Morrison. While he scanned other sports pictures to see if Morrison was mentioned, I checked the three previous years.

"Seems like this Morrison was top jock with the Crimson. Although he was highlighted for his football abilities, he was also on the men's lacrosse team and, it appears, their baseball team."

"He was also spotlighted in the '94, '95 and '96 yearbooks for his participation in various sports, with heavy emphasis on football. In all the pictures I've looked at, he's got one or more pretty girls hanging on his arm."

Sal went back to Matthew Morrison's senior sports pictures. "Yep, he's got the girls all right."

"What does it say under his individual class picture?"

Sal flipped to the front half of the book. It listed very few academic achievements. The inscriptions concentrated on his football prowess. "A future with the NFL—next stop Foxboro."

I leaned back and crossed my arms over my chest. "I've got a friend, Eli Manzy, in the Patriots' front office. He's been there longer than I've been on this job. I'll give him a call. If he's going to be around today, we'll take a road trip."

Sal stood. "While you make your call, I'm going to see how Sophie is doing with Wayne."

"I'll join you in a few."

I took the yearbook Sal was working from and opened it to the page where Morrison was spotlighted, then put Tessa's sketch artist rendition and Mario's images next to it. It was impossible that all the likenesses were the same person. Our jock died eighteen years ago, and our perp is alive and very active. I leaned forward and buried my face in the palm of my hands. "This is a fuckin' mess," I whispered.

I scanned my contacts for Eli's number. He answered on the second ring.

"Were you sitting on the phone waiting for your newest hot prospect's agent to call?"

"Your name came up. I could have answered on the first ring, but I decided to let you wait." Eli's sense of humor hadn't changed. "You old dog, what the hell you up to? You looking to retire and want to know if the chief of security position is open?"

"When I retire I'll be sitting on a beach in Naples, sipping whatever makes me happy with whoever makes me happy."

"Then, why the call? Season's over so you can't be looking for tickets."

"I need information. I'd rather not discuss it on the phone. You going to be around later this morning?"

"Sitting right here in my cushy, oversized desk chair with piles of wannabe applications from money-grubbing agents trying to set up a meeting with the upper management of the best team in the NFL."

"Sorry I asked."

"What time will you be here?"

"How's 10:30 sound?"

"I'll let them know at the front door." Eli hesitated. "Got another call coming in."

I hung up and walked to Wayne's office to join Sal.

Wayne was putting the finishing touches on Sophie's sketch. "The features both girls remembered are remarkably similar."

I looked at Sophie. "Did you and Tessa talk about this customer any time within the last week?"

"You told us not to, so we didn't," she said emphatically.

"Okay, I had to ask."

Wayne showed Sophie the finished product. "Is there anything you want to change or add?"

"That's him. Definitely him."

We're looking for a ghost.

CHAPTER 49

There was little conversation in the car when we gave Sophie a ride to Harvard Square. I knew she didn't like the implication that she and Tessa may have innocently had a conversation involving their customer.

When we pulled up in front of the boutique, Sal got out of the car and opened the door for her. "Thanks for coming down to the station. We'll be in touch."

"I hope I was some help."

"More than you know."

I waited until she got inside before we left.

"I talked to my friend at Gillette Stadium. Told him I needed some information, but I didn't want to talk on the phone. He said he'd be in all day." There was no easy way to get to the football Stadium, especially at this time of day. "We'll take the Pike to 95 and, as long as we don't hit a jam, we should be in Foxboro in an hour."

"You're driving."

Eli was waiting for us.

I introduced Sal, then the three of us took seats around Eli's desk.

"Remember the first time you came to my office?"

I did a three-sixty of the room. "I certainly do."

He turned toward Sal. "Mastro was a cocky kid who thought he could play football with the best. I agreed to see him as a favor to an old buddy of mine, Johnny Higgins, God rest his soul." His speech stalled. "Mike played for the University of Massachusetts—wasn't bad, but wasn't good. I sent him out in one of the third string practice sessions." Eli looked at me. "You were hurtin' when you hit the shower."

"Who you kiddin'? With a little coaching, I would've been great."

"A little coachin'?"

"Yeah, yeah, yeah. I didn't come down here for you to let old secrets out of the bag."

Eli had a shit-eatin' grin on his face. "No, detective, I expect you didn't."

I took my briefcase from beside my chair, set it on his desk, and took out the yearbook, artist's sketches and Mario's images. I stood and arranged them so he could see them all at one time, except the yearbook. I wanted him to study the other pictures first. He looked down the line several times. On the last scan he picked up Wayne's artwork. "This face—I'm sure I've seen it before." He set the pictures back down. "What's with the '97 Harvard yearbook?"

I didn't say anything, just opened it to the page I had marked.

It was as though Eli had seen a ghost. "What's this all about?"

"Do you know who this person is?"

"I do. Matthew Morrison was one of the most promising quarterbacks on the college scene. His name was put into the fishbowl for the Heisman Trophy. We were looking at him." Eli took a deep breath and slowly let it out. "He was good and he knew it. I don't think he was going to graduate Harvard as a Rhodes Scholar, but nonetheless he was going to get a diploma."

"What happened to him?"

"Don't know exactly. What I do know is he liked the young ladies. I never heard of any drinking or drug problems, but they said the night he was killed in a car accident, the girl driving had a blood alcohol level of .125, and tested positive for cocaine. His test showed much lower than the legal limit and no drugs."

"Do you know anything else about the accident?"

"Since we'd been looking to draft him, we took a higher than normal interest in the incident. He was a good kid." Eli cupped his hands around the back of his neck and started to rock in his chair. "If I remember correctly, they were coming back from a party somewhere on the North Shore."

Sal made a note to check it out when they got back to the station.

"I think it was organized by the Gridiron Groupies."

"The who?" I asked.

"You've never heard of them? They've been around, in some form or another, probably since football's inception." Eli leaned forward on his desk. "Umm, let me figure out how to describe them other than whores sporting a D Fence tattoo. I know they're staples around all the stadiums in the United States. If you know where to look, you can't miss them. Next season I'll treat you to a viewing. They're much like band groupies or roller blade groupies or whatever groupies. They're looking to latch onto an up-and-coming player." He looked at Morrison's yearbook pictures again. "The girls don't necessarily know each other. They party together, but they're looking out for themselves, so I don't suspect they get overly friendly."

"Do you still have a personnel file on Morrison?"

"There might be something on the computer in archives, but that was, let's see…eighteen years ago."

"Do you remember anything about his family?"

"No. We usually don't get involved with the player's family background unless we sign him." Eli looked at me over his glasses.

"Why are you asking all these questions about a kid who died eighteen years ago?"

"See those other sketches and pictures you just looked at? That person is alive and kicking, or should I change that to alive and killing."

"What the fuck you talking about?"

"A serial killer, who looks exactly like our dead man. We're either dealing with a ghost, or this Morrison guy has a twin who likes Gridiron Groupies."

"Now I'm really confused. You didn't even know about the sports girls' special society until I mentioned it. How many are there? Do you know their names? Or where they're from?"

"There are four that we know about, no to their names, and no to where they're from, but you just confirmed their group affiliation."

"How's that?"

"They all had a D Fence tattoo."

Eli stood and walked to a window overlooking part of the stadium. It felt like an eternity before he spoke. "Mike, let me do some askin' around."

"Anything—names, addresses, whatever—you can get for me will be appreciated. The only thing I ask is that you don't let anyone know why you're asking. If word gets out, and our perp thinks we're getting closer to finding out who he is, he'll either go into hiding, or worse, he'll kill again."

Eli escorted us to the front lobby. "We'll talk soon."

CHAPTER 50

The ride back to Boston became a private session for throwing out ideas, trying to incite a meaningful discussion leading to new avenues for investigation.

I checked in my rearview mirror, then eased over into the slow lane. "Thinking and driving don't mix."

Sal agreed.

"Gridiron Groupies. I've seen band groupies—both male and female. Some of them will do anything to personally latch onto their idols. Why should we think these Gridirons are any different?"

"They aren't, but, no matter what their intentions, they didn't deserve to be murdered."

"Our perp doesn't agree with you." The wheels in my head were turning, but the thoughts going nowhere. I pulled past the station and headed for the Boulevard and Benny's.

Sal gave me a puzzled look. "Do I dare ask?"

"Doesn't my forehead neon sign flash 'clam roll'?"

He laughed.

Our conversation lightened over lunch, but I couldn't help looking out over the Boulevard, and imagining our killer riding by—taunting us—daring us to find him. I looked down at my empty plate. "We're going to get you." I whispered so only I could hear.

"What?" Sal asked.

"Nothing, just talking to myself."

"Did yourself talk back?"

"Not yet."

CHAPTER 51

Sal and I decided to do some independent web crawling and reverse cyber stalking when we got back to the station, in hopes we could each find a clue that would mesh together to produce one valid step forward.

Before we got started I got a call. "You've got a visitor."

"Who?"

The duty officer hesitated. "Vinny Balducci."

"What the fuck does that scumbag want? Never mind. I'll be right down."

"What was that all about?"

"Vinny Balls is in the lobby wanting to talk to me."

"Do you want me to come with you?"

"No. That way you won't be a witness as to where I might tell him to go, and if he needed any help getting there, I'd be glad to oblige him."

"Be careful."

I pretended to twirl a Snidely Whiplash mustache. "Don't worry."

Vinny Balls was sitting in the far corner of the lobby, reading one of the six-month-old magazines reserved for visitors. He pretended he didn't see me walk in his direction, and didn't stand until I was directly in front of him.

"Forget to put glasses on those eyes on the top of your head?"

"What are you talking about."

"Nothing. What can I do for you?"

I stayed standing. He sat back down.

"I was wondering if you could give me any new information on the dead girls."

I laughed loud enough for the desk officer to hear me. That way he'd think we were having an amicable conversation, when I was just about to tell him I was going to cut his balls off if I read another word about our Doll case in *The Chatter* or any other publication that would buy his crap.

"No reply. So, detective, you're hitting a brick wall?"

"You're not called Balls for nothing. If you printed the truth, I might think about talking to you, but you've never penned anything in your slimy career as a so-called journalist that even resembled the facts. I doubt you even know how to spell the word integrity."

"Such a kind endorsement coming from one of Revere's finest."

"Leave this case alone. If you don't and we have another victim, I'm going to hold you personally responsible and see to it that you're charged as an accessory."

"Never happen."

"Don't test me." I walked away and loud enough for Vinny to hear, I let the duty officer know that Mr. Balducci was ready to leave.

Sal looked away from his computer as I came back into the office carrying a steaming cup of fresh coffee. "Smells good."

"I just made a pot."

He stood up. "I'm going to get myself one. You weren't gone long."

"Didn't need to be. Our conversation was short and to the point."

"And, am I right in saying you're not going to share it."

I nodded. "You're right."

After Sal headed for the breakroom, I called Maggie. "Afternoon."

"What happened to good afternoon?"

"Half good afternoon. Does that work?"

"I'll take it. Did Sophie show up this morning?"

"She did. The sketch Wayne drew from her description and Tessa's were almost identical. They did a great job."

"She'll be pleased she could help."

"They helped more than you know. And, by the way, you're no slouch in the help department. If it wasn't for your recollection of the Kors items, we wouldn't be at the point we're at now."

"Does that mean you've got something concrete to go on?"

"Working on something."

"I won't ask. When you're able, you'll tell me. You will—right?"

I took a drink. "Right. Can you pencil me in for date number two tomorrow night?"

I heard a giggle. "Pencil you in? How about I cyber you into my iPhone."

"Technology. Whatever happened to the free calendars and a Bic pen."

"I've got a customer. Tomorrow night." The phone went dead.

I typed Mathew Morrison's name into the search box. Nothing came up. I know he died eighteen years ago, but something should still be visible. My skills at digging into metal file cabinets for abandoned paperwork were much more adept than electronically shuffling pages to find archived information. I rested my elbow on my desk, supported my chin in the palm of my hand, grasped my cup with my free hand and stared at the screen. There was nothing I hadn't already seen.

I looked up when the office door closed.

Sal walked over behind me. "Matthew is spelled with two t's."

He didn't wait for a reply and I didn't give one. I changed the spelling and pages of Matthew Morrison's came up. I scrolled down, stopping at each one. It was a common name, so unless I found a reason to open the entire article, I continued to the next one. I figured Sal had already run the name, but I might catch some little thing he missed. We're going to need every *t* crossed and *i* dotted and *x,y,z* probed to get information on this guy. Third page was an obituary. I opened it. It was definitely our guy. The picture looked like one of the ones from the '97 yearbook. I sent it to the printer.

Sal looked out from beside his screen. "I'm assuming you found the obit."

"I did. It's time for a team effort." I took the copy of the obit from the printer and moved to the conference table.

Sal took other articles he'd printed and set them down beside the obit. "You might find these interesting too."

It listed information we already knew about how he died, no details, just an automobile accident. The obit didn't list the name of the girl who was driving. When I finished, I'd check our files, unless Sal already had.

"Shows his address, other than Harvard, was in Danvers. Lists his mother and father as living, and also lists a brother, Kevin." I highlighted the three names.

Sal flipped through the pile of papers he'd already printed from computer articles. "Check this one out." He handed it to me. "It's an obit for the father—two years after his son died."

"Did you find out anything more on the mother?"

"Not yet."

"What about the brother?"

"It's like he disappeared."

"We've got to find both of them." I eyed the paperwork. "Anything else I should pay immediate attention to?"

"The *Globe's* article on the accident. Read it, then we can discuss it."

I leaned forward in my chair and started to read the article.

Sal didn't say anything until I finished. "It's pretty much the same accounting Eli gave us earlier, with a few added details. It gives the location, but it doesn't give a name for the girl who was driving. It also says they were returning to Boston after attending a beach party on the north shore."

I glanced up from the article. "Didn't Eli tell us that?"

"Party, yes—beach party, no. The bodies of our four murdered Dolls were left on a beach."

I pointed at Sal. "What are you getting at?"

"I don't know. It's almost like somebody is playing a game, and in some freakish way it's related to football."

"Did you look up the Gridiron Groupies?"

"I was about to when you came in." Sal moved back behind his computer. "Give me a minute."

The silence on the issue was deafening. I could feel the fine hairs in my inner ear vibrate with the slightest change in air pressure.

"Gridiron Groupies are more commonly known as jersey chasers, but then we already knew that. There's nothing designating organized chapters, and none that have adopted a team related name. It's more or less how Eli described them."

"Tag-a-longs in search of securing a dream." I leaned back in my chair and studied the ceiling hoping, by some miracle, our ghost would speak to us from the grave. "Without more creditable evidence to research, the computer isn't our friend. Since the obit said Matthew was originally from Danvers, I'd say we pay their PD a visit."

CHAPTER 52

In forty-five minutes we were at the Danvers Police Department. The captain in charge, Russ Stark, remembered the family well, especially Matthew. "He was popular amongst his peers, particularly the girls. If there was a party, he was there. But, he wasn't a problem. He did volunteer work for various organizations in town that promoted youth activities. The day he died, part of Danvers died."

"Do you remember anything about the accident?" I didn't want to tell him what we'd already found out. I wanted to hear everything he might have to say.

"I know he was coming from a party, but wasn't driving. The driver was a female. I'll never forget. The car looked like it had been spit out of a crusher. The speedometer stopped on impact at one hundred-four miles per hour. I've only seen a couple frozen speedometers and this was one of them."

"Do you know who the female was?"

"We weren't able to identify her, and nobody came forward. We checked missing persons nationwide, but with little to go on, we came up with nothing. The remains were cremated and buried in the public cemetery. Both bodies were mangled and burned beyond recognition. It was Matthew's car, a fire-engine red Corvette, an early graduation present from his parents. He was identified through dental records. The ME was able to determine the driver's use of cocaine and alcohol. Matthew's blood level was under the legal limit, and he had no drugs in his system."

"What about his family? The obituary listed his parents and a brother."

"The father couldn't cope with his son's loss. Two years after the accident he committed suicide. The mother became a recluse and suffered from deep depression. She finally had to be put into a nursing home. I believe she died a couple years ago."

"That leaves the brother," I said.

"His identical twin brother, Kevin, disappeared off the face of the earth after the mother died."

My voice rose to a heightened level of surprise. "His twin brother?"

Sal's mouth opened, but nothing came out.

A puzzled expression appeared on the captain's face. "Yes, he was the brother listed in the obit. Obviously, you didn't know Matthew had a twin."

My surprised look about said it all. "No sir, we didn't."

There was a pause in the conversation. My mind was spinning in umpteen directions, not stopping to examine any one of them.

The silence was broken when Captain Stark spoke. "Your reaction to the discovery of a twin has spiked my imagination. Are you able to share your interest in the Morrison family?"

I glanced at Sal. "We're working a homicide. A young woman, presumed to be in her early twenties, was found dead on Revere Beach last week."

"I read about that."

"We believe this death is the fourth one committed by a serial killer. The first one was ten months ago in Quincy. Our investigation has led us to Matthew Morrison. Yesterday, we found out about his accident. We have partial images from security cameras and our PD sketch artist's renderings from two witnesses, not to the murder, but another aspect of the case. These are an aged match to pictures in several of the Harvard yearbooks, ending in 1997—the same year Matthew died. We were literally searching for a ghost, until you told us he had a twin."

The captain stood and paced his office. "Kevin was never the same after his brother's death. Don't know if you knew Matthew was slated to sign on with the Patriots after his graduation from Harvard. Kevin was into sports, but was never as good as Matthew. Kevin was the studious one, much quieter and never in any trouble. I forget where he ended up going to college, but I can find out for you. It was one of the Ivy League schools or another of the same caliber. The Morrison family had money."

"Money … as in big money? Enough where Kevin could disappear and live comfortably?" Sal asked.

Captain Stark nodded. "Absolutely."

CHAPTER 53

Sal and I left the Danvers Police Station on Ash Street and headed toward the town hall on Sylvan. Captain Stark had given us the address of the former Morrison property. From real estate records at the assessor's office, we found the property had been sold almost two years ago. The seller in the transaction was Kevin Morrison.

Sal sighed. "The entire proceeds went to Kevin. It sounds like all this happened soon after his mother passed."

I asked the clerk if there was any other property in town with Kevin Morrison's name listed as a principal.

The clerk pulled up a database on the computer. "This will tell us if his name is listed on anything else, also if he's registered as a voter, or if he holds some kind of license—example, dog, hunting or fishing." She looked at a couple more screens, then turned to us. "Nothing."

We thanked the clerk and headed for the parking lot.

"One mystery solved. Our perp is off the radar screen, but very much alive." I beeped to open the car doors.

We tried to decide our next move.

"There's nothing we can do here, and unless you have any new ideas, we might as well head back to the station." I started to back out of the parking space. "Call in and ask them to run Kevin Morrison's name through every database available."

Sal pulled his phone from his pocket, and hit number one for the duty officer at the station.

"Kevin Morrison—where the fuck are you?" I said out loud.

"One thing we know is that he's still in the area or, at least, somewhere close."

"Think about this," I said. "We now know he was an identical twin, which probably means they were best friends. I've read studies that living without their other half was too much for one or the other to handle."

"Our living twin could be taking revenge against the elements he figures stole his brother—his best friend."

"Captain Stark said Kevin was very studious. He could have been planning this ever since his father and mother died. Remember, the father committed suicide as a result of Matthew's death, and the mother died from a retreat into a deep depression—basically a broken heart. The nucleus of his family existence was crushed when Matthew died." I pulled into the right lane in anticipation of our exit.

Sal stared out the side window. "The girl driving—a Gridiron Groupie. The cocaine and the alcohol. *She* killed his brother and, in Kevin's eyes, *she's* responsible for his father's suicide and mother's early demise. I have no doubt he's going to strike again."

"Not if we can help it." I parked in front of the station. "It's four o'clock, records should still be here. They've had time to run the reports you asked for."

"I'll get them and meet you in two."

I grabbed a coffee from the breakroom. After the first sip there was no way I was about to drink this mud, and I didn't feel like making a fresh pot. I was just ready to head to room two when my phone rang. It was Maggie. "Hi."

"Busy?"

"Not right at the moment."

"I have that information you wanted about the company who uses the D Fence logo."

"Let me get something to write on." I took a napkin from the counter and sat down at the table. "Ready."

"Its main office in the United States is in New York, with branches in Miami, Chicago and Los Angeles. The logo has the initials of the company, PC, on the bottom of the last fence slat."

"What does the PC stand for?"

"Philip Cotton."

I threw my free hand in the air. "And, who is Philip Cotton?"

"A very expensive designer, originally from London, now expanding—hence the locations in the United States. It's nothing I'd carry. Way out of my league."

I didn't remember seeing initials on the Doll's tattoos. But as far as I was concerned, the jacket logo and the tattoos were tied together.

"Thanks for the info. Gotta go, give you a call later." I hustled back to room two to check out the tattoo pictures.

Sal was waiting for me.

"Maggie called. The logo on the jacket belongs to a high-end designer. Our boy knows his fashions—Michael Kors and, now, Philip Cotton. He'd have been less conspicuous if he'd dressed himself and the Dolls with something off a rack at Walmart. I guess 'money' doesn't think that way."

"And according to Captain Stark, he has more than lots."

I took the picture of Revere girl and Hull girl and pointed to their tattoos. "There's no initials on the Doll's tattoos."

Sal looked puzzled.

"Maggie said the designer logo had initials on it, like the Michael Kors—MK in a circle. Philip Cotton uses PC in a box." I took my magnifying glass to zoom in on something in the bottom right corner of the logo. "There's definitely something there, but I can't say what. I'll have Mario check it out."

A quick phone call to IT confirmed there were, in fact, the initials PC on the jacket logo.

"Now what?" Sal asked.

Before I could make any suggestions, my phone rang. "Detective Mastro."

"Mike, its Eli. I did some checking for you. You know those Gridiron Groupie tattoos I mentioned? There's a guy in Attleboro who does some of the tattooing, at least around here. His name is Terry Holmes. The place is *Specialty Tattoos*. Remember, I told you this 'club' is nationwide, so apparently this is our local guy."

I thanked Eli, and assured him I'd get back to him, then dialed the number he'd given me for the tattoo artist.

"*Specialty Tattoos*, how may I help you?"

"Is Terry available?"

"This is Terry."

"My name is Detective Michael Mastro, with the Revere Police Department. We're conducting inquiries related to an investigation we're working. We'd like to talk to you. Are you available this afternoon?"

"I'll be here until seven. Can I ask what it is you're looking for?"

"It's nothing to do with your business. We'll be there in an hour."

I hung up and rushed to catch up with Sal who was already out the door.

CHAPTER 54

Specialty Tattoos was on Pine Street, not far from the Attleboro Police Station. When Sal and I entered, a door chime rang. Terry was not in sight. A few seconds later, he came out from the back room.

"Give me about ten minutes."

"No problem," I said.

I was impressed with the tattoo store. It was tastefully decorated with samples of what I presumed were tattoos he was most proud of. There were three binders of his artwork resting on the counter for new customers to peruse. While Sal checked the wall hangings, I sat down with the binders.

I caught Sal's attention, and whispered. "This certainly is levels above the places we checked out in Boston."

Sal raised his eyebrows and nodded. "You've got that right."

There it was. "Take a look." Halfway through the second binder was a picture of a D Fence tattoo, just like the ones on our Dolls. It showed the naked back of a girl with long blonde hair pulled to one side to display the artwork. The next picture was one of the same tattoo, but different body location, different model, and different pose. There were five more. From what I could see, all the models were extremely well put together. All but one had long hair, different colors, but the same style—long and straight, like our Dolls.

Sal's expression reflected my thoughts. We spoke quietly, so as not to share our conversation.

We moved to the two chairs furthest from the door to the backroom. I looked around. "Judging by the looks of this place, Terry seems like he's running a successful business. I don't know if he's required to get certain information, per the health department or because of his license, but anything is more than we have right now."

Ten minutes turned into fifteen before Terry checked back with us. "Sorry, I misjudged my time. There are some things you can't rush. My customer's getting changed. Once she leaves, except for possible walk-ins, I'm free for a couple hours."

"This won't take long." I lifted the binders. "Are all these your artwork?"

"They are. I'm a one-man shop. That way I can control my quality."

"Nice work," said Sal.

"Thank-you." Terry went behind the counter and appeared to be writing up some kind of slip.

Customer information?

We waited until his customer left before we approached the counter.

He reached forward to shake my hand. "Let me formally introduce myself. I'm Terry Holmes, proprietor and resident artist of *Specialty Tattoos*."

"I'm Detective Mastro, and this is my partner, Detective Petruca. As I told you on the phone, we're out of the Revere Police Department. We came here looking for a particular tattoo. When I looked through your binders, I found it being modeled by five young ladies." I opened the book to the D Fence tattoos.

Sal took the pictures of the Dolls from my briefcase and handed them to me. I cleared the counter off and slowly laid our four pictures next to the ones in Terry's binder. I watched as he studied them. Then I took the two pictures of the tattoos we found on the Revere and Hull girls and gave them to Terry.

He appeared uncomfortable. He set the pictures down and tapped his finger on the tattoo photos. "These are my work."

"What about the girls. Do you recognize any of them?"

"All four."

"Do you keep records of who you ink?" I asked.

"I do. There are parlors that don't, but I'm licensed and reputable. I require a signed release form with all their information, including what they want done. The customer also has to furnish a legal form of identification. Most times it's a driver's license. If the person is under eighteen, a parent has to sign." He hesitated. "These girls were not minors. I have records for all the girls who got this tattoo. Only once did two come in together. Other than that, I don't know if they even knew each other."

I glanced at the pictures. "Why do you say that?"

"Let me show you what I have." He turned and headed to the backroom.

I shrugged, threw my hands up, and sighed all at the same time.

A minute later, Terry returned carrying a manila folder containing paperwork for seventeen girls. "The first dates back five years, right after I bought the business. When I said the D Fence tattoo was my work, I want you to know I'm not unique to the design.

"Meaning?"

"There are tattooists all over using this same design. A couple of the girls told me the motif symbolized membership in the Gridiron Groupies. When I asked what she was referring to, she told me they follow football players, much like band groupies follow bands. Apparently, they congregate around pro-football stadiums." He handed me the folder. "There's a packet for each girl. I understand the previous owner of my shop was a Patriots season ticket holder. And, that's why the girls came here for their artwork. He's since passed."

I took one off the top of the pile. There was a picture of a girl, and one of the D Fence tattoo, stapled to a copy of her driver's license, and the information-release form, filled out and signed. I shuffled down through several more. “None of these girls are from the area.”

“Keep going.”

Two more down there was one with a Vermont address. It belonged to Revere girl. “I’ll need copies of all these.”

“Give me five minutes and I’ll have them for you.”

CHAPTER 55

As we rode back to the station, Sal thumbed through the folder containing all the information on the girls with the D Fence tattoo. "You learn something new every day. What bothers me is how they kinda just fell off the grid, and nobody's been looking for them."

"They weren't minors." I blasted the horn at a metallic blue Ferrari that cut me off.

Sal pushed his hands against the dashboard. "Not the thing to do to any car, let alone a cruiser."

My grip tightened on the wheel. "That fuckin' track toy shouldn't be allowed on public highways. I ought to pull him over."

Sal waved his hand at me. "Let it go. Back to the girls."

I eased my grip on the wheel. "Okay. Get the paperwork on Revere girl."

"Got it." He read it over.

"What was the name of the town in Vermont she was from?"

"Poultney."

I gave Sal a quick glance. "The same town where Martin Rucci's flunkie, Richard, and his two underage house guests came from."

"The address on her license and information form aren't the same. The license has a Vermont address, but the form has a Boston address. And, if I'm not mistaken, it's Rucci's."

"Check the rest of the forms for same address."

Sal pulled out four more packets. "Bingo. There's five altogether."

"Rucci was their perverted, surrogate father. We need to find out if the girls were underage when they first came to Boston and moved in with Rucci. If so, and the authorities found out, his little bed and breakfast would have gotten closed down, and he'd be spending the rest of his years sleeping on a federally purchased twin bed and shitting in a stainless-steel bowl."

Sal put the five packets back in the folder. "I figured we were through with Rucci and Richard when we delivered them to lock-up. Looks like we're about to become their worst nightmare."

"We might be able to get Richard to roll on Rucci."

It was five-thirty when we pulled into the parking lot behind the station.

Sal handed me the folder. "I'm heading home."

"I want to make a few notes before we question Richard. His answers will determine how we handle Rucci. If you think of anything that can't wait till morning, I'll be leaving here around seven, then home."

Sal headed to his car.

There wasn't anyone in the detective bureau. I spread the packets on my desk, then recorded each name, address—both if the driver's license showed a different one—and date of birth. Just because they were of legal age when they got their tattoo, didn't mean they were of legal age when they chose to become a groupie. I leaned forward on my desk, and studied the girl's faces. They stared back, but not one of them spoke to me. I stopped when I came to the packet for Revere girl. Her name was Jeni Johnson. If the addresses on the licenses are good, we can at least notify the families of our four dead girls.

I called dispatch. "Paulie, do you know who's working second shift in the control room at County?"

"Usually it's Officer Gemme. Do you want me to call?"

"I've worked with him before. If there's a problem, I'll let you know." I dialed the number for the Sheriff's Department.

"Suffolk County Sheriff's Department, Officer Gemme speaking. How may I help you?"

"Officer Gemme, this is Detective Mastro, Revere PD. I'm looking for information on a hold."

"What's the name?"

"Richard Landon."

"He's here. Couldn't make bail. He's listed as indigent. According to his file, he's had no contact with anyone outside the facility. He tried to make a couple collect calls, but the person or persons on the other end wouldn't accept it."

"We need to question him about a case we're working. Detective Petruca and I will be at your facility around 9:30 tomorrow morning. Can you note that in his file, and leave instructions for the day officer to have him available?"

"Done."

"Before I go, do you still have Martin Rucci as a house guest?"

He answered without hesitation. "We certainly do."

I knew he wanted to say more, but couldn't because of the recorded line. "Thank you, Officer Gemme. Have a good rest of the night."

Chapter 56

Thursday

I got to the station early. Everybody was mulling around the fresh pot of coffee in the breakroom, not wanting to be the one to take the last cup, thus having to brew a new pot. I took time before the morning briefing to make a quick call to Maggie. Last night, my mind was washed out. I fell asleep on the couch, and didn't wake up and move to the bed until two a.m.

"Morning detective. When I didn't hear from you last night, I thought you got cold feet about having another date with the same girl."

"Very funny. But now that you mention it, my feet were pretty cold when I woke up from my cat nap."

"Guess I'll have to get you a warm pair of socks." Maggie laughed, "What time are we stepping out, and where are we going, so I can dress appropriately? I wouldn't want to wear a teddy if we're going to—let's say—Abe and Louie's."

"Now that you've decided where, I'll pick you up at your apartment at seven."

"That works for me."

I liked talking to Maggie first thing in the morning. I also liked talking to Maggie afternoons and evenings.

I hung up, just as Sal walked in. "You got our schedule for today lined up?"

"At least the morning one. Richard is still being held at the County Jail on Nashua Street. I talked to the control room officer last night. He noted we'd be paying Richard a visit this morning. If he listens to the stories the seasoned inmates tell him, he won't want to be sentenced and moved to 20 Bradston Street. Most of those guys don't like it when a piece of shit like Richard Landon messes with underage girls. They perform their own methods of punishment."

"Didn't they assign him bail?"

"They did, but he's listed as indigent, and the people he called didn't want to know." I was glad. "Fortunately for us and unfortunately for him."

"What about Rucci?"

"He's still at Nashua Street. I guess nobody wants to be a part of him and he doesn't have enough in his legit bank account to make bail. He's being kept away from Richard." I took a drink of coffee. "If Rucci gets to him, we have a problem. We've got to move fast. If Richard, in fact, did transport those girls across state lines, he could be rooming at a federal facility, and those guys don't care. And if Rucci was deemed an accomplice in those federal charges, our two boys might find themselves roommates."

"I don't think Richard could handle that."

"Exactly, so we need to convince him we're on his side—at least until we get the information we want." I stood and put the paperwork from the tattoo parlor back into my briefcase. "Once we've verified what Richard told us is true, he's off the Christmas list."

Sal's smirk said it all.

CHAPTER 57

The tier officer brought Richard to interrogation room five, where we were waiting. "Good morning," I reached out to shake his hand.

He reciprocated in silence.

"We've got a few questions for you."

"Aren't you supposed to ask my lawyer or, at least, have him or her here while I'm answering?"

"If that's the way you want to have it, we'll leave, contact your legal representative, and make arrangements to come back when he or she is available. Or, you can listen to what we have to say before you make that decision. Your choice." I sat back in my chair and crossed my arms. If he spoke first, I won. If I spoke first, he won.

Sal's elbows were on the table, his chin firmly secured on his raised knuckles, and his eyes focused on Richard while the quiet minutes grew heavier.

I looked at my watch. It would take a while for his pea brain to process what he'd just heard. I stood to give him the impression we were contemplating leaving without a goodbye.

Finally, he broke. "I'm ready."

"Ready to talk or ready to go back to your shared six-by-eight?"

"Talk. You said you wanted to talk."

I sat back down.

Richard put his cuffed hands on the table in front of him.

"The girl that was found on the beach, you told us you didn't see her. I'm going to ask that again. Did you see the body of the girl who was lying dead beside the bathhouse?"

He hesitated and fumbled with his fingers. "I did."

"No more lies. This is the time for truth or consequences. Had you ever seen that girl before that morning?"

Richard was silent.

I leaned in closer and repeated the question. "Had you ever seen that girl before that morning?"

Richard ran his tongue across his bottom lip. "I didn't have anything to do with her murder."

"I didn't ask about the murder. Where did you first see her?"

"At Pinky's Powder Lounge. She was a dancer."

I let the fact that we knew they were from the same town in Vermont stay our secret, at least for the time being.

Sal riveted his eyes on Richard. "Did you see her anywhere else?"

His tongue rimmed the full oval of his mouth. "At Martin Rucci's house," he said in a voice below a whisper.

Sal's voice elevated. "I can't hear you?"

Richard upped his tone. "At Rucci's house."

"That's better," Sal leaned back in his chair.

I took the picture of Revere girl from my briefcase. "This girl?"

"Did you know her?" I waited for his response.

Richard's leg started to quiver, his knee jumping above his toe. "Yes."

"Were you sleeping with her?"

He snapped his head back. "No, Rucci was. He slept with all the girls from the bar, even the underage ones. You already know that."

"Yeah, and I already know you slept with those two underage girls we met at Pinky's last week too."

I had no intention of giving this asshole a break. "Who killed her? Did she have a boyfriend?"

"How the fuck should I know."

I wanted to slap him into answering me, but held back. "Cause you lived with her, like brother and sister. Wouldn't you know who your sister was bonking?"

Richard drew in a deep breath. "When Jeni told Rucci she was quittin' the bar, he kicked her out. She didn't care, 'cause there was a guy she'd talk to at the bar, and I think they had a thing going. Anyway, she quit dancing, moved out and the next time I saw Jeni, she was dead."

"When did this all happen."

"She moved out about five days before they found her on the beach."

I took the sketch artist's renderings and slid them across the table. "Do you recognize this person?"

"He's the guy. That's the one she hooked up with." His nervous-hot breath caused condensation on the glossy finish. "That's him."

I pushed the blown-up yearbook picture of Matthew Morrison toward Richard.

"Same guy?" I knew he had no idea it was the twin brother.

"Same guy. And, something else. In the picture, this guy was a football jock. Jeni was into football big time. She even had a football related tattoo. Sometimes, when she wasn't working, she'd bum a ride to Foxboro and hang around the stadium on game day. I think one time it was this guy who picked her up, but I can't be sure of that."

"How'd you know she had a tattoo?" I asked.

CHAPTER 58

I pulled into the convenience store down the street from the station to pick up a copy of *The Daily Chatter*. "My check to see if Vinny Balls heeded my warning."

"You never shared his conversation with me."

I nodded. "You're right."

"I listed the names and addresses, and attached a copy of driver's licenses along with a picture of the girls who Terry inked. I'm going to have records run them through missing persons' data bases and the DMV. There are seventeen, one positive hit could be a break. Meet you in room two."

I scrutinized the paper. "Balls can live to see another sunrise."

"Records said they'd have the information within the hour."

"I want to check it out before we talk to Rucci. He and Balls crawl out of the same bucket of slime every morning. I don't know which one to trust less. Rucci might talk, but who knows if he's telling the truth. And, Balls will lie about his genuineness to get a story." I tossed *The Chatter* in the center of the table. "It's all yours."

"Since it's full of shit, it'll make good bathroom reading."

"It's only a matter of time before Kevin Morrison gets edgy and tries to kill again, especially if he figures we're closing in. We also have to make sure Sophie and Maggie are safe. We know they don't fit the profile of his victims, but he could feel they're a threat.

If he's planning to continue his quest to rid the area of Gridiron Groupies, he won't let anything or anyone get in his way."

"Amen, brother. You read my mind."

"I'm seeing Maggie tonight. I've told her bits and pieces, but I think she deserves to know more. She needs to be on her guard. And, that goes for Sophie too. I don't want to scare them, but they both should be aware of who might be sharing their surroundings."

Sal grimaced. "Sophie appears stronger than she really is. When you're ready to talk to her, I'd like to be the one who does it."

"I understand."

"I'll get pleasure watching Vinny Balls take pictures and yell questions when we lead Morrison on a perp walk through the most public place allowed by law. Swapping his fancy-dancy designer clothes for a bright orange jumpsuit, and being visibly restrained in front of the media, isn't going to make him happy." I sat back and folded my arms. "As for me, I'll make sure he sees my pearly whites."

My thoughts of Morrison's perp walk were interrupted, when one of the girls from records knocked on the office door. Sal signaled her in.

She handed him the folder. "The information you requested."

"Appreciate it. Thanks."

We pulled out the four packets for the Dolls and set them aside, then briefly checked the remaining thirteen. Eight matched up, three had new addresses and, it appeared two were amongst the missing.

I pointed to the Doll paperwork. "We'll deal with notification as soon as we make sure the rest of these girls, at least the eleven we have addresses for, are alive. I hope the two that are unaccounted for skipped town without leaving a forwarding address."

Chapter 59

Maggie and I had seven o'clock reservations for dinner at Abe and Louie's. I'd requested a table away from the bar where we'd be able to talk softly and enjoy each other's company. She was standing in the doorway when I pulled up in front of her condo. Before I could get out and walk around to greet her, she had the passenger door open and was getting in.

I tilted my head and glanced in her direction. "You do know that chivalry is not dead."

She leaned over and kissed me on the cheek. "You'll have plenty of chances later to convince me."

"I look forward to it, but right now I'm hungry."

She reached over and pinched my thigh. "Me, too."

We were early, so we headed for the bar. Maggie ordered a chocolate martini and I got a dirty martini minus the vermouth.

I held up my glass. "A friend of mine used to say,

Here's to it,
Those who get to it
And don't do it,
May never get to it,
To do it again.

"I like it."

We clicked and took a sip.

“Look at me.” I tried to act lovingly smug. “A second date with the same girl.”

“Something in common. You’re married to your job, and me to my store. I gave up on the opposite sex a long time ago. I didn’t seem to have the time and, frankly, the guys I got involved with weren’t worth keeping company with.”

I gave her a slanted look.

“Don’t worry, I still like men.”

We laughed.

“Well, Miss Maggie Smith, looks like I’ve got my work cut out for me. A cop, a boyfriend and a lover—it’s been a long time.”

I was so involved with Maggie, I didn’t see the hostess step up beside me. “Mr. Mastro, your table is ready.”

We followed her to our seats.

“Perfect, thank you.” I held the seat for Maggie. “I told you chivalry isn’t dead.”

She pursed her lips and smiled, mimicking a proper lady. “That’s a good beginning.”

We weren’t in a hurry, so we ordered an appetizer to pick on while we talked.

“Sophie called me today. She wondered if I knew what this whole thing with the guy who bought the Michael Kors clothes was about. I told her I knew nothing more than she did. I don’t like to lie, but actually I don’t know much more.”

“It’s complicated, and the only thing I’m completely sure of is, the guy we’re looking for is a murderer. I already told you each of his victims had a D Fence tattoo. And, thanks to you, I’m ninety-percent sure I can connect the jacket with the D Fence logo that our person of interest was wearing, to the tattoos the girls had. At this point, I’d rather you didn’t know any more. I promise I’ll share when I’m able to.” I lifted my glass in a mini-toast, then took a sip.

Maggie reached across the table and took my hands. “I’ll hold you to that, and maybe a few other things.”

Our clams casinos arrived. We ordered dinner and a bottle of Merlot.

"It never entered my mind I'd meet a Maggie Smith while investigating a case."

"When we're looking, it doesn't happen, or it doesn't work out. I'm glad, Detective, that you weren't looking."

"I like you, Maggie Smith."

"I like you, too, Detective Mastro."

"Let's enjoy dinner, then decide whether to head to your place or mine."

CHAPTER 60

Friday

Friday morning was a repeat of Wednesday. I dropped Maggie off at her store and I made it to the station in time for the morning briefing.

Sal was waiting outside the door. "Later than usual and no coffee?"

"Hit the snooze alarm?"

"Bet you did." He smirked. "We have to work up that report for the chief."

"I know. After the briefing." I walked past Sal, into the squad room and took a seat near the back. He sat beside me.

The captain reminded the uniforms of several residential break-ins involving property theft. There were also complaints of kids congregating along the Boulevard during school hours. There were several other directives that didn't concern Sal and me. The last thing Captain Bosworth did was remind all officers to keep their ears and eyes open for information regarding the girl murdered on Revere Beach, and if they heard or saw something, to get in touch with us.

We were in the hallway when the chief walked by the briefing room.

"See you around three with your report." He walked away.

"Let's work in room two again, and get this thing done."

Sal agreed.

We listed everything relating to the case, including what we'd already told him. Sal took copies of our original reports, pictures of

Revere girl, along with Hull and Quincy girls, Mario's IT images and Wayne's drawings.

"I'm going to read the list to make sure we've included everything."

Sal followed from a copy, ready to suggest changes.

I leaned back and took in a deep breath. "If we put a narrative with each heading, it should satisfy him.

1. D Fence logo on the back of our guy's jacket
2. D Fence tattoos on our dead girls
3. Sketches done when Sophie and Tessa met with Wayne
4. Discovery of a look-alike in an eighteen-year-old Harvard yearbook,
5. Meeting with Eli Manzy in Foxboro
6. Eye-witness account of an incident near the bath house where Revere girl was found
7. Rolex,
8. Gridiron Groupies
9. Tattoo parlor in Attleboro
10. Meeting with Captain Stark at Danvers PD."

"You throw out the information. I'll type a draft."

Halfway through, my phone rang. Unknown caller lit up on the screen. "Detective Mastro."

"Mike, it's Eli. I've got something that might interest you. This weekend there's an open scrimmage for the second- and third-string teams. It's a strong possibility there'll be groupies hanging around. A couple of local school groups are coming to watch, and usually we get a decent amount of spectators too."

"What time?"

"I'll meet you at the Bank of America gate at nine."

"You're the man, Eli. See you at nine."

"What was that all about?" Sal asked.

"Going to Gillette Stadium tomorrow morning. I could use an extra set of eyes. If we're lucky, our perp may be working the groupies."

"I'm with you."

"Pick you up at seven-thirty at your house."

Sal nodded. "I'll be ready. I'd love to nail this prick right there. Maybe we could tackle him during the scrimmage. Make the headlines ourselves."

CHAPTER 61

Saturday

It was eight-thirty when Sal and I pulled into the parking lot at Gillette Stadium. I could see Eli standing with another guy at the Bank of America gate. When he saw us, he checked his watch. "You're early. I want you to meet Drew, our head of security."

We greeted our new acquaintance.

Eli caught my sideward glance. "Drew, why don't you and Sal head down to the area designated for spectators. Mike and I have a little catchin' up to do."

Once they were out of earshot, I asked, "Does Drew know why we're here?"

"Don't worry, I didn't tell him anything, except you're an old friend who wanted to rekindle past memories of almost being a New England Patriot."

"You are a ball-buster, but a good one." I patted him on the back.

"People are starting to arrive. I haven't been to the field yet, but your groupies should be starting to congregate. If you weren't here on a mission, you'd find it amusing. But, that's for another day. Let's walk down to the viewing area."

"I brought pictures of the guy we're looking for, and some of our girls."

Eli and I were steps away from our destination, when three girls, dressed in head-turning outfits, crossed in front of us. Eli waved his hand inviting them to pass. "And, here they come."

They shared no conversation, and didn't acknowledge each other's presence, as they continued down to the front of the spectator seating. Two of them appeared to be looking for someone, and the third continued to a front row, aisle seat.

I scanned the same area as our groupies. The two schools on field trips were already settled in their seats—some clutching footballs as though they'd just caught a game-winning pass.

I was one of those kids once, guarding my football in hopes of securing an autograph. Didn't make any difference if the player was a first stringer or not, he was a New England Patriot.

Eli caught me watching the kids. "Those were the days."

I nodded. "Only we didn't realize it at the time."

"Another fifteen minutes and this place will be swarming. Let's move down with Sal and Drew."

Since Drew had no idea why we came to Foxboro, I told him we had information that a person of interest in a case we were working frequents the stadium.

I took the perp's pictures from my pocket and handed one to Eli and one to Drew. Sal had taken one before we left the station. "This is the guy we're looking for. He's Mr. Suave, but if he thinks we're not here to watch the game, he could become paranoid and disappear. Imbed his image in your brain. If you think you've spotted him don't make any move in his direction. Keep him in your sights and call me on my cell." Eli and Drew put my number into their phones. "You two work this area. He's a frequent flyer, so I'm sure he's seen you around. We, on the other hand, aren't familiar. Sal and I will be traveling in different directions, acting like normal guys—cheering the team, drinking beer, stuffing down a hot dog—the whole football experience.

Drew's puzzled look matched his question. "What'd this guy do?"

"We'll fill you in later." I headed toward the concession stand.

Sal went in the opposite direction to the seats next to the tunnel where the players enter the stadium.

The dogs already looked shriveled and overdone. I ordered a pretzel and cheese to go along with my beer. There was a girl, I sized up to be in her early twenties, ordering a beer from the server beside mine. When she tried to pull some napkins from their holder, they fell to the ground.

I didn't give her a chance to bend over. "Let me get those for you."

"Thanks."

"Me and my buddy used to come here all the time, but I moved out of the area and lost touch with my friend, so today I'm reminiscing." We walked away from the stand. "You come here often?"

"Yeah, I love football, especially the Patriots. I met Tom Brady once, and I've bumped into Gronk and his brothers at a bar in Boston a couple times."

"The buddy I mentioned, I heard he's kinda friends with Gronk. The last I knew he was still coming to the stadium all the time. I was in town and heard about the scrimmage. I took a chance he might be here." I didn't want her to ask for a name, so I quickly pulled out the picture of our perp.

"You carry around his picture?"

"No. I made a copy of one I had, so I could show it to someone like you who's always hanging around here, hoping you might have seen him. His name's Kevin, but we called him MB."

She stopped chewing her gum. "Why MB?"

"Crazy, but he was in love with his Mercedes Benz, hence the MB."

She looked back at the picture. "I've seen him here lots of times. I don't know his name. He does drive a black Mercedes. Once he asked me if I needed a ride. I didn't."

"He used to talk with the Gridiron Groupies. I know who they are, but don't know any of them personally. I think they hang around hoping to get close to one of the players, if you know what I mean."

So she wasn't a *groupie*. "It was nice talking to you. Enjoy your nachos and the game. Maybe see you later back at the concession stand."

She nodded and headed back to the field.

There was a half-hour before kickoff. I hung around the concession area hoping to engage in conversation with another young lady, this time, a groupie. I was awkwardly trying to wipe a blob of cheese from my pretzel off my Pat's sweatshirt, when a well-put-together gorgeous blonde came to my rescue.

She reached out for my glass of beer. "Let me hold that for you."

When she did, I noticed a D Fence tattoo on her forearm just above her wrist.

"I've got a buddy who has a leather bomber jacket with that logo on it. As a matter of fact, I was supposed to meet him here today."

She smiled warmly. "That's Willy."

I pretended to be surprised. "Willy? So that's the name he's using now."

"Does he have another one?"

"Kevin," I said. "When he's on the outs with the wife, he has a laundry list of names."

Her eyes shifted from one side to the other. "He's married?" she asked.

"Sure is—for eighteen years—and has three kids, one probably only a few years younger than you."

She stood silent, still holding my beer.

"Just for your ears, don't let him know you know about his life outside the stadium. He gets angry when he reverts back into reality."

"Thank you, I appreciate the advice." When she gave me my beer, a twenty dollar bill fell from her hand.

I reached down, picked it up and handed it to her. "You dropped this."

"I didn't even realize it. Thanks."

"You're welcome."

"If Willy's not here now, he should be soon. He mingles among the groupies. Now I know why. He doesn't care about football, just getting a piece of ass. I'll keep that knowledge locked in my head." She smirked. "Let him promise a never-going-to-happen world of luxury to another groupie. As for me, he doesn't exist anymore."

"Can I ask you something else?" I was afraid she was going to ignore me and take off, but she didn't. "Did Kevin ever take you to his home?"

"If you mean the one he shares with his wife, no. I never would have gone anywhere, let alone a family home, with him if I knew he was married. Fuckin' bastard."

"Where did he take you?"

Her face tightened. "Why are you asking so many questions?"

Any acting ability I could conjure up to keep this conversation going had to happen now. "His wife is my cousin. I'm the godfather to his oldest daughter." I took a deep breath. "I must have been blind not to see this prick was living a double life."

"Look, I don't know you, but you seem sincere."

"I'm sure you're not the first outside of his happy family to be drawn into his web of control. I guess that's what men of great wealth figure they can do successfully without regard to human feelings." I watched the sparkle drain from her eyes.

She rubbed her D Fence tattoo. "He said he had a condo in Boston overlooking the harbor. Said he'd take me there someday, but never did. We went to a suite at the Mandarin Oriental on Boylston Street. It was beautiful." Tears formed in her eyes. "How could I be so naïve?"

I put my arm on her shoulder. "You're going to be just fine. Walk away from all this and don't look back."

"I don't feel like watchin' the game." She stood with her hands in her pockets. "Can I give you my name and number, in case your cousin, Mrs. Willy, needs my help?"

I felt guilty, but couldn't tell her the real reason I was looking for 'Willy'. I told her my name was Gary Brown, and gave her the number to my 'hello' burner phone that I only used for emergency calls, in case she wanted to reach me.

She decided not to stay, but gave me her contact information as I walked her to the parking lot.

On the way back to the stadium, my cell rang. "Detective Mastro, here."

"Detective, it's Drew. I need to see you right away. Meet me inside the Bank America gate."

I ran from the lot, across the vehicle access road, dodging several cars, and into the building. I saw Drew bobbing around, looking for me, while at the same time scanning the area.

"What's up?" I tried to catch my breath.

Drew appeared nervous. "I think I saw the guy you were looking for, but I may have spooked him."

"Why's that?"

"I was looking at his picture while I was walking around the concession area. I caught a glimpse of someone who resembled the image and circled around to get a better look. You blend in better than me. The security uniform and my interest in his person, might have triggered an alarm." He stopped talking for a second, then continued. "A friend of mine saw me and tried to start up a conversation. I told him I was working and would get back to him. When I glanced back down the walkway, your guy, if it was him, was gone."

"You think he saw you observing him?"

"He may have. He looked over his shoulder several times. That's when my buddy came along. I took my eyes off your person for less than a minute and he disappeared. I ran down the walkway in the direction he was headed, but nothing." Drew lowered his head. "I fucked up."

"Keep looking," I walked back to the field to the area where I originally left Sal and Eli. I caught Sal's attention, and he started up the aisle to join me. I didn't see Eli.

"What's wrong?"

"Our guy was here. Now, he's either in hiding, or has left the building and probably the property."

"Explain."

"Drew saw him, or thinks he did."

I turned around in time to see Eli walking in our direction.

"I bumped into Drew. He told me what happened." Eli shook his head. "Good kid, but a little light on experience."

"A thank-you job?" I asked.

"Yep."

"I talked to a couple patrons, both females. One just a football crazy and the other, a groupie, but this isn't the place to talk about my conversations." I turned to face Eli. "Don't you have security cameras?"

"We do. The cameras are located all over the stadium, inside and out. The control room is beside Drew's office. I'll radio him to meet us there."

We followed Eli halfway around the inside perimeter of the stadium, then took the elevator to the third floor. Drew was waiting for us.

Eli instructed Drew to follow my directives.

"Start off with footage from the parking lot outside the Bank of America gate. What we find here will dictate our next area of surveillance."

Drew pulled up the parking lot video. Within a matter of seconds Sal and I counted seven Mercedes, three of them black 550's.

Sal moved closer to the screen and pointed. "Drew, zoom in on the plates of those Mercedes."

The numbers were visible on two, but the third one was parked, maybe on purpose, at an angle that didn't let us view the plate. A current shot of the lot showed the car in question gone.

Sal walked back to the desk. "Run the footage and stop the first time you notice the Mercedes is gone."

Drew froze the frame at twelve-twenty-seven. "He's pulling away. I can't get anything from the plate. This son-of-a-bitch knows exactly when and where to turn to stay off the radar."

"He knows you've got cameras on the parking lot. How far out from the stadium does your camera record?"

"Fifty feet, but aimed down to cover the perimeter."

I did another search, but didn't come up with anything more. "Move inside."

Drew ran the footage from the time the gate opened, to the time we noted the Mercedes pulling away.

"Stop." We all looked at Sal. He pointed. "There he is."

It was almost a carbon copy of the Harvard Square pictures. Our perp had his bomber jacket on, and this time a Patriots ball cap pulled down low enough to hide two-thirds of his face.

I looked at Sal. "There's the dimple."

Without taking his eyes off the screen, Eli backed up and rested on the corner of Drew's desk. "There's something about this guy. It's the jacket."

"What about the jacket?"

"He walked by me earlier. I didn't see his face, but I admired his jacket. There was a D Fence logo on the back, near the collar. He walked to where the groupies were." Eli rubbed his eyes. "Drew, go to the camera covering that section."

I took a deep breath. "No question, our guy was on campus. We need copies of those videos."

Sal put the notes he'd been taking in his pocket. "Give us a copy of the frame showing the girls he was talking to. Mike and I will go down and rekindle the conversation they were having with our person of interest."

"I'll see that Drew has those discs ready to travel. Meet me in my office when you're done on the field."

I nodded and took the pictures of the girls our perp was keeping company with.

CHAPTER 62

Sal and I sounded like a gab session at a sports bar on our ride back to the station. We threw around ideas and personal observations, but accomplished nothing. The Gridiron Groupies we spoke to in the stands didn't offer any information. I was sure they had some, but nobody came forward. Maybe because they were in earshot of each other's answers and didn't want "Willy' to think they were talking about him to strangers.

"What's next?" Sal asked.

"I'll take you home, then I'm going to ride Atlantic Boulevard and show our perp's picture to the doormen at a couple of the harbor front condos. I'm picking Maggie up at the *Closet* at six-thirty, then we're heading over to Pagliuca's for dinner. You and Becky want to join us?"

"Not tonight. I'd say yes, but she made some special dish she saw on the Food Channel, and I'm her guinea pig."

"That's why you're still married."

"Yep."

"Also, the Mandarin isn't far from Newbury Street, so before I see Maggie, I'll have time to check with a friend who works the concierge desk on weekends. If we're lucky, he'll recognize our perp or one of his arm huggers."

The doorman at Harbor Towers was beside my car before I could turn the key and get out. He backed away when I flashed my badge. "I'll only be a few minutes." I didn't wait for a response.

The concierge was sitting behind his counter, I assumed deeply involved with whatever was on his cell. I startled him when I cleared my throat.

"Hello, sir, may I help you with something?"

I presented my badge.

"I'm Detective Mastro from the Revere Police Department. We're scouting the area for a person of interest in an investigation." I took our perp's picture from my pocket. "Have you seen this man?"

The thirtyish, spit-shined and polished errand boy studied it for only a few seconds. "No, sir. He's not at all familiar to me. Do you have a name?"

I wanted to slap him up side of his head. "I was hoping you could provide that for me." I looked him straight in the eyes. "And of course, if you did know, I'm sure you'd tell me. Right?"

"Of course, sir."

"Good," I handed him one of my cards. "Then, I can count on you for a phone call if he happens to walk through your lobby."

"Yes, sir."

Either this wind-up toy was programmed not to give out any resident information, even to the police, or he was telling the truth. I wasn't sure. His performance was too shaky for my liking. But, for all I know, he had an overdue parking ticket in his pocket and was afraid it might come flying out. Nothing here.

I continued the couple miles to Waters Edge Condos. They were off Hanover, only streets away from my place. Their newness, size and water views valued them in the two plus million dollar category, whereas mine was valued at eight hundred twenty-nine thousand, the last time I looked. Far cry from what I paid twenty-three years ago.

I knew the concierge at Waters Edge. We dated a few times. It didn't work out, but we remained friends. The doorman didn't rush as quickly to assist me. Probably because he recognized me and knew I wasn't going to slip him a twenty to watch my car.

"Afternoon, Phil." I walked by him and into the lobby, not waiting for a response.

Gina was at the concierge desk, just far enough from reception to ward off any unwanted eavesdroppers. She was good at her job, and because of it, was generously rewarded by residents and visitors alike. She saw me, came across the lobby and greeted me with a hug. I leaned down and sealed her welcome with a quick kiss on her cheek.

"Been a long time, Mike."

"It has. How's life been treating you?"

She held up her left hand and tilted her fingers to display a diamond that would blind you if it caught the sun. "Yep. I'm finally going to settle down. I figure thirty-nine's a good age to give it a try."

I gave her another hug. "Who's the lucky guy."

"Not a local. I met him here at the Waters Edge. He works in banking. Travels a lot, but once we're married and I give up this job, I'll be his companion. He wants me to go with him now, but you know me. I have to be sure. I am, but a little scared too." She took hold of my left hand. "And, what about you? That ring finger's still bare."

"You know the story. Once was enough. A cop's life doesn't lend itself to happy everaftering, and dinner being served at six."

Gina nodded. "I'm sure you didn't just stop to shoot the shit. What brings you to my castle?"

"I'm looking for a guy in a case I'm working. We have reason to believe he owns, or possibly rents, a condo in the area." I sighed. "Problem is, we don't have a name or, for that matter, anything else. He may be using an alias." I took the picture from my pocket and handed it to her.

"He could look familiar, but not because I've done work for him. I'm on a first name basis with all my clients and he's not one of them. I may have seen him cut through the lobby on occasion, but I can't be sure."

I felt a rush at the possibility Gina may have seen our perp.

"We've got people living here that sometimes never use the front door. If they've got a car, most of them self-park in the garage, then use the residence entrance. Also, I'm usually out the door by six-thirty. A lot of our residents don't get back here from wherever, until well after that."

That was a dead end. "Keep the picture. If anything jogs your memory, give me a call. If you happen to see him, don't, and I repeat don't, mention the fact that I'm looking for him. In fact, I suggest you have nothing to do with him. It would be better if you keep anything regarding this person to yourself, and that includes no sharing with your fiancé or any other Burrough's employees."

She gave me a serious look. "Mike, I know you well enough to know you're not just spouting words. I'll be on the lookout, and I'll be careful."

I checked my watch. "I'll be in touch. And, congratulations." I pointed to my ring finger, then to her.

One of her clients was headed toward her desk. "Bye," she whispered and hustled back to work.

I had just enough time to swing by the Mandarin before meeting Maggie. The closest open parking spot was five spaces from the front of the hotel. I put my official police placard on the front dash.

Greg Burquest was sitting behind the concierge desk. Fancy brochure holders lined the right side and professionally framed pictures of Boston landmarks and must-sees filled the opposite wall.

Three chairs were evenly spaced, waiting for takers. I sat in the middle one.

"Mr. Mike, what the hell brings you uptown? You lookin' for some show tickets?"

"Not this time, but I'll keep you in mind."

"You know I'll take care of you."

"Yeah, Greg, I do." I looked around the lobby. It was a Saturday, and check-in time, so there was steady activity at the registration desk. "I'm looking for someone."

"As long as it isn't me, I'll try to help."

I slid the picture of our perp across the desk. "Does he look familiar? You may have seen him in the company of a girl in her early twenties. Actually, several girls."

"At the same time?"

"No, only one at a time."

"If you've got a name, I can check registration."

"If I had one, I'd give it to you. That's the problem. We think he goes by several different names."

Greg studied the picture again.

"You can keep that. Don't share it." I kept my eyes on his. "Here's my card."

CHAPTER 63

My cell rang as I pulled up in front of *Maggie's Closet.* "Detective Mastro, here."

"It's me. I just got off the phone with Sophie. Where are you?"

"In front of your store."

"I'll be right out." Her voice was elevated. The phone went dead.

Two seconds later Maggie was at the passenger door. "We're meeting Sophie at the Grafton Street Pub and Grill, down from her boutique."

"I know where it is." I pulled away. "Calm down and tell me what's going on."

"She closed the store and walked down to the Pub to get dinner. She'd just finished giving the server her order, when she saw him leave the bar and head for the front door."

"Stop. Who's him?"

"The murderer, the guy, you're looking for."

I couldn't believe what I was hearing. "I told you way too much. You didn't say anything to her about it, did you?"

"No, but she's pretty shook up. She knows something's wrong."

"When we get there, I've got to rely on you to stay cool." *What the hell's he doing in Harvard Square?* "Why didn't she call me?"

"She told me to call you because she left your card on her desk and didn't want to leave the Pub to go back to get it."

"Good move."

I used the wig-wags to get down Mass Ave., then shut them off, so as not to attract any unwanted attention.

Sophie was at a table in the back corner of the Pub. She waved. An untouched burger and fries were sitting in front of her.

Her eyes were open wide, her forehead furrowed. "Detective Mastro, I saw the guy you're looking for. I'm absolutely sure it was him. He was sitting right over there." She pointed to the bar. "He didn't have his hat on. When he got off the bar stool, he turned toward me. That's when I saw his face, and I know he saw mine. It was him."

"I'll be right back." I left the girls at the table, walked to the bar and signaled the bartender.

"Can I help you?"

I pulled my jacket open so he could see my badge. "A guy, about six-two—in good physical shape, sharp dresser, perchance wearing a leather bomber jacket. He was alone. Left about twenty minutes ago. Did he use a credit card or pay cash?"

"He had a sandwich and a beer. He paid cash."

"Have you seen him around here before?"

"Yeah. He started coming in a couple weeks ago. He's a big tipper. You remember those people."

"Do you know his name?"

"No."

"Does he live around here?"

"No idea. Always goes out the front door, so maybe he does. Usually if somebody drives here, they park in the back and use the back door."

"Here's my card. I don't want this conversation repeated. Do you understand? If … when he comes back, I want you to call me immediately. If he leaves before I get here, I want you to put his silverware and glassware into a plastic bag, don't compromise the prints, and hold it for me."

He nodded. "I understand."

I walked back to the table and sat down.

"Sophie has something to tell you."

I glanced across the table. "I'm listening."

"Nobody told me. I figured it out. The guy you're looking for had something to do with the murder of the girl found on Revere Beach, didn't he?"

"What makes you think that?"

She leaned forward. "Did you see this morning's edition of *The Chatter*? It mentioned a Michael Kors skirt. It said there may be more girls with matching skirts." Sophie got quiet and stared at the table. "Those skirts came from my store, didn't they?"

I was fuming inside. If I could get my hands around Balls' neck, he'd be dead. "This is what we're going to do." I looked at the girls. Maggie had her arm around Sophie. "We're going to swing by your condos. Throw some clothes and toiletries into a bag. You're both staying at my place tonight."

CHAPTER 64

Once inside my condo, Sophie handed me her copy of *The Chatter*. Vinny Balls conceivably penned a death sentence for another groupie, by letting our perp think the cops had solid information relating to the case. The only concrete thing Balls reported was regarding the Kors skirts, and where he got that information, I don't know. Fortunately, he didn't play a guess-the-clues game, trying to draw our perp out with false evidence.

"I'm gonna get us a pizza. It's just around the corner." I started out, then, turned back. "Don't answer my phone or the door."

I didn't call the order in because I wanted the walk time to call Sal without the girls listening. "We've got a problem. Sophie saw an article this morning in *The Chatter*."

"Vinny Balls?"

"Yep. Don't stop me." I filled him in on Sophie's call and her perp sighting. "The girls are staying at my condo, at least until Monday. I'll arrange for a twenty-four hour security detail." I placed my pizza order and went back outside to continue my conversation. "Sophie's boutique is open tomorrow. Meet me there at nine-thirty. Maggie's place isn't open, so she'll be with us.

"*Sophie's Sophisticates* at nine-thirty, I'll be there."

"Vinny Balls may have put himself in danger. Him I could give a shit about, it's Maggie and Sophie that concern me. We'll discuss that in the morning."

I picked up my pizza and headed home. I looked over my shoulder several times to make sure I wasn't being followed. I patted the Glock securely tucked into my waistband and walked past my front door. At the end of the block, I doubled back and cut through the alley beyond my condo and stopped behind a dumpster. The pizza was getting cold, but I had to make sure my trail wasn't hot. Convinced I didn't have company, I walked one building down, to the sidewalk, then circled back to my condo.

The girls were waiting. I sensed a feeling of uneasiness.

"There's beer in the fridge."

Without words, Maggie got three bottles of Boston Lager while I got the utensils and plates. Sophie moved over to the table and I doled out the pizza.

While we ate, I presented a plan for the next course of action. "Well, ladies, here's the scoop. The guy we've been looking for—the one who bought the Michael Kors skirts—visited Sophie's boutique and was sighted at the Grafton Street Pub. Apparently he frequents Harvard Square. We don't think he lives in the area. We think he has a connection, but that's only conjecture."

Sophie put her pizza back on her dish. "Are you looking for him because he's the one who killed the girl you found on Revere Beach? Was the article in *The Chatter* right?"

"The person who wrote that article likes to instigate. Most of the time he writes half-truths or embellishes what he thinks to be fact."

Sophie spoke with her mouth full. "What about this time?"

Maggie spoke up before I had a chance to reply. "Mike, what's next?"

"You girls will stay here until Monday. We've got leads we're working. Until he's caught, we're going to have undercover police watching both of you. Sophie, Detective Petruca is meeting us tomorrow morning at the boutique."

She took a deep breath. "What does this guy think we know?"

"He thinks you know too much, when you really don't."

She took a drink of beer. "All I did was sell him skirts."

CHAPTER 65

Sunday

Sal was waiting for us outside *Sophie's Sophisticates*. He held a cardboard holder with four coffees and a mini-box of donuts. It was too early for foot-traffic, too early for our perp to travel incognito amongst the Sunday morning strollers. I wasn't positive, but pretty sure, he'd seen me at Gillette Stadium yesterday, but didn't know who I was. I hustled the girls and Sal inside. While Sophie and Maggie were working on their donuts and coffee, I pulled Sal aside.

I made sure our conversation wouldn't be overheard. "It's a strong possibility this asshole followed us from the stadium yesterday. This guy's no dummy."

"And you dropped me off at my house."

"So, the hunted is now the hunter."

"I don't like that game."

"And, it's one we're not going to play. If he did follow us, he knows we're cops. Unmarks are readily recognized by reprobates. I don't think he'd be foolish enough to screw with a cop's wife, I'll put a watch on your house." I looked back at the girls. "You stay here while I head in to arrange the surveillance."

On the way to the PD, I called Chief Pozzy's cell. "Chief, Detective Mastro. I'm on my way to the station."

He knew I'd never call him at home unless it was important. "What do you need?"

"Undercovers, to do house and people surveillance."

"Get what you need. Any problems call me back." His cell went dead.

I arranged for round-the-clock surveillance for Sophie, Maggie and Sal's wife, Becky. Since I was going to insist Maggie stay with me, my house would be under the watchful eye of a ninja, too. I cringed at my next step, trying to figure out something to replace it. There was nothing. I dialed the number I had for Vinny Balls.

He answered on the first ring.

"Vinny, Detective Mastro here."

"To what do I owe this pleasure, or are you checking on my well-being?"

I clenched my fist. "We need to meet. Now."

"Is this about the article in *The Chatter* yesterday morning?"

"Indirectly."

"Vague answer."

"It's time to stop playing with your dick and meet me in a half-hour at the Dunkin's on the corner of Beach and Shirley."

"You do have a way with words, detective."

I hung up. The last thing I wanted to do was work with Balls.

I was at a corner table in Dunkin's, when Vinny Balls came in. I had my coffee. He could buy his own.

I rested my elbows on the table and nested my chin on my folded hands.

"Detective, you look like you're about to pray."

"I read the story you wrote for *The Daily Chatter*. Who's your informant at the station?"

“I don’t have to tell you anything, and trust me, I’m not going to. As a journalist, I don’t have to reveal my sources.”

“We’ll deal with that later. Right now, I’m going to help you write a story, and you’re going to see it gets in the paper…actually two papers. *The Chatter* could be one, but the other will be the *Globe* or the *Herald.* Can you pull it off?”

“If I like your story, *The Chatter’s* no problem. The *Globe* or *Herald* might take some greasing.”

“You will like my story. And in reference to the greasing, buy yourself a can of Crisco, because the second paper is going to be either the *Globe* or *Herald.”* My facial expression let him know I meant business. “Capeesh?”

“Fuck you, Mastro.”

“I understand you writer-types have certain protection, but you don’t want to play ‘let’s piss off the cops’ more than you need to.”

Balls took a drink of coffee and looked around before answering. “When do you want this to happen?”

“I’ll meet you back here at four. That’ll give you time to contact the papers and make arrangements for the story to run in tomorrow’s edition. I don’t want one running Monday and one Tuesday. They have to appear the same day.”

“That’s easier said than done. If I agree, what’s in it for me?”

I moved my hands from my mouth and rested them on the table. “Your life.”

A puzzled look came over his face. “I don’t understand.”

“Of course you don’t. You act before you think. The article that appeared in yesterday’s *Chatter* could produce enough nails to seal your coffin. If the person who murdered the girl from Revere Beach reads it, he may figure you have more information. He may come looking for you to find out exactly what you know.”

“Detective, you know me. Sometimes I write things that lean to the left or maybe a little to the right. Maybe, I stretch words into new meanings, but most of the time I know very little.”

"I've known that for years and you've denied it for years. But, that doesn't mean shit, if this guy thinks you know something."

"So, you're going to use me to flush this guy out?"

"Exactly."

"Will I get protection?"

"As much as I hate to say it, yes."

CHAPTER 66

Maggie stayed with Sophie at the boutique. I assured them there were undercover cops watching the area, so they had nothing to worry about. "Tonight we'll go to Legal Seafood for dinner." I gave Maggie a hug and whispered, "If you need me, call."

"Hmmm," said Maggie. "Legal—lobster—sounds good to me." She smiled, trying to get Sophie to relax.

Sundays at the station were quiet. Sal and I took up residence in the detective bureau while I caught him up on my meeting with Balls. "We'll meet him at four with the article he's going to submit to *The Chatter* and either the *Globe* or the *Herald*."

"He agreed?"

"I didn't give him a choice."

Sal took his jacket off and hung it on the back of his chair. "How'd you pull that one off?"

"Told him his last article may have been read by the killer who might think the reporter knows too much, so if he wanted protection, he'd better agree to help."

"Does he want compensation?"

"He asked what was in it for him, I told him 'his life'. That's when he began to pay attention."

Sal put his hands on the keyboard. "I'm ready."

"Since Balls' first article mentioned Revere girl wore a Michael Kors skirt, we should maybe say something like the police department has information indicating the girls murdered in Quincy ten months ago, and the girl found on the beach in Hull, were all dressed in the same style Michael Kors skirts, only different colors. This would make the information a continuation of what was reported yesterday, and would leave the perp wondering what else Balls knows."

"What about the cause of death?"

"Balls could write that his sources indicated the cause of death in the four murders was cocaine overdose. That's how we should leave it." I sat back to think for a minute. "We don't want to feed our perp so much information that he has no reason to come after Vinny."

"Balls as bait sounds good to me."

"Sometimes this job does have its perks. I don't want to mention the D Fence tattoo or the Gillette Stadium correlation, at least not yet. For now, that's our ace in the hole. There's one more thing that would hit home if Kevin Morrison is our perp."

"I can read it across your forehead. The Harvard connection."

"Yep. But, not the actual connection. Briefly mention the fact that a person of interest has been seen frequenting Harvard Square and leave it at that."

"You know he'll link that tidbit to Sophie."

"We've got her covered." I stared out the window overlooking the parking lot. "He's dangerous and we're running out of time. If he thinks we're closing in on him, I'm afraid he'll try to kill again."

At four, Sal and I sat in Dunkin's with our backs to the wall. We watched as several cars pulled into the lot. I checked my watch. It was ten after four and no Vinny Balls.

I called Maggie. "Just checkin' in. How's everything going?"

"Fine. It's been busy."

It was four-fifteen, Sal pointed out the window toward the T station. Balls was hustling across the parking lot.

"Maggie, gotta go."

He came in huffing and puffing.. "I couldn't hail a cab." After a gulped inhale, he added, "I took the T."

"Did you make your calls to the newspapers?"

"*The Chatter's* fine with it. It took some talkin', but I finally got the *Herald* to agree as long as I deliver the article to them by seven. I assured them it would be there."

I handed him a copy of the article I'd put together.

I glanced at Sal, then at Balls. "Coffee?"

Sal nodded.

Balls looked up from his reading. "Cream and two sugars."

At five-fifteen, we dropped Balls in front of the *Herald*. "I'll retype the article and email a copy to *The Chatter* as soon as I get home. Detective Mastro, you do have someone looking out for my well-being?"

"Would I risk such an important resource?"

Without answering, the three of us walked out.

CHAPTER 67

I parked four spaces up from the boutique. Sal and I scanned the area as we walked back to *Sophie's Sophisticates*. Any of the bench sitters or sidewalk strollers could be our undercovers, I didn't care who they were, as long as they were there.

Sophie was getting ready to close. She snapped around when the bell above the door jingled.

"We're back. Anybody hungry?"

Maggie grinned. "I'm always hungry."

"I made reservations for five at six-thirty."

Sal addressed the puzzled look on the girl's faces. "My wife, Becky, is going to join us." He walked back to the door. "I'll meet you at the restaurant."

I caught the look on Maggie's face. "He was supposed to pick her up at six. He's late. Cops wives get used to that, at least some of them do."

Sophie planted her hands on her hips. "You know I'm open 'til six-thirty."

I looked from Maggie to Sophie. "Oops."

"I've got no customers, so you get a pass this time." She went to the back of the store to lock up and get her and Maggie's purses.

"How's she doing?"

"Being a trooper."

"I'm back. You can stop talking about me now."

I cupped my hand around my ear. "I hear Larry Lobster calling our names."

CHAPTER 68

Monday

I dropped Sophie at the boutique, then brought Maggie to Newbury Street.

"I noticed Sophie took her overnight bag with her this morning."

"She wants to go home."

"What about you?"

"If you still want company, I'd like to stay in the North End."

I kissed her cheek. "I'd like that. Give you a call later."

I waited for her to unlock the door and go inside, before heading for the station.

Sal was waiting for me in the parking lot. "*The Chatter* and the *Herald*." He held them up.

"Have you looked at 'em?"

"I was on my way in to do just that."

We skipped the morning briefing, and went directly to the detective bureau. Sal kept *The Chatter* and handed me the *Herald*.

I found the article on page three, top right. "Got it. Just the way we wrote it. Nothing cut and nothing added."

"Same with *The Chatter*."

I'll make a copy of both. "As soon as the chief's back in his office, we'll meet and let him know our strategy."

Sal read the article again, pacing the room as he did. "If I were Morrison, I'd surmise the authorities know more than is printed. He's going to be running offense."

"You may have something there. He'll be bobbing and weaving, so he doesn't get tackled. We don't have to worry about Gillette Stadium. Eli is going to have every gate covered. If he's spotted, he'll have the local PD pick him up."

"The thing we can't control is his ability to contact one of the groupies."

"That could be a problem." I put the paper on the desk. "We didn't mention the stadium or the groupies in the article. But, by the way he evaded me and took off, I have no doubt he knows he's being watched. He's got to figure we have a security detail watching Sophie and Maggie. But, Vinny Balls? We want Morrison to think no police department would assign a babysitter to a grunge like him."

Sal appeared uncomfortable. "I explained the situation to Becky last night. She's not happy, but is trying to understand. I assured her, she was safe."

"Now it comes down to you and me. He's either going to assume we're on a fishing expedition, or that we know too much. Either way, these articles will rattle his cage."

We headed to the chief's office. I handed him a copy of the report stating everything we had to date.

"We've baited our perp, using Vinny Balls." I gave him a copy of the article I'd written for Balls to have published under his name.

The chief looked at us over the rims of his glasses. "Do you think our perp will go after him?"

"Strong possibility. Actually, I'm hoping so. I think our perp will figure Balls is working on his own—like he usually does—and, was afforded no police protection. At this point, my bet is on the perp going after another girl or even us."

"The 'us' being you and Sal?"

"Exactly."

Chief Pozzy leaned forward on his desk. "I don't like it."

"We've got ninjas watching both of us, Sal's wife, Maggie, Sophie, and Vinny Balls." I gave it a minute for the chief to put what I'd just told him in perspective, then continued. "And we need more." I reached across the desk and took the packet containing information on eleven girls we had current addresses for. "These girls may be in danger. We got their names and information from the tattoo parlor in Attleboro who did the D Fence tattoos. *Specialty Tattoos* did a total of seventeen, these eleven, our four dead girls, and two with whereabouts unknown. Most of the eleven live near Gillette Stadium, a couple around the Quincy area and one closer to the South Shore."

"I'll call the respective chiefs and have their departments check out the residents at these addresses without setting off an alarm. I'll let you know as soon as I hear back."

CHAPTER 69

"There's too many ears in the bureau. I'll grab us a couple coffees and meet you in room two."

Sal was staring out the window when I walked into the room.

I set the coffee on the desk. "Where's your mind?"

"Nowhere good. I can't get inside Morrison's head." Sal paced while he talked. "It's bothering me how Balls knew about the Michael Kors skirts?"

"That's why we can't meet in the bureau office. Somehow, information on this case was leaked. Whether it was done on purpose or just in conversation is anybody's guess."

"The only person we shared information with is Mario. He knows about the skirts and a whole lot more."

I took a deep breath. "I've worked with Mario as long as I've been in Revere. That's going on eleven years. I've never doubted his trust."

"What about his office?"

"We need to check." I dialed Mario's number.

"Detective Mastro."

"Mario, are you alone in the office?"

"I am. What's up?"

"We need to talk."

"You need me to do more cyber stalking?"

"Maybe."

Mario looked up over his monitor as we walked in. "How's the case going?"

"Going." I looked around to see if there was anyone else in the office. There wasn't.

"What can I do for you two?"

I didn't want to go this route, but I didn't have a chance. "We have a problem."

Mario's shrugged. "Bring it on."

"Did you discuss the information on the Doll murders with anyone?"

"Mike, you know me better than that."

"I do, but, how about someone in your office?"

"I wouldn't unless you'd given me the okay and if it was for research purposes."

"That's what I wanted to hear." I leaned back in my chair. "The other people who have access to IT's data bank, would they have access to your files and research?"

"No. I have everything that's pertaining to an open or working case passworded." Mario stood and moved to the corner of his desk. "Where is this all coming from?"

"You ever heard of Vinny Balls?" Sal asked.

Mario made a grimacing face. "The free-lance wannabe journalist who writes for *The Daily Chatter*?"

"The one and only." I rolled my eyes. "He did an article for *The Chatter* last Saturday about the Revere Beach Doll murder and mentioned the Michael Kors skirts."

Mario folded his arms across his chest. "We talked about that, but nothing left this office. Did you mention it when you were at the ME's office?"

I looked at Sal.

"Not that I recall."

I paced back and forth trying to come up with an answer. Maggie and Sophie knew something about the skirts, but if Balls had approached them, I would have known.

"Mike, the only other people that I know who knew about the skirts were Detectives Scully and McGinnis."

That crossed my mind. "Mario, keep your ears open."

He acknowledged my request. "Will do, boss."

Sal and I headed back to the bureau. Everyone was gone, so there weren't any ears to pick up on our conversation.

"I don't want to think Scully and McGinnis are that stupid, but information was leaked from somewhere." I punched in the number for the Quincy PD and asked to be connected with their detective bureau. "This is Detective Mike Mastro from Revere. Is Detective Scully or McGinnis in?"

"Not at the moment, but they're due in within the hour."

"Please leave a message for one of them to call."

"Do they have your number?"

I knew they did, but I gave it to the officer on the other end of the phone anyway. "Thanks," I hung up and looked at Sal. "Now we wait."

The call from the Quincy detectives didn't offer any concrete information as to the Michael Kors leak.

My next call was to Vinny. "Balls is either screening his calls, doesn't want to talk to me or is tied up in a chair being tortured." I held up my hands, palms facing Sal, and cocked my head. "You didn't hear that."

Sal stood and headed toward the door. "Let's pay him a visit."

CHAPTER 70

There was moderate foot activity on Vinny Balls' street. I casually glanced around wondering if any of the passersby were working ninjas. We didn't want to draw any attention, so we didn't stop to talk, just walked up the five steps and through the front door into the little foyer in Balls' building.

"Six mail boxes. Balls has neighbors. I wonder how close they are." I pushed the buzzer that had Vinny's name below it. No response. I tried again, this time leaning on it. Nothing.

Sal looked out the window to see if we'd drawn any attention by parking the unmarked out front. "Since he hasn't got a real job, there's no place of employment we can contact."

I took out my cell and called his number again. Nothing. "We need to talk to his undercover." I called the station.

Fifteen minutes later, we were sitting in a busy Dunkin's near the station. We took two tables beside each other, away from the front door and windows. I set a coffee and newspaper on one, then Sal and I took our coffees and another newspaper and sat at the other. A couple minutes later, a guy with just-got-out-of-bed hair, dressed in holey jeans, heavy sweater and a navy-blue vest sat down beside us and started reading the paper.

I looked over at him. "Black coffee?"

He looked around the edge of the newspaper and nodded.

I turned my attention back to Sal and spoke in a whisper, but loud enough for our neighbor to hear. "Vincent Balducci isn't answering his phone or his door."

"Balls, as you call him, hasn't left since I reported at five-thirty this morning."

"Did the guy before you say anything about a visitor?"

"Nothing."

"Is there only one person watching him at a time?"

"Yes."

"So does that mean he could have slipped out the back?"

"Since he has no idea who we are, I find that unlikely."

"Why?"

"We blend in with the locals. We become part of a building. You could, and have, walked by us and have no idea we're watching. He's a man of habit. Easy to follow. Same routine every day."

"What time does he usually leave his place?"

"Nine o'clock."

"But not today?"

"No, not today."

"Do you know what window in the alley behind the building belongs to him?"

"Second floor. The one to the right. Has a shade, but no curtain."

"Question—you're here. Is there someone watching his place as we speak?"

"He's being watched twenty-four hours."

"We need to get inside his place."

He got up from the table, picked up his coffee and tucked the newspaper under his arm. "Meet me there in a half hour."

The ninja we'd just left, buzzed us into Vinny Balls' building. The door to Vinny's apartment was cracked open. An undercover was waiting inside.

I looked around. "Where's Balducci?"

The undercover was noticeably uneasy. "There's no way he could have gotten by any one of us."

"Obviously, he did."

Sal walked around the rest of the apartment. "There's no sign of a struggle. His clothes are in the closet and drawers. There's plenty of food in the fridge. I don't see any indication he skipped town."

My mind flashed to Maggie, Sophie and Sal's wife, Becky. "Call your counterparts who are watching Maggie Smith, Sophie Glover and Becky Petruca. I want to know they have eyes on them as we speak."

The undercover made the calls. "Yes, sir, the three girls are visible."

"Make sure it stays that way. The person we're looking for is a serial killer. He's killed at least four girls. He'll try to kill again. If he thinks anyone could stand in his way, he'll eliminate that person too. He doesn't care if it's a cop he takes out or a scumbag reporter like Vinny Balls. What I'm saying is, watch your back as well as ours."

"We were briefed, sir."

I looked at the undercover, then toward Sal. "Call your central control and find out the last time Balls was sighted."

Sal and I walked away while the undercover called in.

"Could he be in one of the other apartments?" Sal took a deep breath. "Be right back. I'm going to check to see if there are names under each buzzer."

The undercover ended his call. "Detective, the log shows him coming home at eleven-forty three last night, but nothing about leaving this morning."

"And, was he alone?"

"Yes. The log noted the undercover on duty waited until the lights came on, then walked around to do a back alley check."

I turned as Sal came through the door. "Names under every buzzer. One did appear new, but nothing out of the ordinary."

I handed the undercover two of my cards. "Here's my cell number. Write yours on the other one. If you need me for any reason, any time, call."

He reached out to shake my hand. "Yes, sir. And visa-versa."

Sal and I left the undercover to lock up, and leave the same way he arrived.

As we walked through the foyer, Sal looked again at the names. "Give me a minute. I want to copy these down. One's for the super. We might have occasion to talk to him."

Chapter 71

It was almost noontime when we got back to the station. There were a couple officers milling around the bureau, so Sal and I headed to room two.

"Balls' disappearance is a mystery. If we're right, our perp knows the girls are being watched, but doesn't figure Vinny or you and I are. He confirmed that by taking Balls, assuming he's behind the disappearance. Our perp, no doubt, knows we've been in contact with Balls. He also knows we've been scouting Gillette Stadium. So, he knows that we know who he is. That makes us vulnerable, too. I think Morrison is using Balls in his sick game. I'm not sure how, but he is." I paced the room.

"You said one of the names below the buzzers at Vinny's building looked like it was new."

"Yeah, only 'cause it was clean. Not yellowed with age."

"What was the name?"

Sal checked his notes. "GG Morris."

"That fuckin' bastard." I pulled my cell out and dialed the number I had for the undercover. "Meet us at Vinny Balducci's apartment building." I turned to Sal. "Let's go."

Sal shook his head. "What's happening?"

"GG Morris. Gridiron Groupies Morrison. Vinny is inside this apartment."

The undercover was waiting in the foyer when we pulled up.

I pushed the button for the super. "Revere PD, we need to get into apartment 4B."

The undercover already had the inside foyer door open. The super was halfway up the stairs. "Hurry up." I yelled.

Sal and I stood, with guns drawn, on opposite sides of the door. As soon as the super turned the key, I pushed the door open and ran in. The living room was empty except for two folding chairs, a card table, and another small table a flat screen called home. The kitchen was the same as Vinney's place. I looked across the room at a closed door I assumed led to the bedroom. I instructed the super to stay put. My heart raced. I pulled my gun and stood to one side, then turned the knob and pushed the door open. There was no return greeting, so I rushed into the room. Vinny Balls laid sprawled out on the only piece of furniture—a full-size bed.

Sal searched the rest of the apartment.

I checked Balls. He had a pulse, but barely. I called for an ambulance. His ankles and wrists were secured with fancy knotted rope and pulled together behind his back as tightly as possible. Moving straps anchored his body to the bed frame, so he couldn't roll off and try to signal a downstairs neighbor. His mouth and half of one nostril was covered with wide, black electrical tape allowing only a small stream of breath.

I pulled the tape from Vinny's mouth, but no sound came out. Sal, the undercover and I maneuvered the ropes and straps to release him from his Houdini hold.

I leaned in close. "Vinny—it's Mike Mastro. You're okay now. Talk to me." I raised my voice. "Vinny, can you hear me?"

His lips tried to move, but couldn't.

"Hang in there. I'm not leaving." I watched as color started to creep back into his face.

The faint wail of the ambulance got louder.

With Vinny in the ambulance headed for Mass General, and two uniforms scheduled to be posted at his door with strict no unauthorized admittance instructions, I turned to the building super. "Who's this apartment rented to?"

"Some guy, last name Morris, came in three days ago. Said he saw the sign in the window and was looking for a place for a few months. The unit rents for nine hundred a month if the rental term is less than a year. He paid me twenty-seven hundred dollars—all hundred dollar bills."

I took the folded picture of Morrison from my pocket. "Is this the guy?"

"Yeah, that's him. Big guy—I'm five-nine. He was at least five inches taller than me. Looked like he worked out. Sharp dresser, too."

"Did he fill out an application?"

"No, but he gave me his cell number and an address in New York City. Said he was consulting with State Street Bank on a project."

"Give me the cell number and address." I was agitated at the stupidity of the super. "Didn't you find it odd that he'd want to stay in this section of the city? State Street has downtown condos on retainer."

"No, I didn't. Looked like a good rental and the money was up front. It was none of my business why he chose this area."

"Did he have a car?"

"Sure did. One of those big, fancy Mercedes."

"Black?"

"Yep." The super rocked nervously. "He didn't park it here though. There's an indoor garage two blocks north of here that rents space. Out of sight of some of the neighborhood undesirables, if you know what I mean."

"Here's my cell number. If he comes back, call me immediately."

"Will do."

"And, don't mention our conversation to anyone." I looked him in the eyes. "Do you understand?"

"Yes, sir."

I dialed the cell number Morrison gave the super. It went to a canned voice mail.

The undercover and Sal were in Vinny's apartment making sure they'd left nothing unturned.

"Did you guys find anything out of the ordinary?"

Sal took another glance around. "Nothing."

"This prick's treating his life like a video game. He needs to step it up to keep it interesting. That's where we come in. He's conquered everything up to this point. We're the next level."

The undercover walked outside with us. "If there's nothing more you need right now, I've got to report to central command. After that, I'll be back in the line-up."

Before Sal and I left for the hospital, I instructed a uniform to stake out Vinny's building.

"I don't put anything past this guy."

CHAPTER 72

Vinny drifted in and out of consciousness. He whispered hospital, then closed his eyes. The attending doctor came in ten minutes after we got there.

"I'm Doctor Atkins. Mr. Balducci is one lucky man. Two of his fingers on each hand and one of his toes are broken. They're all a clean snap. Somebody did it on purpose. There's also what appears to be cigarette burns on his back, and a fresh carved symbol that I can't make out, on his shoulder." The doctor pulled back the top of the hospital johnny to reveal a primitive attempt at a version of a D Fence logo. It was red and raw, and obviously very painful.

I stepped back and motioned the doctor to join me. "Did you find drugs in his system?"

"We took blood, but the test results aren't back yet. I put a rush on them. I'll call the lab." He checked his watch as he left the room.

"Thanks." I turned to Sal. "Do you have more of Morrison's pictures?"

He nodded.

"Good. Drop one off at the nurse's station, and get hospital security to circulate them. We'll give one to each of the uniforms when they get here. Our perp still thinks Vinny knows more than he does, otherwise he would have killed him."

The uniforms hadn't arrived so I stayed with Vinny while Sal left to distribute the flyers. I sat so I could see every person who walked by. A female walked by exceptionally slow, craning to see inside the room. When she saw me get up on her second walk-by, she stepped up her pace and disappeared around the corner at the end of the hallway. I made a mental picture of her features, then sat back down.

Just as Sal came back into the room, my burner rang. "Hello," I answered, as I motioned for him to close the door.

"Is this Gary?"

"It is." I held a finger to my lips so Sal wouldn't speak.

"It's Suzi Dayton. I met you at Gillette Stadium."

"Yes Suzi, I remember you well."

"I need to talk to you." She hesitated a second, then continued, "Willy called me. I didn't let him know about you."

I hadn't told her I was a cop. She still thought I was an old friend, pissed at what Willy was doing to his wife—my cousin—and his kids.

My heart stopped. "What did he want?"

"To go to dinner tonight. I had all I could do not to ream him a new asshole, but that would be less painful than what you might have in mind for him."

I raised my eyebrows. "Did he say where?"

"Yeah. The Top of the Hub at the Prudential on Boylston Street."

"What did you tell him?"

"I told him I'd love to."

"Is he picking you up?"

"No, he said he'd send a limo to my house around six." She sighed. "Said it was a special occasion. All I could think of was your cousin and the kids. That's why I called you."

"You did good. Where do you live?"

"The house across from where Hatch comes onto East 8th Street in Southie."

"I'll be at the Prudential. Don't worry if you don't see me right away. I'll be watching. Just go along with his 'little' party." I took a deep breath. "Do you think you can do this?"

"I'll be fine."

I had to hold my enthusiasm under wraps. “I’ll see you tonight.”

“Oh, one more thing, he told me to pack an overnight bag. When I asked him if we were going to his place overlooking the harbor, he said I’d find out later. He didn’t want to ruin the surprise.”

CHAPTER 73

I looked back at Vinny. There was no movement. I leaned up close and whispered his name. Nothing.

Sal was leaning against the inside of the door when a knock brought him to attention. He turned to open it. I stood and motioned the two uniforms in. Sal stationed himself in the open doorway to observe the passing traffic while I spoke to the officers.

"I'm Detective Mastro and this is my partner Detective Petruca." I nodded in Sal's direction.

The older of the two spoke. "Sergeant Butler," he pointed with his head, Officer Reynolds."

I faced the two uniforms. "What do you know about this case?"

Sergeant Butler answered, "The victim we're watching is possibly a failed homicide attempt by a person-of-interest in a murder investigation."

"That's it in a nutshell. Except for one thing. The person-of-interest is devious and dangerous. If anything appears out of the norm, you're to call me immediately." I handed each of them a picture of Morrison. "This is the guy we're looking for. If he comes by, call the station directly and don't let him out of your sight. He's a master. He could be disguised as anybody—a doctor, lab tech, janitor—anybody. Here's a list of people allowed in this room." I quickly reviewed it with the officers. "Other than the ones listed, nobody else is allowed in unless authorized by Dr. Atkins or me. I'll introduce you to Dr. Atkins."

“We’re here until midnight. Do you want me to call you when we leave?”

I thought about it for a minute, then realized I might be off the radar if I was involved with our perp and Suzi Dayton. “I’ll call you. If you don’t hear from me, instruct your replacements.”

CHAPTER 74

On the way back to the station, I called the chief and asked him to meet us there. We only had a few hours to get a plan into place. Suzi Dayton figured to be his next intended victim.

I let the duty desk officer know Sal and I would be in room two. Sal set up the computer to project the Prudential lobby, the Top of the Hub Restaurant and the area surrounding the Pru.

The chief walked in. “Fill me in.”

I told him about Vinny Balls. “I’m sure he was targeted because our perp thinks he knows more than he does. We’ve got tight security on him, so he should be all right for the time being.” I leaned forward on the table. “We’ve got a bigger problem. Our perp has lined up his next victim.”

The chief gave me a puzzled look.

“Her name is Suzi Dayton. I met her Saturday when we were at Gillette Stadium.”

“Continue.”

“She’s a Gridiron Groupie, knows Morrison by the name of Willy and has dated him. After I finished making him out to be a womanizer with a beautiful wife, who’s my cousin, and three kids, one being my godchild, she wanted nothing more to do with him. Even offered to expose him, if he tried to tie up with her again.”

“I understand the groupie girls don’t practice the highest of standards. Why was she so open and honest with a cop?”

“She doesn’t know I’m a cop. She thinks I’m trying to protect my cousin. That I’m disgusted with the lifestyle ‘Willy’ chooses to live behind my cousin's back." I shrugged. "Who knows, maybe Suzi's been burned herself or she's interested in me. I got a call from her while we were in Vinny's room at the hospital. Her 'Willy' called her this morning and wants to take her to dinner at The Top of the Hub. Told her to bring an overnight bag."

"Give me the particulars."

"I don't want to pull the undercovers that are watching Maggie, Sophie, and Becky, but I'm okay with pulling the ones watching us. Suzi told me Morrison is sending a limo pick her up at her house in South Boston around six to bring her to the Pru. The driver is supposed to escort her in the elevator to the restaurant, then Morrison will take it from there. I want surveillance at her house when she's picked up, then I want her followed until she meets Morrison. We have to have eyes on her at all times. I want the plate number of the limo run. I don't even want her riding the elevator up the fifty-two floors without one or more of ours beside her—a couple going to dinner and a single person like her. That shouldn't draw unnecessary attention. Morrison knows who Sal and I are, so we can't be anywhere near open areas where he could spot us."

"Are you planning on arresting him at the restaurant?"

"No. We need a solid case against him. That's where it gets touchy. He didn't leave any tracks or physical evidence that we can definitely tie to him. We're still waiting for the crime lab to extract DNA that might be on the Rolex our homeless person found on Revere Beach. Truth is, we don't know if the watch even belongs to our perp. If Morrison is our perp, he comes from a lot of money. We don't want him going to court and having the judge set bail. No question in my mind, he'd bolt."

Sal let us know he was ready to present the plans of the Pru and the restaurant.

"I want two undercovers outside where the limo driver will park to bring Suzi in, then five more mingling with the crowd by the elevator doors, three into the elevator with her and the driver." I used a pointer to identify the areas I was talking about. "There should be four in the restaurant. The couple that comes up with her should have a table waiting for them. I'd like it near Morrison's, but we know he doesn't go by his real name and without his phony name, that might be impossible. I know the maître d'. Maybe, we can figure it out when I call him to set this whole thing up. The single undercover should have a barstool reserved. The fourth should already be seated in the bar area."

Sal came back and joined us at the table. "We got shit we can't control. When he arrives, without his name, we can't dictate where the restaurant will seat him."

"Question. If you're not going to arrest him at the restaurant, where is it going to take place?"

I took a deep breath. "Remember I said when Morrison set up his little soiree with Suzi, he told her to bring an overnight bag. At one point in their relationship, he told her he had a condo overlooking Boston Harbor and that someday he'd take her there. When she asked him if that's where they were going after dinner, he said it was a surprise and would neither confirm nor deny the location. We don't know which building he was referring to. That's where Sal and I come in. We'll follow them when they leave the Pru. All I'll need is one of the undercovers to let me know what garage he's coming from. Once we know the condo location, I'll call for backup."

"Then I suggest we have more undercovers hanging around for a few hours before the limo arrives. We have about two hours to set up before we play the waiting game." The chief picked up his cell and punched in a number. "Lieutenant, I need you to come to room two immediately."

Forty-five minutes later, more than half of our players were in place. Sal and I signed out one of the non-descript undercover cars—a tan 2012 Taurus.

I called the hospital to check on Vinny. Sergeant Butler said everything was quiet. Vinny's condition hadn't changed. He hadn't moved or made any attempt to speak. I told him I'd check back later.

I slid our paperwork into my briefcase. "Gonna hit the head, then we'll swing by Mickey D's and grab something to eat. It's going to be a long night."

CHAPTER 75

We holed up in an alley off Dalton Street across from the Pru. It allowed us a clear view of any cars that took the corner off Boylston heading toward the main parking garage.

I reached around the back of my seat for the bag of burgers. "When you're hungry, Mickey D's hits the spot." I took my double-cheese and handed Sal the bag. "The Top of the Hub or McDonald's."

Sal rocked his hands like the scale of justice. "On a cop's pay, it's definitely McDonald's. I took Becky to the top of the Pru once."

"Once?"

"Once."

"I know someone who works there and I've never been. Anyway, I'll take Abe and Louie's anytime."

"When all this is done, Abe and Louie's it is. Becky will love that."

I watched a few cars turn the corner but pass the entrance to the garage. None were a black 550 Mercedes. "Most of the clientele that frequents The Hub valet their vehicles. That means Morrison won't know the car's location for a couple hours, and not be able to retrieve it quickly."

"Morrison more than likely regularly uses a valet, but not tonight."

It was five-forty-five, when I saw a black Mercedes make the corner. I nudged Sal and pointed. "Check it out."

It slowed at the entrance to the garage, then, drove past it.

He shook his head. "Looked like a female driving."

"Whoever it was can't get very far, very fast." I pulled out and headed in the direction of the Mercedes.

"It's making a right onto Belvidere."

I sped up slightly, keeping the vehicle in my sight.

"Another right onto St. Cecilia. Since it's a one way and the light just turned red, I'm going to pull up beside it."

Even though the windows were slightly tinted, we could tell it was definitely not Morrison. We circled the block, then pulled back into our hideaway off Dalton.

Ten minutes passed. My cell rang. "Detective Mastro."

"Officer Kline, here. The limo just pulled away from the Dayton house. Depending on traffic, we should be at the Prudential Tower by six-thirty. I'll let you know when we get close."

"I'll wait for your call." I turned toward Sal. "I'd feel more assured if we were part of the inside team, but we can't chance being spotted."

Another ten minutes passed.

My cell rang. It was a frantic Officer Kline. "I lost them. I was one car behind, then a pick-up cut me off, the light turned red, I was boxed in and by the time I could get free, the limo was nowhere in sight."

"Follow the route you'd take to the restaurant. He should have to slow down when he gets to Boylston Street. Whatever you do, don't use your lights." I threw my hands up over my face. "What the fuck."

Sal sat quiet.

I called the undercover stationed in the area next to the elevators. "Mastro, here. Do you have eyes on the limo?"

"Nothing, yet."

"Casually take a walk. Make like you're having a conversation with someone, look around, then laugh and head back to the lobby. I'll stay on the phone."

A few seconds later, he gave a phony laugh. "Don't see anyone or anything that looks out of place."

"Get back inside, but check the door every once in a while. It's six-twenty five, the limo should be pulling up momentarily. Call me immediately when you have eyes on it."

Sal's head pivoted from side to side, scanning the area before and after the garage. "Not good."

I called our undercover bar sitter. "Any Morrison sighting?"

"Not yet."

Not yet wasn't what I wanted to hear. "There's no doubt, he's made a change in plans." I looked at Sal. "He didn't intend to take Suzi to the restaurant. He's taking her to his condo on the harbor. He knows we're onto him, but doesn't know how much we know about him, so he can't chance a public place like the Mandarin."

"Suzi's in trouble if he figures out she talked to us."

"She's in trouble even if he doesn't." I headed toward the harbor. "We'll check Harbor Towers first."

I pulled over a block before the Towers and called the chief. "I may have read Morrison's plan wrong. His intentions to wine, dine, kill, and rape Suzi may not have included dinner at The Top of the Hub. He may have lured her with the idea of a dinner date first." I hesitated, then continued. "On the other hand, we may have hit the nail on the head and, when he realized it, he changed his game."

"Where are you and Sal now?"

"A couple blocks from the Harbor Towers. It's time to kick it up a notch. We need to know if he's there. Keep our undercovers in place, in case I'm wrong, but have personnel ready to back up Sal and me."

"I'll wait for your call." The chief's cell went dead.

I took a deep breath. "Ready, partner?"

"As ready as I'm going to be."

There weren't many people in the lobby and none at the front desk. I took out my badge and showed the clerk. "Is your supervisor available?"

"I'm in charge. What can I do for you?"

"Step down to the end of the counter."

Sal and I didn't wait for a response and moved to the farthest end, away from any incoming residents.

I took Morrison's picture from my pocket. "Do you recognize this man?"

The clerk studied Morrison's face. "Doesn't look at all familiar."

"You're positive," Sal asked.

"I've been here ten years and have had interaction with all residents. Yes, I'm positive."

"Thank you. Here's my card, should you need to contact me. Otherwise, forget this ever happened."

We left Harbor Towers and drove the two blocks to Waters Edge. Gina was still at her desk. She gave me a puzzled look.

"You're still here?" I introduced her to Sal. "I need your help. The guy I asked you about Saturday. You said he might look familiar."

"I did, but I've looked at his picture many times since you were here, and still nothing jogs my memory. I see so many people."

"Did you see anyone arrive in a limo within the last half-hour? Would have been a young, well-put together blonde."

"No, but if she was visiting a resident, she could have met him at the resident entrance in the back by the water. We don't have a valet stationed there, so I can't tell if that's what happened."

"I need you to take me to someone who has access to resident files."

She didn't hesitate. "Follow me." She brought us down a hallway, past several offices before we stopped. She knocked, but didn't wait for an answer before she walked in with us in tow. "Eric, this is Detective Mastro and Detective Patruca. Eric is our general manager."

He stood. "What can I do for you?"

"We haven't got the luxury of time. We're looking for this individual." I handed him Morrison's picture. "We don't have a current name he's using, but we have reason to believe he's a resident."

"He is." He opened his computer and punched in a name. "Jeffrey Stewart has owned number 502 since two-thousand-twelve. Quiet guy, never any complaints or demands."

"I need the location of his assigned parking spot in the garage."

"What's happening? Is something wrong? We have panic buttons installed in every unit for the safety of our residents. Did he call the police department?"

"Eric, I need that information now. And, get the code or a key or whatever it takes to get inside number 502. "

He printed out a copy of what showed on his screen. "I'll take you there."

"Is that the fifth floor?"

"Yes."

"Sal, check out the garage first. If Morrison's car's there, he should be home."

"His name is Stewart, not Morrison."

I ignored Eric's comment.

Sal moved beside Eric. "Do we go up to the garage from the lobby?"

"No, it's underground."

I turned to Sal."You go with Eric. I'll meet you by the elevators on the fifth floor. Gina, stay in the lobby. I'll need you to direct my back-ups to condo 502."

Sal, Eric and Gina walked ahead of me, Sal setting the pace.

"Chief, we've located the condo owned by Morrison. Send back-ups to the lobby at Waters Edge. The concierge, Gina DiMari, will be waiting to direct them to our location. I don't know if

Morrison is inside, but Sal's checking the garage for his Mercedes. Did Kline get the plate number on the limo?"

"You're not going to want to hear this."

"You're right." I was steaming at the incompetency of Officer Kline for not getting the plate number, but I'd deal with that later. My concern was for the safety of Suzi Dayton and the capture of a serial murderer.

I rode the elevator to the fifth floor, fortunately alone. Morrison's condo was at the far end of the building. I stayed out-of-sight of anyone leaving their condo. I gambled on them using the residents only exit. Of course, if they chose to use the main elevator, I was a sitting duck. I was an outsider and didn't want to engage in a conversation with anyone asking who I was and how could they help me. My thought ended when the elevator door opened and Sal and Eric came out.

Sal leaned in. "His Mercedes is in the garage."

"The back-up team's on the way. When they get here, we'll walk to 502. Eric, you knock on the door and announce your presence. He'll look through his peephole to make sure it's you. If he doesn't open the door, instead asks why you're here, tell him a courier left an envelope that had to be delivered immediately." I pulled an empty number ten envelope from my pocket and wrote Jeffrey Stewart on the outside. "Hold it up so he can see it. We'll be here, but out of viewing range."

"What if he tells me to leave it in front of his door?"

"Tell him you signed for it, making you responsible and you don't want to do that."

"What if he tells me to take it to the front desk and he'll pick it up later?"

"Then back away and say 'okay'."

Sal held out his hand. "Give me the code card or the master key to his condo."

Eric reached in his pocket. "It's a code card. Slip it in the slot and pull it out quickly."

The elevator opened behind us. Gina stood by the control buttons. I made a keep-it-quiet gesture with my finger and motioned the chief and the four officers to fall in behind me. I told Gina to go back to the lobby and not let any residents or guests use the elevator until further notice. I rehashed Eric's part in the operation and if Morrison didn't open the door, we had the code card and were going in.

Chief Pozzy's eyes were cold. "Have you been able to determine if the girl's inside?"

"No. Since we couldn't trace the limo tracks, we can't say for sure." I took a deep breath. "My guess is she is."

The chief brushed his hand over his Glock. "Do you know if he has any firearms?"

"No, I don't. Without a name, the one he's using anyway, we couldn't run records. But, that doesn't mean anything. He could have illegal firearms." I turned to the team. "The one thing we have going for us is Suzi Dayton knows who I am. She doesn't know I'm a cop, but she's the one who called me. That requires a level of trust."

Sal studied the officer's faces.

"We have to move fast. There's no room for error. I want two of you on each side of the door, five feet back, hugging the wall. Morrison's killed at least four girls, and we believe the girl with him now is his intended fifth victim. Let's get her out safe and him into custody." I signaled the team to move into position.

Eric took his spot in front of the door. He looked at me for his cue to knock.

I shook my hand toward the door and mouthed go.

The knock echoed through the hallway.

A voice acknowledged Eric's presence through the speaker below the peephole. "Eric, what can I do for you?"

"A courier left an envelope. He said it had to be delivered immediately."

"Leave it outside the door."

"Mr. Stewart, I signed for it, so I feel responsible for it."

Morrison's voice elevated. "Look, I'm busy. Leave it at the desk and I'll pick it up later."

"Yes, sir." Eric turned and walked toward the elevator.

I gave him a thumbs up. We waited two minutes to let Stewart get back away from the door before I gestured the team that we were ready to move. Figuring there'd be a security chain, I motioned the first team to do a shoulder push to gain entry. I took the code card from my pocket, reached out and slid it into the lock.

Within seconds, we were inside, and had Morrison down and cuffed. I saw two half-empty glasses of wine on the coffee table, but Suzi wasn't in the room.

Sal was already checking the rest of the condo.

I got into Morrison's face. "Where's Suzi Dayton?"

I didn't need his answer.

Sal yelled from a bedroom. "Mike, she's in here."

I ran to his voice. She was laying half clothed, out of sight, between the bed and closet door. I detected a faint pulse. There were signs of a white powder around her nose. "She's breathing, but barely. Call for a bus, possible overdose." I leaned down beside her face. "Suzi, can you hear me?" I repeated it several times, each time a little louder. Nothing.

"Sal, keep talking to her. Keep checking her pulse."

I walked back to the living room. I wanted to beat the shit out of Morrison, but knew I had to control myself. I kept my eyes glued to his. "You have the right to remain silent. Anything you say can and will be used against you in a court of law. You have the right to an attorney. If you cannot afford an attorney, one will be appointed for you."

He smirked. "You think you're pretty smart, don't you?"

"Much smarter than you." I looked at the two officers flanking him. "Take him to the station."

"You got nothing on me. The girl was a druggie. Went into the bathroom and did some coke. I was just about to call for help."

"Get him out of here."

"You're nothing but a bunch of pigs." He spit, missing me, but hitting a uniform.

Once he cleared the door and was out of earshot, I called for a CSI team.

Chief Pozzy stopped for a second. "I'm taking one more of the officers and following the car with Morrison."

"Once we get Suzi stabilized, I'll meet you back at the station." I instructed one of the remaining officers to accompany the EMTs from the lobby to the condo, and the other two to handle any resident questions or manage nosy reporters, then walked back to the bedroom to join Sal.

He shook his head. "No change."

It didn't appear Suzi's bra and panties had been altered, but her clothes were in a pile on the floor above her head. Either he didn't have time to strip her completely, or he had another step in mind before he raped her.

I could hear Sal repeating her name, over and over again, trying to draw her into consciousness.

I checked my watch. *Where's that bus?* I opened the door to the condo at the same time the elevator doors opened. I directed the escorting officer to stay outside the door and not to offer any information to neighbors who might ask what's going on. I held the door long enough for the EMT's to push the gurney inside, then pointed to the bedroom.

Sal and I walked back to the living room to play the waiting game.

Since I'd stuck a rolled-up magazine between the jamb and the door the CSI team didn't wait for me to introduce myself. They joined us in the living room.

I recognized one of the CSI's from a case I'd worked a few years ago. "Andy Menta, this is my partner, Detective Petruca."

Sal extended his hand. "I worked with you years ago on the Beacon Hill Rapist murders."

"I do get around." He surveyed the room. "What's happening here?"

"I'm sure you heard about the girls found dead ten months ago in Quincy, the one two months ago in Hull, and the one a week and a half ago on Revere Beach."

"I have."

"We have his intended fifth victim being attended to as we speak."

"Alive or dead?"

"At this time, she's alive, but barely."

Andy turned to the CSIs. "Take pictures of the girl and her surroundings first before the EMTs move her. I'll be right with you."

We know she has cocaine in her system. What, or if, she was given anything before that, we don't know." I shrugged. "The other girls died of an overdose of cocaine, but the ME found traces of another drug, possibly administered by dissolving it in alcohol, in this case, wine." I pointed to the two glasses and an open bottle of 2008 *Spottswoode* Cabernet Sauvignon on the table. "Once this drug was in the girl's system, she was rendered helpless. Our perp intended to have the cocaine finish her off."

"What's with the black rose beside the wine bottle?"

"I'm assuming it's symbolic. A black rose symbolizes death, similar to the color black."

Andy lifted his hands up. "And, you know this why?"

"I know this because there was a bouquet of black roses at a funeral I covered."

Andy grinned. "Must have been one of the North End "boys" being laid to rest."

"It was. I asked about the choice of flowers and was told they're commonly used when someone wants to make reference to the death of a friendship or relationship. What kind of a friendship or relationship, I wasn't about to ask."

Sal walked over to see if the rose was real. "Morrison blamed his brother's death on the Gridiron Groupie who was driving Matthew's car. She died too. The black rose must have represented the darker emotion of the sorrow Kevin felt with the loss of his twin."

I looked at the glasses of wine and the single rose resting, out-of-water, on a frayed piece of white satin material. "Kevin was on a self-imposed mission to eliminate however many groupies it took to satisfy his brother's death."

CSI Menta through his hands up. "A sick mother."

One of the EMTs came out of the bedroom. "We've stabilized her and are taking her to Mass General. She's got a ways to go, but she's breathing on her own. Are you going to station an officer outside her door?"

"I am. I'll arrange for one to meet you in emergency."

I gestured to Andy as they wheeled Suzi out of Morrison's condo. "Retirement's looking better and better."

Andy agreed, but said, "Neither one of us is going nowhere."

Sal and I walked out into the hallway, while Andy and his crew took pictures and swept the condo. Only one neighbor came by. A lady, who appeared to be in her early seventies, asked if Mr. Stewart was all right. "Such a nice guy, I wouldn't want him to be sick or something more." She put her hand up to her mouth and giggled. "He's popular with the women. Has lots of visitors—pretty ones. I remember his housekeeper, Hazel, telling me about his white satin sheets." She blushed. "He sure knows how to treat a woman."

I told her he was fine, but I'd let him know she was concerned. It was a way to get her name and number in case I'd need her as a witness to identify some of his other victims.

"We've found a couple things you guys need to take a look at." Andy rubbed his chin and rolled his eyes in the direction of the bedroom.

Sal and I followed him. The closet door was open. It was empty except for two Michael Kors skirts, same pattern, different colors, and two white jerseys hanging as outfits in the center of the bar.

I stared at the outfits. "One of those was for Suzi." I glanced at Sal.

"The count is off."

Andy walked over to the dresser on the opposite side of the room. The top drawer was open. "Take a look."

"Got an extra set of evidence gloves?" I asked.

Andy handed both Sal and me a set.

Inside the drawer were six envelopes carefully nested in a blanket of white satin. "Each one is numbered and sealed with a candle wax stamp of a black rose."

Sal took a deep breath. "Six sets of the Kors' clothing are missing and now we have six envelopes."

"Andy, take extra pictures of these." I unsealed the envelope marked number one. "Dead petals from a black rose." I checked the other five. I slammed my hand on the top of the dresser. "Same fuckin' thing."

Sal took one of the envelopes and looked inside. "Suzi wasn't number five. She was number seven."

The silence was deafening.

I bit my bottom lip and fist punched my hand. "We've got him, the son of a bitch."

CHAPTER 76

Sal and I stopped by the manager's office and told him an officer would be stationed outside of Kevin Morrison's condo. He reprogramed the entry code and gave us a new key card.

"I told the chief we'd go by the hospital to check on Suzi, then head to the station." It was ten-thirty when I pulled up in front of Mass General.

She was still in intensive care.

Since I didn't recognize the officer stationed outside her room, I flashed my badge to identify myself. "Evening, officer. Detectives Mastro and Petruca."

"My lieutenant said you'd be by. The only person that's been in to see her is the doctor." He checked his notepad. "Dr. Atkins."

"We'll be right back." I motioned Sal to join me in the waiting room. "Check with the desk. If Dr. Atkins is still on duty, have him paged. If he's not, then I need to talk to the attending physician. I'll meet you back in Suzi's room."

Suzi was conscious, but very listless. She tried to turn her head when I walked in. Her voice was weak. "What happened?"

"You're going to be fine. I'll explain it all to you tomorrow. Right now you need to rest." As I turned to greet Dr. Atkins, my jacket opened, exposing my badge.

Suzi opened her eyes as wide as she could. "You're a policeman?"

I took a deep breath. "I am."

A faint smile came over her face. "You saved my life."

I looked toward Sal. "We did."

It was two a.m. when I unlocked the door to my condo.

Maggie was lying on the couch, wrapped in a blanket, watching a rerun of Castle. At the sound of a key turning, she glanced toward the door. Her smile said it all.

I walked over, sat on the edge of the couch and gave her a kiss on the cheek. She scooched back on the couch as much as she could.

I slid my shoes off and cuddled in beside her, cradling her in my arms. "I'm home."

"I'm glad."

I was still hyped from Morrison's capture. And, Maggie appeared uncertain from not knowing what was going on.

I leaned back far enough to see her face. "I could use a drink. How 'bout you?"

"Thought you'd never ask."

"Sam's Boston Lager and popcorn?"

"As long as it comes with a side of conversation."

"It does." I handed her an open bottle of beer. "Glass?"

"I'm good." She took a drink. "Tell me you got the guy."

"We did. If he'd had his way, he would have claimed his seventh victim tonight."

"Seventh?"

"Yep. There are two more out there … somewhere." I washed down my words with a slug of beer.

"His intended victim's name is Suzi Dalton. Right now she's at Mass General, but she's going to be fine—at least physically. It may take her a while to come to grips with what happened and the fact she'll be a live witness at his trial." I got the popcorn from the microwave. "Once they match what DNA we have to the Quincy,

Hull and Revere girls, they'll be able to put him away for the rest of his life."

Maggie set her beer on the table and leaned forward to grab the remote. "Detective Mike Mastro, I really don't want popcorn and I've seen this episode of *Castle* more times than I want to admit."

I took her hand. "Then, can I interest you in a cop, a boyfriend and a lover?"

If you enjoyed, **A BLACK ROSE**, the first book in
The Detective Mike Mastro Mystery Series,
please post a reader's review on Amazon.com.

And…be sure to check out
The Casey Quinby Mystery Series:

Empty Rocker (November 2012)
Paint Her Dead (October 2013)
Caught With A Quahog (October 2014)
A Tale of Two Lobsters (October 2015)
18 Buzzy Lane (October 2016)

I can be reached by email at judiciance@gmail.com
Or, visit me at my website, **judiciance.com**
Don't forget to sign up to receive my newsletter.

Made in the USA
Middletown, DE
20 June 2017